The Cosmic Cucumber

By
Matthew Sowden

For Natasha and Theo. My retirement plan relies on one of you being successful.

CHAPTER 1
THE WORST CAB EVER

It was 3pm and that meant it was time to make the store 'Fab for Four', the initiative where everyone who wasn't on a till spent an hour tidying up the shelves and taking all the empty cardboard packaging away. Mark always tried to turn his brain off during this hour, in case he was driven mad by the banality of it all and went screaming down the escalator toward the front doors, stripping off his uniform as he did so. He was convinced that the length this hour felt like was proof of what Einstein was on about when he said time was relative. It was almost as bad as the time his ex-wife had made him spend watching *Mamma Mia!* and he was sure that he felt blood coming out of his ears when that was happening.

Of course, the only problem with turning his brain off for the hour was that customers would make him turn it back on again by asking him questions.

These questions could range from the sublime ('have you seen my son, I left him eating a jar of Piccalilli in aisle 5'), to the ridiculous ('Have you ever had a Bishops Finger?'). The customer who coerced him forcibly into reactivating his lobes at this moment, was definitely in the latter category.

"Why have you stopped doing Tropical Squash?!" the man exclaimed, feverishly hopping from one blue deck shoe to the other.

"Oh, I'm sorry sir, I didn't know we had," said Mark, as cheerfully as his brain would let him at 50% of the way through restarting, "Let's go and have a look at the drinks aisle, shall we? Follow me".

Mark led the yellow-trousered worrier back to the Drinks aisle, which was the next one over from the Biscuits aisle he had been Fabbing. They stopped at the Squash section and both scanned the shelves. Mark's scanning was definitely more Tortoise-like than the golden-jeaned Hare next to him.

"See?! See?!" said the posh man, pointing frantically yet limply, which Mark thought was quite a trick, "No Tropical Squash!"

Mark's heart fell when he realised that there was indeed no Tropical Squash on the shelves. 'Surely there'd be an alternative' he thought, scanning again.

"Ten years!" shouted the man, his cheeks reddening to match his polo shirt, "Ten years it's taken me to find a Squash that I like! And you go and discontinue it!"

'Ten years to find a suitable squash?' thought Mark, looking at all the 'NEW' signs that littered the recently-changed section, 'and to think you could have used all that time to get a life!'

Mark was eternally grateful that telepathy was not a human trait, or he would have been sacked from his people-focused job a long time ago. Probably right around the time the customer asked him the Bishops Finger question and he telepathically answered with 'No I haven't Sir but let me get my friend as he used to be a choirboy.'

Much to Mark's relief, his eyes finally settled on what would surely be a suitable replacement.

"Ah, here we go sir, this is what's replaced it," he said, grabbing a bottle of dark-orange squash from behind one of the 'NEW' signs and giving it to the man, "This one is Passion Fruit, Pineapple, Mango & Guava".

The man stared at the bottle with all the intent and consideration of a man choosing which treatment regime to undertake for a cancer diagnosis. It was at least a minute until the customer made his momentous decision.

"I'm not sure…" he pondered, shaking the bottle gently and turning it over and over in his hand, as if surveying it from every angle, "I'm not sure it's going to be Tropical enough for me".

For a split second, Mark wondered if this was one of those candid camera-type mickey takes.

'Not…Tropical…enough' he thought to himself, looking around slyly for the hidden cameras. He didn't say what he wanted to say next, but if he had, this is what he'd have said…

"Firstly, 20% of the world's population haven't got access to clean drinking water and you're worried your squash 'isn't tropical enough' and secondly, if it's really an issue I can show you where we keep the little frilly drinks umbrellas!"

But instead, he smiled politely. The crimson-cheeked customer continued to twirl the bottle around as if he were looking for the secret code word written on it by his spy contact at Robinsons.

"I wish they wouldn't keep discontinuing things!" said the man, forlornly, as if he'd just had a death in the family.

'I wish a lot of things,' thought Mark, from behind his fake smile, 'I wish I'd tried harder at school; I wish I hadn't dropped out of university after the first year; I wish I'd kissed Michelle Evans at the Sixth Form Leavers Disco. Maybe then I wouldn't be stood here, taking bits of cardboard off a shelf and wasting time talking to you!'

"I know, it can be frustrating can't it?" sympathised Mark, nodding as genuinely as he could, "Hopefully this one will be okay".

"Well, we'll see," replied the angst-ridden shopper, as he turned and walked back to his trolley. Mark widened his eyes in exasperation for a moment and went back to Fabbing the Ginger Nuts.

-

It was time to go home and as usual, it was raining. Plymouth was one of those places where the main difference in the seasons was the temperature of the rain. Mark stood in the doorway of Drakes Circus Mall, waiting for the latest downpour to ease off, so he could make a run for the bus stop. Well, 'run' might be over-stating it.

Actually, 'light jog' would be over-egging it. Mark had tried running and really enjoyed it. For two weeks at a time. Then his knees would swell up to twice their normal size and that would be that for two weeks. Ask any Olympic runner; "fortnight on, fortnight off" is not the way to get any benefit out of jogging. Don't ask some of them though, or you'll end up pooping in the street.

He was especially annoyed that he'd mixed up the date of his MOT and his day off, meaning he'd had to catch the bus to work today. But Mark was even more annoyed that he'd rushed out of the house this morning, without his cap. He could quite happily walk in the rain if his cap was covering his balding head. Without it, it was a no-go.

'I'll just wait,' he thought, deciding to look at Facebook while he waited for the rain to ease. Before he had a chance, his phone rang. It was Dad calling. This would be a computer question. It was *always* a computer question. He was the 'person who knows about computers' in his family, which meant he had everyone's passwords on various notes on his phone. That way, his family could use him as their personal reminder service, when they forgot them.

"Hellooo…no, just finished, just waiting for the rain to stop before I walk to the bus stop," he leaned against the window of *Build-A-Bear*, which was warm because of the stuffing machine's exhaust the other side of it, "What's up?"

Mark listened to his Dad's query, as the sharp-faced shop assistant tapped on the window and told him to stop leaning. He nodded compliantly, then turned around so his whole back was one against it.

"Well, you just have to…I know, it's confusing, I know…have you got your email password there…the pass…for the TalkTalk account, yeah"

He relaxed as the warmth of the window spread across his back. He tried not to look at the amazing arse walking past in yoga pants, but his eyes were drawn from the floor.

"It's in your password book, isn't it…no, that's your account login…no, your phone account, not your email account…yes, it is confusing, I know…"

He did the age-old trick of looking at the same spot on the opposite window and let the yoga pants with a woman attached walk through his field of vision. 'Just checking out the bargains' he lied to himself, in case someone of a higher power was listening.

"It's definitely there, I remember writing it in the last time I was…got it? Under the other…yeah, that's right…944, yeah that's the one. Okay, no worries, see you tonight".

Just as he finished the conversation with his Dad, his phone showed him the low battery warning and went off. Now what was he supposed to do? Stare blankly at people until he got arrested?! 'Well, it's one way to get a lift home, I suppose', he considered briefly, before deciding against it. He concluded that he'd have a good stare at the patterns the rain was making in the shop window and wait for more yoga pants to walk past.

He'd just made out two sheep fighting (in the window, not in any clothing), when a Taxi pulled up at the pavement, ten yards away from him.

'Oh sod it, I can't be bothered to wait for the bus,' he determined, 'I'll get this cab.'

'Can't be bothered' - That was a phrase that had followed him around like a bored younger sibling.

He had used it most of his life. He told himself not to do something, rather than try and do it and end up failing. Right from his school days, he had always taken the easy option. He got his exams with the bare minimum of revision; he had fallen into his job at the supermarket; he had fallen upwards into one of the manager jobs at the supermarket due to his aptitude with the computer systems; he'd never taken the difficult chances presented to him, but it was easier to tell himself that it was through lack of effort rather than fear of failure. Now, here he was, 40 years old, divorced, approaching his 25 years' service in the same shop and getting in a cab because he was too lazy to walk the extra five hundred yards to the bus.

"Moorland Road, please mate", he said to the driver, as he scrambled into the back seat,

"No problem," replied the driver, "Good day at the supermarket?"

Mark wondered how the driver knew he worked in a supermarket, but assumed he could tell by Mark's uniform, "Ugh, not really. One of those days where you question your life choices, you know?"

"Oh yes mate, I know all about choices". Mark heard the locks engage on the doors.

"Everything okay?" asked Mark, as he brushed the rain off his non-existent hair. To think he tried to grow his hair once during his Heavy Metal phase and just ended up with a "Jew-fro".

"You've never fulfilled your potential, have you Mark?" asked the driver, ominously.

"Sorry?" replied Mark, his hand coming to a stop on his head, making him look like he would start rubbing his belly with the other hand any moment.

11

"Always taking the easy option, aren't you Mark?" continued the driver.

"How the hell do you know who I am?" Mark panicked and started to try to open the doors. They were locked tight and the windows were locked shut.

"You couldn't even keep a brace on your teeth could you?"

Mark froze. He was 15 when that happened. How long had this Taxi driver been watching him? It's one thing to know what your customers want, but this was ridiculous. Mark ran his finger down his crooked front teeth and remembered how he had talked his parents into letting him have the braces removed because it felt funny when he ate. He'd regretted it as an adult, along with a lot of other things.

"What if I could help you fulfil your potential, Mark?" asked the driver, glancing at him in the rear-view mirror. The driver had the brightest green eyes Mark had ever seen, although he didn't spend a lot of time looking into men's eyes, so he couldn't really claim a large sample size.

'Blimey', Mark suddenly thought, 'The Jehovah's Witnesses have certainly embraced the hard-sell tactics'

"I'm not going door to door" Mark's voice trembled, half in anger and half in fright.

"I work for an organisation called Universal Corrections. We've been watching you Mark. We think you have the right stuff to be this Galaxy's last line of defence against total destruction".

"Right," said Mark, raising his eyebrows sarcastically, "I suppose this Taxi is a spaceship is it?"

"It's really more of a *Time* ship than a space ship, but you know…its all relative" said the driver, with a smirk. Mark's eye was caught by a glint out of the window. It was the cloud level falling below them.

It was then he noticed the timer flick down to zero on the dashboard and he was suddenly in space. Not just above the clouds, but properly in space. And they were next to the biggest space station he'd ever seen (and he'd watched Babylon 5).

"I'm afraid you haven't really got a choice, Mark" said the driver, turning away from the steering wheel, resting his denim shirted arms on the back of the seat and sliding back the glass partition. "You've been chosen, the galaxy is depending on you"

"Well okay, but I've got work at 09:00 tomorrow" Replied Mark, expecting to wake up at any second. But he didn't. Wake up or make his shift the next day, that is.

The space station they were heading towards looked like a massive wheel, silently rotating in space. The outer edge was constantly moving around six fixed spokes that met at a central hub. It was this centre point that they seemed to be headed for. The rim of the wheel was covered in windows, lights and open areas, through which Mark could see all manner of flora and activities. One thing he couldn't see was any Humans. All of the beings busying themselves looked they were a dizzying array of sizes and shapes, with varying amounts of arms and suits. One creature he spotted through a window just before the Taxi entered the station looked not only to have ten arms but appeared to be playing five games of table tennis simultaneously. It came as a strange momentary comfort to him that they had ping pong in space.

"What's going to happen to my family?" asked Mark, leaning over the front seat, with one eye on the driver and one eye on the landing bay they were about to land in.

"Don't worry, the Cromulites will explain everything during Orientation," Replied the driver, suddenly looking in his rear - view mirror, "Hey, you've taken your seatbelt off!"

Mark was shocked at being told off and went to sit back in his seat, when he stopped and realised what he was doing.

"Right, so you've just abducted me and taken me away from everything and everyone I love, but I'm the naughty one?!" exclaimed Mark, leaning forward again, "What are we going to hit out here?"

Without saying a word and with only a sigh, like he'd been questioned in this way a thousand times, the driver's foot pressed down on one of the pedals and the Taxi stopped. Very abruptly. Its forward motion ceased, and it travelled the remaining two feet of vertical clearance in less than a second. Mark ended up in the front seat, upside down. His legs were waving about like a dog's ears when it hangs his head out of a car window. His face was less than six inches away from the floor of the footwell.

Mark admired the assortment of sweet wrappers and old betting slips (the driver clearly had a problem) for a few seconds, while he decided how he was going to get out of the vehicle with any shred of dignity intact. He resolved that he probably couldn't and that ignoring this little scenario had ever happened was probably the best way forward. So with a selection of grunts and moans, this what exactly what he did. Or didn't do, as it never happened of course.

He opened the rear door of the Taxi and got out into the brightly lit and surprisingly quiet landing bay. There were clearly space ships coming and going all the time, but when he looked at them, they seemed to be doing so in almost complete silence. The walls of the landing bay were completely white, so much so that doors and window were hard to make out. On the other side of the Taxi from him, Mark watched as a space ship that looked like a classic 'Flying Saucer' landed silently and the front opened into a ramp. Two aliens disembarked and Mark was surprised to see what they looked like. The aliens resembled what he would consider 'proper' aliens to look like. Like those aliens you see hillbillies describing on a History channel program. Aliens that would rather stick a probe up your bum than just ask you a question in a proper manner.

The aliens had long, slim heads and large, grey eyes, like two ovals set at opposite 45-degree angles either side of its recessed nose. The aliens were tall, taller than Mark by about a twelve to fifteen inches, but slender with long, graceful arms. Their legs and body were covered with fitted white gowns that reached down to their feet. The aliens were each wearing sashes stretching from their right shoulders to their left sides where their belt would be. One had a green sash, the other red. He had a little giggle to himself as he wondered if the red-sashed workers had a similarly reduced life expectancy as the 'red shirts' on Star Trek.

He gawped at the oblivious aliens as they made their way towards the side of the room and disappeared into a hole on the wall that had serenely slid open and then closed behind them. He had watched a lot of science fiction and to be fair, this sort of landing bay was exactly how he would have imagined one to be. It was pure 70s, Battle Beyond the Stars type of a deal. At least the bits with the white robotic race in that film. Not the warrior woman with the big boobs. He was still hoping to meet her somewhere else on the ship, probably in the bar.

He was so deep in thought about the warrior woman, that he didn't notice another two of the same aliens walking towards him. They caught his attention when they were close enough and smiled, holding up their right arms in a greeting as they did so. These aliens were both wearing purple sashes.

"Greetings Mark, we have been watching you for quite a long time," said the alien on the left, in a monotone yet warm voice. Mark was briefly taken aback, as he expected all aliens to talk like the Martians on *Mars Attacks*. He almost felt like he was owed a few "Ack acks!"

"Oh, ur, yeah, Fred Housego over there said that as well". Replied Mark, pointing over at the Taxi driver. The quizzical looks on the aliens' faces made him realise that obscure 1980s Mastermind references would probably fall on deaf ears in outer space.

"Indeed," said the alien on the right, his smile widening as if to pretend he understood Mark's reply, "I'm sure our TTAXI pilot has also told you that we are an organisation named Universal Corrections. And that we believe you are the best choice to be this universe's last line of defence".

"Yeah, he said that too," agreed Mark, nodding suspiciously, "But what Fred didn't tell me was the last line of defence against what exactly?"

The aliens each moved to one side, creating a path between them. Behind them, Mark could see a door noiselessly opening in the wall. They both motioned towards it and bowing slightly.

"All questions will be answered at Orientation," said the left alien, "It is time to show you your new life as the Universe's defender".

-

As they walked down the corridor, which was a little dimmer than the landing bay but still very white, he saw another hole open up and another brightly-lit room up ahead. It looked as if there was another Taxi cab in this room, along with several aliens of the same race as his welcoming committee, who were still walking alongside him. They had remained silent throughout the walk from the landing bay. But they exuded such an aura of calm and serenity that the silence had not been awkward like it would have if this was three Humans walking together. Even the elevator ride had been a silent, pleasant experience, which would be unheard of where he came from. In Britain, a lift ride full of strangers is silent, admittedly, but only because everyone is trying not to fart.

They reached the room and were greeted by another two aliens, this time wearing blue sashes. They gave the same welcoming greeting as the landing bay delegation had. This time, Mark pretended like he knew what he was doing and reciprocated the greeting.

"Greetings, Mark and welcome to your orientation. This shouldn't take long". Said the left hand one of the blue-sashed aliens, as his purple-sashed colleagues back through the door before it closed,

"First let us introduce ourselves. I am Chief Correction Officer Tarkir and this is Assistant Galaforg. We are Cromulites, part of the oldest civilisation in the known universe. We are here to show you the tools you will use to fight the forces of chaos".

"Yeah, about that," Mark interrupted, "What am I going to be fighting exactly?"

"You are going to be stopping the forces of Anti-Matter from deleting all normal matter in this reality. We call them the Wardz and they represent the greatest threat this universe has yet seen".

"Great!" Mark nodded as bravely as he could, trying to pretend his stomach hadn't just done a somersault.

The room lights dimmed, and a display screen lit up on the wall.

The video that started playing and Tarkir's commentary did not help Mark's stomach situation one little bit.

"For aeons, entropy has been a natural force. Stars burn out, planets lose temperature, beings die, energy dissipates. Eventually everything will be empty". Tarkir began, calmly waving his hand at a video of all the apocalyptically bad things happening that he'd just mentioned.

"Have you ever thought of going into motivational speaking?" asked Mark, sarcastically. Silence. "Tough crowd," he whispered.

"But just as matter has evolved into sentient life, so it would appear that Anti-Matter has done the same. And with the invention of Wormhole Anti-Matter Drives, the Wardz have found a way to cross into our reality, for limited periods of time". Tarkir continued, as the video changed to scenes of six-armed demons attacking cities with ray guns and black holes with creatures pouring out of them. All the scenes had 'artists impression' written in the bottom right hand corner of the screen.

"As they are comprised of Anti-Matter, Wardz would not be able to interact with our reality, were it not for the protection of their suits and the Wormhole. Don't let them hear you calling them 'Dark Matter' though. You can get in all sorts of trouble. Also, don't call our reality "normal" around them either – to them we are the anomaly. As Dark Matter and Dark Energy comprises of 95% of the known universe, they probably have a point. Their goal is to remove the 'anomaly' completely, so that eventually everything is cold, dark and free of intelligent life. Like a night out with a Gedren. The Anti-Matter Wormhole Drive harnesses the power of a black hole to create enough matter for Wardz to spend a few hours in our reality. A few hours in which the try to remove as many things from existence as possible with their Entropiser weapons. It will be your job to disable these threats before they can do too much damage wherever they appear in the universe. You will also be charged with the removal of any high-profile target who we believe are aiding the Wardz".

"Is that all?" Mark laughed sarcastically, "anything else?"

"Yes, the Wardz invisible and the high-profile targets are extremely difficult to get to," said Galaforg without a trace of humour, "which is why you will need SARDOC and your Nano Byte suit".

Assistant Galaforg motioned his hand in the direction of a large tube on the table behind him. The glass cylinder was home to a swarm of floating metal, undulating wildly like the angriest cloud Mark had ever seen. Next to it on the bench was a small clear cube, about twelve inches in diameter, with a plethora of LEDs, wiring and circuit boards inside. As it started to talk, the LEDs illuminated in time with its syllables.

"Please to meet you, sir!" said the cube in an upper-class English accent, "I am your Sentient Adaptable Roaming Digital Organisational Companion, or SARDOC for short. I will assist you with your base, your Nano Byte suit and in any other way I can to make our missions successful. Thanks to my proprietary technology, I am able to go wherever and *whenever* you go".

'Like a flea on a dog's back.' Thought Mark, happy to keep his humorous comments to himself for the moment until he could find a more receptive audience.

"Hello, er, SARDOC," said Mark, lightly patting the disco cube with one hand and tapping the glass tube with the other, "and I suppose these are the, er, Nano Bots?"

The metallic cloud did not seem to like the sound of the tapping, as it moved away to form a recess from Mark's finger.

"Nano *Bytes*," corrected Tarkir, quietly pushing Mark's finger down and away from the glass, "and yes, this is your new suit. It is comprised of thirty billion individual, microscopic, artificial lifeforms, all working together as one hive mind. They are controlled by SARDOC, to a point, but will react to danger instinctively if required. They will not only protect you from Anti-Matter exposure, but also allow you to see the Wardz in the field. They are also able to replicate any being in the Galactic Database, meaning you can infiltrate most planets without alerting the local population".

"Cool". Replied Mark, in his ongoing attempt to win 'most inappropriate reaction of the year', "So can I, you know, fly through space in it...er, in them?" Ten minutes in and he was already imagining pretending to be *Iron Man*.

"Unfortunately not," reported Galaforg sadly, "We have not yet developed the capability in the Nano Bytes to permit flight".

"However, the interstellar distances you will travelling would preclude using this as a mode of transport in any case," added Tarkir, somewhat defensively, "This is why you will need a TTAXI like the one you see behind you".

"Oh right," said Mark turning around, "You call it a Taxi too, do you?"

His question was met with confused faces from the usually implacable Cromulites.

"TTAXI is the acronym of the vehicle's name," said Tarkir, "It stands for Time Travelling Archite-Xevron Imploder, which refers to the fusion reactor that powers the vehicle. But the humour of the acronym is not lost on us".

"Oh thank god, I was starting to think you guys didn't know what humour was!" said Mark, relieved, "Because this *really* looks like what we call a Taxi on Earth!"

"I can assure that any resemblance to a Terran vehicle is purely coincidental, Mark," corrected Tarkir, looking even more confused than before, "this vehicle is designed as such because it was the most efficient design available. We are referring to the fact that 'Ttaxi' is the Cromulite word for what you would call a Haemorrhoid. The junior officers find this most humorous".

Galaforg's giggling proved that this was indeed the case. Tarkir shot his Assistant a demeaning look and continued.

"The reaction between the Archite and Xevron molecules within the reactor produces a consistent Tachyon output. These are necessary for the TTAXI to travel anywhere in the universe, instantly. This is achieved by travelling to the chosen destination at 98% the speed of light and then using the collected Tachyons to 'rewind time' to the point that you left. This is because Tachyons travel backwards in time. This method gives the illusion of instantaneous travel. Any beings inside the TTAXI are sheltered from any unwanted ageing effects or memories by an anti-time bubble generated within the cab. Although, on some occasions, the passengers or driver have reported being left with what you would call 'a mullet'. The craft are also fitted with a holographic projection which allows them to blend in as seamlessly as your Nano Byte suit".

"Sounds okay," agreed Mark, nodding, "anything else?"

"Oh yes, to protect your family from any...unwanted attention, your code name from now on will be Agent Abel".

The mention of his family made him stop in his mental tracks. Mark suddenly felt a pangs of guilt coursing through him. His head had been filled so full of his glorious future in the last few minutes, that he'd forgotten to ask about what he was leaving behind.

"Oh god yes, what about my family?" he asked, turning back to face Tarkir, "What happens to them? You can't just leave my kids without a Dad, even if it is for the good of the Universe!"

"Do not worry, Mark," said Tarkir calmly, as if it was a question he got asked all the time, "you have already been replaced with a Automaton that mimics your appearance and personality in every way. Your family will never know the difference. It has even been programmed to spend 2 hours a day in the toilet, despite not having any use for it".

"Clever, that would have given the game away," agreed Mark, quite impressed that the aliens had clearly done their research. Maybe the kids would be better off with a robot-version of him. It would probably have more energy than he did.

"Alright, I'm in".

"Excellent," said Tarkir, smiling, "Come, we will show you to your base. We believe it will be to your liking. We have tried to make it feel as comfortable and as homely as possible".

"Sounds good, one final question though…"

"Yes?"

"Can I have a Cat?"

CHAPTER 2
DEAD MEN DON'T WATCH VIDEOS

"Oh, I'm dead", thought Abel, as he tried to move his head to look around the room, "Could be worse I suppose, could still be alive".

"How is that worse than being dead?" chimed an incredulous voice from somewhere in his psyche. Abel presumed this other voice was his conscience, which made him wonder why it was only showing up now. Where was his moral compass when he was massacring the Flundo Legions of Betamaj V, or setting fire to the King of Narp's beard? When he had been chosen to kill the Great Confluence of Traubfire III (while it was still a baby), his guardian angel had been unavailable for comment.

But oh no, now it was too late to prevent a descent into whatever eternal damnation awaited him, his conscience shows up large as life and starts giving advice, like a man stood next to a fireworks factory, talking to the manager and offering, "I don't think you should have allowed smoking in the canteen".

Abel decided against arguing with his Johnny-Come-Lately Soul and set about finding out who was whistling. He hated whistling. Who ever thought whistling was a good idea? It's the musical equivalent of sneezing without putting your hand up to your face. Fair enough, you've got a crap song stuck in your head, but now you've spread it to my head too. In fact, Abel was so angered by the whistling, that he'd forgotten he was dead and tried to move his head in the direction of the sound.

"Bugger," he thought, remembering his current state, "I'll have to wait for the sound to come to me".

As his whistling-induced anger subsided, he started to realise that the back of his head was cold. Not just the back of his head, but the back of his whole body. It was even cold considering he was a corpse. Not that he knew what being a corpse felt like first-hand until now. Maybe it was one of those 'Is it cold or is it me?' type situations that old people were always going on about.

Despite being an intergalactic assassin, Abel hadn't seen many cold corpses. They were usually still warm, convulsing and venting blood when he left them. Tidying the bodies and erasing them was the purview of Dispatches. He sometimes felt a bit sorry for some of the messes he left behind for Dispatches. Especially if he used the Gutsalizer, the only gun on the market that doubles as a soup maker. At least with the Wardz targets, the bodies ended up as solid blocks of purified matter-foam.

"Oh, I'm not just dead," he said to himself, "I'm in a Morgue".

The realisation was cut short by the whistling getting louder. From out of the corner of his eye, there appeared a pair of glasses, wearing a lady. A human lady, by the look of it.

"Could be one of those 50/50 FemBoy bots", said his conscience, "You don't want to be making that mistake again".

"Shut. Up". Thought Abel, who would be metaphorically grabbing his conscience by the throat if he wasn't still dead. "That was an honest mistake, they sent me the wrong one and…. anyway, what would a FemBoy bot be doing working in a morgue?"

"Overtime?" Suggested his conscience.

No, this lady was definitely Human. The glasses were a nice touch though. A *very* nice touch.

"Can corpses get aroused?", he wondered quietly, hoping old Nanny State wouldn't hear.

"We have drained the body of blood". Said the lady, into a dangling microphone.

"Well there's your answer", said his conscience, sarcastically. Abel was depressed that even his good side was a prick.

"The deceased is a white male, 50 years old, in average physical condition,"

"Who are you calling average, love?" thought Abel,

"He appears to have died from multiple puncture wounds to the chest"

"Amateurs," Abel thought, knowing that if this were a professional job, it would be one laser wound to the back of the head and he wouldn't have a face left to look at her. Either that, or he'd be Abel Soup in a bucket in the corner.

"I am suspending the autopsy at 17:58…"

"Phew, at least she's not going to cut me up!"

"…and prepare the body for dissection tomorrow".

"Bugger…"

As the lady moved out of Abel's peripheral vision, he could feel the slab start to move upwards. As he started to move, he began to feel strange. Even stranger than being dead. He'd gotten quite used to being dead over the last few minutes. Like how you get used to being in a cold swimming pool once you've been in it for a while and your bits have slid back up inside your body.

But this was stranger than that. He soon realised that he could now *see* his body, the lady and even some of the room. But more importantly, he could see where his body was being pushed. It was being pushed into the storage drawer and some reason, this was the moment that being dead *finally* hit him. It hit him like a bag of cement would hit a builder's apprentice if he didn't notice his workmate throw it at him because he was too busy watching *Busty Flaps VI* on his phone. Right in the chest. He began to panic and not even the thought of watching *Busty Flaps VI* could pull him out of it.

As his body slid further inside the cold store, he began to scream his imaginary lungs out. Imaginary sweat coursed down his imaginary brow and his imaginary heart felt like it was going to beat out of his imaginary chest. As he lunged toward the drawer, the door slammed shut in front of him. He came face to imaginary face with a big sign…

"Abel – deceased".

That's when he woke up….

-

UNIVERSAL CORRECTIONS COMPOUND, UNKNOWN LOCATION, EARTH YEAR 2018

Abel woke up with a jolt, the kind of jolt you get when you fall asleep at the wheel and drift onto the bumpy bits at the side of the motorway. In a flash he was wide awake, but unlike in the movies, he didn't sit bolt upright. It would take something much more momentous and frightening than a nightmare about being dead to make his body get upright that quickly. Not even waking up to his bed being on fire would make him spring to a vertical axis; he'd probably just use it to light a cigarette. He wasn't the 'jump out of bed and give me twenty' kinda guy; he was more of a 'slide out of bed and hack up green stuff in the sink' type.

As the memory of the nightmare began to recede, he decided it was probably best to get up and watch some TV to take his mind of it further. Actually, Colin decided it was time for Abel to get up and watch some TV after feeding him. Colin was a typical Cat, which meant he didn't give a toss about what you wanted, unless what you wanted was to feed him or provide a warm lap to sit on for an unspecified period of Colin's choosing.

"Good morning S," he attempted to say out loud as he trudged stiffly out of the bedroom. What came out was a series of what can only be described as 'deep squeaks', if that's even possible. He coughed and tried again, with more success this time.

"Good Morning Agent Abel", replied SARDOC, his warm voice filling the room from its multi-point speakers, "Shall I begin to prepare the usual beverage?"

"You know it, S," Abel said as he wrestled with the Cat Food pouch, "Easy open my arse", he said quietly to himself.

"Sir, you are aware that I can be requested to feed Colin for you on a set timescale", SARDOC offered, as the sound of the Hologiser spinning up came darting through the kitchen.

"I know S, but I like to keep this one for myself, go a bit old school," Abel finally found the little notch on the side of the packet, "besides, it reminds me of home. And Colin likes me to do it," he crouched down, emptied the packet into the bowl and held his hand at the right height so that he stroked Colin as he barged in for his breakfast, "don't you, mate".

Colin, truth be told and as previously mentioned, couldn't give a toss.

As he struggled painfully to his feet, his knees let out a noise that sounded like he was eating crisps. He wondered every morning why the Cromulites that controlled Universal Corrections had chosen him when he was 40, just as his Arthritis was beginning to kick in. Sure, the Nano Byte suit that he wore for missions did most of the physical work, but surely a younger specimen would be better suited to all the leaping and killing.

He ambled to the other end of the kitchen area and picked up the coffee from the Hologiser. He blew on it, but it didn't stop the steam from making his nose run. He sipped a nervous sip, as his tongue was still recovering from the "I thought I'd asked for Orange Juice" debacle of a few days earlier.

"Shall I prepare your protein-enriched Flarg Nuts, sir?" asked SARDOC.

"Oh yes please S, I can't wait to taste the Flargy goodness for the two thousandth day in a row!" said Abel glibly, forgetting that SARDOC had learned to ignore his sarcasm.

"Very well," replied SARDOC, "I'll have it transmitted to the living room table when it's finished Hologising".

"Hooofff!", Abel made that noise that old people make when they reach for things as he sat down, "Let's see what's going on in the Galaxy shall we? Engage the display wall please, S".

"Of course, sir", the wall opposite Abel's seat began to swirl with colour, as if a very slow-burning firework had suddenly been lit. The three-dimensional picture coalesced into the figures of Marv Blatworthy and Pfffffft N'Zerb, the hosts of Good Morning Milky Way, the number-one Breakfast Show in the known universe. And in one house in Hull, where Phil Smith had misaligned his satellite dish and accidentally started picking it up.

The sound kicked in a few seconds later, meaning Marv could only be understood if you were skilled in lip reading and Pfffffft could only be understood if you could read mandibles.

"…in a three-ship wreck," Blatworthy's booming voice suddenly filled the lounge, "that meant a jam on trade route Epsilon 359 in the Glarvington system at the height of rush hour. One of the ships shed their load of Flermtwats and emergency services were dispatched to deal with the suck wounds".

"Oh great," sighed Abel.

"Were we planning a trip to the Glarvington system today, sir?" enquired SARDOC.

"No, I just hate it when Marv's on with Pfffffft," exclaimed Abel, "he tries to flirt with them and it's creepy".

"Is it the Sildonian auto-flirt response you object to?" asked SARDOC. N'Zerb was indeed Sildonian, meaning they were actually three creatures in one, standing on each other's shoulders inside a host skin.

Each three-way creature took it in turns to be on top, meaning their mandibles all get equal exercise. They are attached mouth to anus, to ensure when one eats, they all eat. They also have an auto-flirting response, which is to regurgitate their last meal. To be fair to Pfffffft, she did a good job of holding it in when needed.

"No, not necessarily," said Abel, thoughtfully, "It's his choice of ties I can't stand. They make me want to throw up on him and I'm not even Sildonian. I much prefer Zadjin, I like the cut of his jib". Zadjin was from a planet of thinking machines and was a former crane engineer, meaning this wasn't a metaphor.

"Your Flarg Nuts, sir", said SARDOC, as a shimmering bowl of breakfast cereal began to materialise on the table in front of him. First the bowl, then the cereal would appear, in a cone of holographic light swirling in a rising helix, leaving a trail of wholesome matter in its wake.

Thankfully, the latest models of Hologisers produced the receptacles and the food separately, thanks to their double-transmitter design. Before this, more than a few people had reported ordering a bowl of cereal and being left with a pile ceramic-infused crispies and a trickle of milk dripping off the table and onto their slippers.

"Thanks, S", Abel put down his coffee, grabbed a cushion from next to him on the sofa, placed it on his lap and reached for the bowl.

"In breaking news," continued Pfffffft, her clicking vocabulary being automatically translated through the speakers by SARDOC, "more disappearances are being reported in the Igonid cluster, with three villages being reported missing on Igonid 3 in the last two hours alone. More details in the lunchtime news".

"Sounds interesting, S" Abel delved his spoon deep into the Flarg nuts, which had now softened in the heat of the milk to form a substance similar to purple porridge. "I wonder if today's mission will be around there. Whole villages going missing. Sounds like something…oooaaa…uuueeei…oooia", Abel had not expected the Flarg Nuts to be so hot. They were so hot in fact, that they had burned the consonants out of his mouth. The spoon clattered back into the bowl as he waved his hand in front of his mouth. He sucked in and out until the mouthful was cool enough to swallow. He continued his sentence now that the consonants had returned.

"Sounds like something the Wardz could be involved in," Abel took a swig of his coffee, which now felt cool in comparison to the supernova Flarg Nuts.

"Indeed, sir," SARDOC did his assistantly duties by hologising a glass of cold milk to the table, to help with the wildfire in Abel's mouth. "Shall I request an adhoc TTAXI?"

"Check I don't have a scheduled defence patrol today," Abel poured half the glass of newly-Hologised milk into his bowl to cool down the purple lava at its source, "and then order one, if one isn't already on its way".

"Very good sir, I'll contact them immediately".

Abel was just finishing the last mouthful of Flarg Nuts, when SARDOC came back with an answer.

"You do not have a scheduled defence patrol today sire, so I have taken the liberty of calling you an adhoc TTAXI,"

"Don't tell me, it's just around the corner at the top of the road," sniggered Abel, starting the back and forth rocking that would eventually lead to him getting up off the sofa.

Abel didn't think that joke would ever get old.

SARDOC quietly added a 1567th entry to the joke count file.

"Hoooof", there was the old man noise again.

Abel turned to walk back into his bedroom, hobbling the first few steps before the blood got flowing round his arthritic knees. He was more or less completely upright by the time he reached the doorway. Colin sauntered past him, hopped up onto the bed and began to clean himself. 'Not an arthritic joint in sight, the swine' thought Abel.

As he entered the doorway, SARDOC opened the wardrobe door containing the Nano Byte tube. Abel turned around, arms straight down his sides and backed into the opening in the tube. As the glass slid shut in front of him, the friendly swarm of shiny metal descended from its orbit at the top of the tube. It gradually began to attach itself to his body, the Nano Bytes working as one organism to cover him from head to toe. First his chest felt the warmth of the Nano Bytes as they branched out towards his extremities like the best Thermal vest he could possibly imagine. As the suit began to spread over his boxer shorts, he thought of how many times it had taken to not feel like he'd wet himself at this point of integration. It carried on down over his legs, arms, hands and feet until he was completely covered in its warm, golden glow. He always knew when the transfer was complete, as SARDOCs voice went from being in the corner of the room, to being right next to his ear, like when his Bluetooth headphones would connect to his phone back on Earth. The Heads-Up Display that appeared in his helmet straight after, soon made the memories of home disperse, replaced with brightly-coloured super-hero style new ones.

One thing the Cromulites had not told him about the Nano Byte suit at Orientation, was that it also contained a miniature hologiser to aid survival. He had found that out from SARDOC. He could sneak up silently, kick the snot out of the enemy and then offer them a Garibaldi. And he was the only person in the universe with one. The suit, not the biscuits.

"All systems online, sir" confirmed SARDOC, as a friendly *BEEP BEEP* cut through the air from outside the window, "It would appear your TTAXI is here".

35

"Let's get to it then", he walked away from the stand, "bye Colin", he held his hand out and let Colin nuzzle against it, which he did. After a few nuzzles, he bit Abel's hand to let him nuzzle time had passed. The joke was on Colin, as biting the ADS felt like licking a battery.

Abel made his way out of the bedroom, though the hallway and out the front door. His base was an exact replica of his Mum and Dads bungalow back on Earth, complete with back and front garden. The whole thing was encased in a large pressure dome, with views of space in every direction. He didn't really mind living on his own. He had SARDOC; and Colin; and he got to hang out with the locals sometimes after missions had finished. Of course, they thought he was one of them, but what better way to get along with people? None of the "stranger danger" if you don't look like a stranger. He had always been what you would call a "social chameleon" on Earth anyway. Yep, he was happy enough on his own, he told himself. He subconsciously sang "All by Myself" as he got in the TTAXI. The irony was not lost on SARDOC, but like any good butler, he said nothing.

He plonked his besuited bottom onto the back seat of the TTAXI and closed the door behind him to seal the anti-time bubble.

"Where to, mate?" asked the driver, turning around and resting his left arm on the top of the seat.

Abel looked at him. Once again, he was dressed in a short sleeved, light blue denim shirt and dark blue denim jeans, with an ID card hanging from his neck. He had never been able to work out whether this was an android made to look like a real London cabbie, or they had actually abducted a cabbie just for his benefit.

Imagine trying to do the Knowledge for the whole universe?! How long would the exam be? But this aural assault of fashion apocalypse *must* mean he was a real person. Surely a race of super-advanced, universe-spanning aliens wouldn't have saddled their android with double Denim?!

He realised he had probably been staring at the driver for an uncomfortable amount of time and decided he had better answer.

"It's an adhoc investigatory mission. Igonid 3 please", as he told the driver, SARDOC uploaded the coordinates to the taxi's databanks.

The driver cranked down a red flag, that was next to a timer in the centre of the dashboard and the readout started counting down the seconds and milliseconds from 30:00. As the numbers diminished, the reactor could be heard beginning to heat up in the front. As it got louder, Abel fastened his seatbelt, the driver turned to face the front and grasped the steering wheel.

"You'll never guess who I had in this cab last time", exclaimed the driver, looking cheekily in the rear-view mirror.

"Me?" answered Abel, barely able to contain his anti-excitements hearing the same joke for the umpteenth time. SARDOC empathised completely.

"That's right," guffawed the Driver, "Ha-ha, ugh, gets me every time that one. Anyway, see the match last night?"

As the timer clicked down to three seconds, Abel thought to himself that the best thing about instantaneous travel is that its cuts out a lot of unnecessary small talk.

He had just finished that thought when the countdown hit zero. With not so much as a by-your-leave, 124,956 years were travelled and instantly untravelled.

In that time, roughly 2 billion generations of micro bacteria had lived and died on the outside of the TTAXI – bacterial civilisations came and went, microscopic empires lived and died. They even invented a toaster at one point, which was weird because they hadn't yet invented bread.

Thousands of generations later, Bacillian archaeologists found evidence of the great, Ancient Toaster and were laughed out of pathogenic universities by their peers, only to be proved right eventually. All this happened in the germic epochs of this one journey.

From Abel's point of view, he was there before he had time to cross his legs.

CHAPTER 3
THE MISSION IMPOSITION

The TTAXI heat shield crackled violently as it entered the atmosphere, bayonets of fire poking past the windows in an awe-inspiring display of what happens when physics meets chemistry, like a nerd fight in a university car park. Abel had indeed had his awe inspired the first few times it happened. Maybe even the first few hundred times had seen his awe's interest tweaked. But not now. He had seen this scenario play out enough times by now, that his awe was sat down in a comfy chair, reading the paper. If it did look up, it was a brief look over the folded down paper corner, like a Victorian father regarding his children before the Nanny took them off to bed.

The Driver engaged stealth mode as the TTAXI cleared the effects of atmospheric entry and the windows cleared. The Igonidian civilisation was still using the Earth-equivalent of Horse and Cart technology, just here the beast of burden was the Glomp. The Glomp was a six-foot-tall, four-legged creature with short, shaggy fur and a long face. Abel had often imagined it looked like a cow trying to get into a 'Llamas only' club by wearing the skin of one, propping up the neck and head using a plunger attached to its head.

Their carts were pretty much the same as Earth carts, as the universe had never really improved on the wheel for land-based, fuel-free conveyance.

This did make for an interesting cloak for the stealth mode though. Abel still got a mild kick out of seeing what the stealth mode CPU would come up with to help the TTAXI blend in with its surroundings. The Igonidian solution was always one of his favourites.

The TTAXI landed in a small clearing, away from the main trading paths and behind a small hill. A perfect infiltration point.

Abel disengaged the door lock as SARDOC prompted the suit to fold back up over his head. He climbed out of the door and knocked his newly configured Antennae on the frame as he did. He always forgot the antennae when he landed on a world requiring them. It was like writing the previous year on things until June of the following one. In remembering antennae terms, he was still only in March.

As he shut the door behind him, there it was. The Stealth Mode had yet again made it look as if he had climbed out of the Glomp's shaggy-furred backside. Quite what the locals would make of seeing one of their own climbing out of the anus of their favourite vehicle, Abel wondered, was anyone's guess. Unbeknownst to him, however, a local would probably have just thought the Igness Festival had come early this year.

"Hold position here," Abel instructed, as his suit's HUD started to fill up with red patches, "I'm picking up evidence of Wardz activity already. I'll call you in when I need you"

"No problem, skip" said the Glomp, as the Stealth Mode had made it look like the Driver's face was inside the animal's head.

'At least the Glomp isn't wearing double denim' thought Abel, as he turned away and headed towards the edge of the hill.

"I'm picking up high amounts of Anti-Matter residue around the other side of this hill, sir," SARDOC said in Abel's ear, "which would confirm our suspicions".

"*My* suspicions, S," corrected Abel, "You were busy roasting Flarg Nuts".

"Of course, my mistake sir," said SARDOC, apologetically. He declined to tell Abel that he had already heard the news bulletin about the disappearances an hour earlier and put in a pre-order for an adhoc mission before Colin had even finished licking his bum and decided to jump on his owner.

As he walked around the corner, the suit's HUD lit up with a plethora of red signatures, all in the place where the village should be.

"Disable the Anti-Matter signatures, S", asked Abel, "I want to get a look at what's left here".

As the measles on his HUD began to clear up, the devastation left behind by the Wardz attack was revealed. Rather than a crater, or anything resembling a bomb blast, there was simply a completely flat expanse where the village should be. Foundations of building were surgically cut at exactly ground level. Plants were dissected at the same point and the wound instantly quarterised, leaving no burn mark or bleeding whatsoever. It was as if the whole area had been chopped down by a mile-long, searing hot rotor blade.

"This is bigger and more planned than a normal Wardz attacks, S" said Abel, shocked. It was a long time since anything had shocked him.

He hadn't been this shocked since that incident on Zepular, when he tried to get in the wrong coffee animal, thinking it was his cloaked TTAXI.

"Indeed sir, there seems to be additional residual deposits leading towards the next village. Should we follow them?"

"I suppose we should..." Abel's voice trailed off, as he was struck by the beautiful sun rise appearing between the mountains in the distance.

His train of thought was violently derailed by the sight of a Glomp and cart beeping and its rear end opening.

The TTAXI followed the residual traces of Anti-Matter to the site where the next village used to be. They discovered the same thing as they did at the first ex-village, as well as more tracks.

As soon as Abel disembarked at the village, he could see the tracks were different this time. Fresher, redder. Redder than a pimple that won't squeeze, but you still spend ten minutes trying to squeeze it.

"I think they might still be here S," said Abel, touching the ground at the beginning of where the tracks headed away from the village site.

"Indeed, sir," concurred SARDOC, "I am reading moving signatures and a possible Wormhole less than 1km away".

Abel looked in the direction of the signature that SARDOC had added to his HUD. He could see the residual trail left by the creature's Entropiser, as well as black hole energy leaking from its degrading protection, "I've just never seen them cause so much damage in one sitting before. Their tech must be improving".

"I concur, sir. The longest sustained Wardz attack on record is 1 hour 57 minutes until now". SARDOC calculated from the databanks, "If they are still here, that makes this one approximately three hours already".

"...and the amount of dark energy they must have used to Entropise these three villages is much more than anything..."

Abel stopped mid-sentence as a small black spot appeared in the distance on his HUD. It looked like the black spot was heading back to the Wormhole, black ribbons of degrading protection spinning away from it. "Got him...engage sprint mode!"

SARDOC commanded the Nano Bytes to comply and the suit sprinted off in the direction of the spot. Even though the suit was doing the lion's share of the work, the bumping onto the ground still made his 46-year old knees hurt. Each time his foot connected with the ground, it was like stepping on Lego, or rather kneeling on it. It was a few hundred bricks worth before the Wardz seemed to realise it was being chased. Abel knew that it would take his target at least half a minute to get back to the safety of the Wormhole and if he could get to it before then, he could successfully Matter them into existence.

"Aim for Patrick's right bottom leg, as usual, S" commanded Abel, as the shape ceased to be a blob and took on the familiar five-legged, Starfish-like appearance. Abel had always thought they looked like a Black Patrick from *SpongeBob SquarePants*.

Without answering, SARDOC mustered the right hand of the suit to become a Matter cannon and fired with a bright, wobbly yellow flash. The glob of concentrated plasma whizzed toward the target and joined itself to the Wardz' leg. It kept trying to run, as the Matter began to weight it down, making it hobble and halving its speed. The Ward was visibly hampered by this experience, as they always were.

"I reckon ten seconds before he's gone," said Abel, through puffing cheeks, "how far before we can crack him?"

"Thirty yards until we can engage the scalpel boost, sir" answered SARDOC, "I estimate a successful first-time boost will complete the mission 1.47 seconds before they reached the Wormhole, sir".

"Then let's make sure it counts, S" said Abel, as his leg felt like he had stepped on a red 3x2, "Boost us as soon as we're in range!"

18 more bricks and he was there.

"Scalpel boost engaged, sir" SARDOC said, as the suit vaulted forward toward the hobbling Ward. While in mid-jump, the Nano Bytes around Abel's left hand formed into a razor-sharp triangular trident. The three prongs snapped together in preparation for the attack, forming a murderous cone. Abel landed on the back of the black spot with a *WHUMP*, the Nano Bytes on Abel's feet wrapping themselves around the Anti-Matter creature to fasten him down for the hard landing was about to come. The trident punctured the beast's suit right between its shoulders. Its prongs flattened and pulled apart, exposing a ten-centimetre hole that began to froth, as the Dark Energy of the Wardz began to react with the outside world. As soon as the hole was opened, the Matter cannon hovered quickly over it and unleashed another glob of yellow plasma. The Ward screamed it usual anti-scream, which Abel always thought sounded like the vacuum of sound left behind when a house alarm has stopped after going off for four bloody hours. As the concentrated plasma mixed with the Dark Energy, everything expanded like the foam you put in a wasp's nest, destroying the Ward from the inside and sending a large plume of matter out through the hole.

Abel and the creature tumbled to the floor and skidded to a halt. Through the dust that jolted up, Abel could see his TTAXI Glomping its way up the path, albeit quite a way back. Abel fell to the side as the weapons in the suit disengaged and became hands again. He was knackered and he hadn't really done anything.

"I'm getting too old for this S," he wheezed as he rolled over, clambered onto all fours and rocked into an upright position. This was always the hardest bit of a mission. The suit had used so much energy in the last few minutes that the Nano Bytes would always go into Eco-mode, meaning it was harder to move around until the microscopic robots had charged their Solar cells.

"Unfortunately sir, this is the life you have chosen sir," said SARDOC, reminding him of his duties, "With great power…"

"Don't quote *Spider-Man* to me, S" snapped Abel, "Don't bloody do that. I'm not being Uncle-Benned by you. Let's just go home, it's nearly time for The Hunt with Walshly Brad".

"Indeed, sir," replied SARDOC, in his best Nanny voice," I believe Flemington Dzz is the hunter tonight".

"Oh well, at least that's something," said Abel, perking up a bit whilst grabbing the bottom of his back, "Might get to see some of them snotted tonight then".

Abel trudged back to his double-denimed chauffeur in the Glomp and cart and thanked himself for a job well done with as much alacrity as you do when you've had a clean poo.

Before too long, he was back at base in his comfortable trousers, happily ensconced on the sofa, sipping a nice cup of tea and watching The Hunt. Colin had joined him to watch people getting snotted.

CHAPTER 4
THE RIP

Abel woke up with what was now becoming the customary shock. He had been dreaming of the lady in the morgue again. He lay there for a minute, on his back, contemplating his life whilst staring blankly at the ceiling. He was bored. If his career officer had told his 16-year old self that this is what he'd be doing in his mid-40s, he'd have snapped his hand off. But after defending the universe for six years, even being an intergalactic super-hero had become passé.

It was the longest he'd ever stuck at anything apart from counting Carrots in a supermarket though, so he was quite proud of himself in the grand scheme of things. He often wondered how his family had taken to his android replacement. He wondered if they had ever spotted the differences, if there were any. They probably hadn't noticed. In fact, the android was probably better at jogging.

Colin decided to break into Abel's thoughts by doing his customary bladder jump. Colin's paws and loud purr were better than any alarm clock.

"Who's a clever boy," asked Abel, smushing Colin's head together at the ears, "Ooo, if I could squeeze out the cute juice and bottle it, I'd be a millionaire!" Abel had long since become immune to how stupid that sentence sounded.

Colin pulled away as he had no wish to be squeezed and bottled. He did, however, want to be fed.

Abel shambled to the toilet and Colin was around his legs as he sat there. He gave a little 'meow' as he reached up and put his front paws on Abel's knees. It sounded cute, but only because Abel didn't speak Cat. If he did, he'd have been shocked at such explicit language.

As Abel bent down to feed Colin, SARDOC activated the display wall.

"I'm getting an emergency report from Yicorth 6" said SARDOC, as the 3D image of the planet coalesced in the lounge, "Another Wardz attack. Similar in size to the last one, sir".

"Okay, ready the suit S", replied Abel, as he squeezed the rest of the pouch into Colin's bowl, his knees still sore from the mission the day before, "No rest for the wicked, I guess".

"I've taken the liberty of already calling a TTAXI, sir", said SARDOC, as two red blobs appeared on the planet image.

"Good idea," Abel walked back to the bedroom and reappeared a minute later, the suit in the process of covering his limbs. Her grabbed the breakfast smoothie that SARDOC had prepared for him as he made for the hallway. He took one sip and blanched at the horrendous flavour.

"What's in this breakfast smoothie?!" Abel exclaimed, wiping his lips with his hand as if trying to delete the taste.

"I incorporated all the elements of your normal Tuesday break fast, sir," replied his digital butler, "Coffee, Mango and Gluten Free Crumpets".

"When I say I want a breakfast smoothie, I mean Strawberries, Blueberries, maybe some Oats!" Cried Abel, his tongue licking in and out in the same way Colin's did when he had a hair stuck in his throat.

"Duly noted, sir".

As Abel opened the front door, the TTAXI appeared in the driveway. 'Trusty old DD' he thought, as the driver lolled a hairy, blue-topped arm against the window.

"Yicorth, in the Ulia system!" shouted Abel as he climbed in. Emergency missions were a bit of a dichotomy for Abel; on one hand he never felt fully prepared for them; on the other it was about the only time he still felt the rush of excitement. He was there in the time he took him to ponder this thought.

-

"I don't think we've been to Yicorth, have we S?" enquired Abel, as the TTAXI began its atmospheric entry routine. "What do we know about it?"

"This is indeed your first visit, sir" confirmed SARDOC, "Yicorth is a modern, class-D society, with energy weapon capability and interstellar space flight. Their society is approximately two thousand years ahead of what you would call '20th century Earth'. They have so far refused any attempts

49

to involve them in the Galactic Alliance, as they don't like the colour scheme. The average Yicorthite will shoot first and not bother with the questions. They should be approached with caution. They are known for their argumentative attitude and their extreme pedantry".

"Blimey, if you want to get my suit to blend in with this lot," offered Abel, "You should disguise me as my ex-wife!"

"I don't believe she had three rows of teeth or back spikes, did she sir?" asked SARDOC, playing dumb.

"Don't worry S," he said as they landed on the outskirts of what looked like a city that was half on the ground and half suspended in mid-air. It appeared to Abel like the city had been built flat and then folded along a horizontal axis to save space. If this megalopolis wasn't called Calzone, they were missing a trick.

"Let's get out and see what we can see".

What they could see was remarkably like what they had seen on Igonid 3. A huge area of the city had been flattened, surgically and carefully.

The Wardz were clearly evolving, both militarily and strategically. Their destruction up to this point had been wanton and random, like a toddler running around a toyshop with a sandwich and getting jam on everything. They usually destroyed as much as they could in the time they had and then warped back to their reality. But this…this was more calculated.

"Send up a Nano-drone and see if we can get an aerial view of the affected sites", Abel commanded, as a few hundred thousand Nano Bytes broke away from his suit, formed a small, rectangular camera drone and ascended into the purple, cloudless sky. It went as high as it could, before it bumped into an upside-down street light on the upper part of the city. No one noticed, except the uniformed Yicorthite police officer who was coming out of the Googolnut shop nearby. The drone began to scan the city for evidence of Anti-Matter activity, unaware it was now being watched. The image from the drone was relayed to Abel's HUD and a pattern was becoming clear. A worrying pattern.

"Oh great," Abel said, astonished. He could see from the shape created by the attack sites, that they were in a large ring around the outskirts, equidistant from each other. All except a gap at what would be South East on an Earth Compass (or Flirp Nock on a Venusian one), "They're trying to Entropise the whole city in one go!"

"I would strongly advise against letting them complete the circle, sir," said SARDOC calmly, "It has the potential to create an anti-matter gateway, the size of which could destroy the whole planet".

"You think?!" exclaimed Abel, rushing back to the TTAXI, "Recall the drone!"

Unbeknownst to anyone, the Yicorthite police officer continued to follow the drone's movements as it returned to its suit. He started his Police Maglev Bike and sped off to question the source of the drone. By question of course, he meant shoot. The Yicorthite police interrogation was generally regarded to be both their greatest strength and their most glaring weakness. Most of the time, the very real fear of being shot would mean suspects blurted out their information very quickly. Sometimes however, the urge to shoot someone in the face would prove too great for the Interrogator and he would be left with only half the information, after killing the suspect in mid-sentence.

51

-

"Head directly for these coordinates", shouted Abel, as SARDOC relayed the data to the driver's screen.

"Too bloody right!" exulted the driver, who seemed genuinely excited to get to do some real driving for a change, "I've never done proper police chase before!"

Abel sighed, 'I remember that feeling' he thought. 'What's wrong with me? I'm chasing an impossible alien in an *Iron Man* suit, with the safety of the Universe at stake. And all I want is a cup of tea and an episode of Paintless'.

But even Abel didn't have time for moping or introspection right now. The TTAXI sped through the access road and onto the highway that connected the vertical halves of the city. The intersections made Spaghetti Junction look like Route 66. If anything, it could have been called 'Headphone cables that have been in a drawer for two years and you need to use them quickly' junction.

"I've plotted the fastest route to the final site, sir", said SARDOC, "It will take us 1 minute and 15 seconds to get there".

"Put it on the dash clock S," instructed Abel. As he did so, a very official looking Yicorthite pulled up alongside the TTAXI and motioned to the driver with his claw to wind down his window. The driver dutifully complied. The next thing Abel knew he was being showered with the driver's brain matter. The Yicorthite interrogation had been really short, even for them.

"What the…?!" exclaimed Abel, vaulting back in his chair, and trying to wipe bits of double Denim's brains off his visor.

"…And don't do it again!", the Yicorthite shouted. He then shot twice more through the dashboard for good measure, before pulling away and disappearing down a side lane.

The TTAXI began to gently swerve off-course as the driver's headless body slid towards the side door.

"Is there an auto pilot on these TTAXIs, S?" asked Abel, suddenly realising he'd never thought to ask before.

"Unfortunately not sir," replied SARDOC, "I can control take-off and landing, but not ground travel or time jumps".

"Fabulous," complained Abel sarcastically, as he lifted his legs up to the window separating the back and front seats.

"That's just frigging fabulous," With one suit-enhanced kick, the plastiglass panel popped out, giving Abel access to the driver's section.

"Intergalactic, time travelling taxis and they can't install a bloody auto-pilot," he tossed the shards of shattered plastiglass into the back seat and clambered into the front passenger seat.

"Actually, the auto-pilot system was taken out after the Bomoa incident, sir" said SARDOC, almost sounding defensive, "It would appear to have been damaged anyway, sir".

"Okay, good to know," said Abel, as he reached across the driver's neck stump and opened the driver's door. With the gentlest of pushes, double-denim became a hairy, two-shades-of-blue speed bump.

Abel shimmied across and took command of the steering wheel. For a few seconds, he even felt like he knew what he was doing. The feeling was dispelled as quickly as the TTAXI lurched towards the other side of the road.

"It doesn't respond like a normal car, S" shouted Abel, as he tried in vain to keep the TTAXI straight.

"Clearly…" replied SARDOC, "…and it appears the route mapping function has also been disabled by the second shot, sir. Without that, we have no way of navigating to the target in time".

"How long do we have?" asked Abel.

"I estimate the next event will happen in 37 seconds, sir"

Abel looked around with his suit HUD and realised the site was almost directly below them. At the same time, a warning light starting flashing on the dashboard. Abel was perturbed, not only because warning lights are never good, but because this one had a skull on it.

"What's that mean S?" shouted Abel, "That can't be good".

"Indeed not, sir," agreed SARDOC, "it would appear the reactor core has been breached. I estimate 35 seconds until it explodes"

"Hang on SARDOC", Abel turned the wheel sharply to the right, "I've got an idea!"

Abel crashed the TTAXI through the sidewall of the (very) high-way and for a few seconds, there was silence apart from the quiet whirring of the suit's faecal recycling systems kicking in.

"Well, it's certainly *an* idea, sir" replied SARDOC, as sarcastically as his programming would let him.

The TTAXI began to pick up speed as it neared terminal velocity. Abel attempted to control the descent as much as he could, but the damaged systems could only do so much. He wrestled with the steering wheel like a fisherman trying to navigate the high seas in a boat called Deidre.

"If this TTAXI explodes, what blast radius are we looking at?" asked Abel, as the red spots grew larger and larger in his HUD. The Entropisation was seconds away now.

"The explosion will destroy anything within 500 metres, sir"

"And are we right on top of the target now?"

"It would appear so, sir"

"Okay, I'm out of here. Get ready with scalpel boost when I need it S!" Abel climbed out the door and scaled up the side of the TTAXI. He stood on the boot and prepared to jump.

"Engage Scalpel boost...now!" he shouted. As he jumped, the boost from his foot boosters catapulted him horizontally for a few seconds, giving him the impression of what this suit would feel like if it could fly. Now he really did feel like *Iron Man*. It was less than five seconds before gravity caught up with him.

Abel and the fatally damaged TTAXI were now both falling side by side as if engaged in a vertical race into the jaws of death. Starfish shaped black spots could be seen in Abel's HUD jolting their head stalks upwards, as if to say "Huh, doesn't it get dark quickly on this planet", before they disappeared beneath the TTAXI.

They both hit the ground at the same time, except that Abel hit with an *OOF* and the TTAXI hit with a very large *BOOM*. The blast incinerated everything in the blast radius in seconds, including the half of Abel's suit that was closest to it, millions of tiny Nano Bytes giving their life to protect their pilot.

The secondary blast picked him up and threw him back as the remaining Nano Bytes frantically tried to compensate for their losses by diverting armour to the areas about to meet the ground.

"Unfortunately, you did not jump quite far enough away from the explosion, sir" SARDOC said from the circle of armour covering the Agent's left nipple.

"Thanks for the update, Captain Obvious," coughed Abel, as he struggled to his bare feet, "at least we stopped the Wardz".

The remains of his suit made him look like he was about to go bodyboarding. As he stood up, he could see what looked like a ten-feet high, glowing mouth, with sparks pouring from it, which had appeared at the centre of the blast.

The mouth yawned open and Abel couldn't quite believe what confronted him. Through the hole, he could see another humanoid, who was definitely not Yicorthite. He appeared to be wearing the same sort of suit as Abel and it was also missing its head protection.

It was clearly another Agent, and he looked very familiar. In fact, he looked like…him. No, scratch that. He didn't *look* like him, he *was* him. Admittedly, a better looked after, physically fitter version of him. But definitely him. They stared at each other for what seemed like forever. The other version of him finally broke the silence.

"Who the hell is that, Sarge?" asked the other agent, 'He even sounds like me', thought Abel. In fact, the mystery Agent's voice was so much like Abel's, that both suits answered.

"Sir, that is Agent Abel, sir!" replied the stranger's suit in an American accent.

"That is Agent Rigsan, sir". replied SARDOC, in his normal voice

Before either agent had chance to say anything else, the mouth closed with a belch. The belch caused another explosion, that lead to Abel's third *OOF* of the last five minutes. Except this one rendered him unconscious…

CHAPTER 5
ONCE MORE, WITH FEELING

**EXETER, UK, TERRA, SOL SYSTEM, MILKY WAY, EARTH
YEAR 2012**

"I don't care what time it is, tell him I want the new renders on my workstation by 9am. And that's GMT, tell him. That's three hours. He's has two weeks to get them ready, tell him to get a shift on. And order more staples. Mark out".

It was always damp in Exeter. Especially this early in the morning. At 6am, everything seemed to be covered in a fine layer of water, no matter what the weather. During the summer days when it was actually warm, it would burn off. Or rather, it would ascend into the air and make it humid. Or 'clammy' as his Mum would say.

'Haven't seen Mum and Dad in a while,' Mark thought, his mind hopping on a tangent as it was prone to do. The logical side of his mind got out it's big butterfly net (as *it* was prone to do), caught the tangential thought and grounded it before it could get away, 'if I've got time, of course. Which I haven't.'

His calendar was indeed always packed. In between running his software company, RockHard Softworks and training for his next Iron Man Challenge, you would struggle to slide a piece of paper into the 'not busy' sections of his life; and that's the really posh paper you can buy at John Lewis. He somehow managed to have his kids once a fortnight, but now they were a bit older they were happy to watch YouTube videos of Cats and other people playing computer games on their laptops, while he caught up with emails on his. He even set his daily alarm for 4:25am, partly because it was the only way to fit everything in, but also because he once read an article saying most successful got up at 4:30 every day and he wanted to be better than them.

His iPhone 4 beeped in his headphones, meaning it was time to rest for 1 minute. He came to stop beside the river and put his fingers on his wrist to measure his heartrate. The sound of the wind rustling through the trees, the ducks quacking gently on the river and water lapping against the embankment, made for a perfect picture of relaxation. Or at least they would, had Mark's headphones not been drowning it all out with *Holding Out for A Hero* by *Bonnie Tyler*. He was fourteen songs into his 'Run Fat Boy' custom playlist and he wouldn't be turning it off until at least *Rebel Yell* by *Billy Idol*. As if it had been waiting for him to stop, his phone started ringing. He pressed the button on the headphone cord and started speaking, fully expecting it to be Deidre, his PA.

"Go for Mark...oh hi Dad," he subconsciously stopped jogging on the spot, as if he had regressed to being a son again, "No, I can talk. You're up early...yes, I know you can't reach me any other time. I don't accept personal calls at work...well I'm normally still at work in the evenings...anyway, what do you want, I'm in the middle of a run".

He listened for a moment and rolled his eyes.

"Well, you just have to…I know, it's confusing, I know…have you got your email password there…the pass…for the TalkTalk account, yeah"

He stretched his legs one at a time and tried to stretch away the frustration of the phone call.

"It's in your password book, isn't it…no, that's your account login…no, your phone account, not your email account…yes, it is confusing, I know…"

As the frustration grew, so did the depth of the stretches. Pretty soon, he'd be bent over double.

"It's definitely there, I remember writing it in the last time I was…got it? Under the other…yeah, that's right…944, yeah that's the one. Okay, no worries, see you whenever….I don't know I'm really busy at work at the moment. Bye!"

He breathed deeply and treated himself to an extra eye roll for good measure. The second beep meant he could set off again. As he did, his third step landed on an errant pebble from the embankment. First his ankle, then his leg, then his whole body buckled beneath him and for a few milliseconds his head felt like it was suspended in mid-air, like when Wile-E-Coyote would run off a cliff trying to catch the Road Runner. The irony of this situation was not lost on the watching Ducks, who quacked their amusement and resolved to tell the other Ducks when they met up later.

"Bloody pebbles!" he screamed his logical side, as he tumbled to the ground," every jogger's mortal enemy"

"Yeah, that and heart failure" laughed his tangential side, before being covered in a large imaginary net.

Mark collapsed to the floor in a heap, rolled over his shoulder and landed on his back, his cap falling off as his head came to rest, like a full stop on a particularly pathetic sentence.

He lay there for a few seconds while he processed what had happened, until his logical side had recovered enough to admonish him, "Get up," it said, "someone will see you!"

As he struggled to his feet, he tried to ignore how much his ankle was hurting. He looked down at it – it had already started to swell up. He left his sock where it was, although if he *had* moved it, he would have seen his ankle beginning to look like a roadmap of Paris, with his ankle bone being the Eifel Tower, about to be swallowed up.

"Run it off. No failures remember?" continued his logical side, as his tangential side glared at him from beneath the net.

Wishing I was Lucky by *Wet Wet Wet* came on his playlist, which was far too happy for his current situation.

'I wish I was lucky, Marty, he thought to himself as he prepared to start running again, 'I wish a lot of things. I wish I'd never got married. I wish people would do as they're told. I wish I'd never kissed Michelle Evans at the sixth form leavers disco!'

He started to run again, trying not make a little "ow" noise every time his right foot connected with the road. Instead, his face began a weird repeating series of expressions which made him look like he was trying to pass a Galia Melon.

'Michelle would have loved this' he thought, between grimaces, 'she never liked my running anyway'. Indeed, Michelle hadn't liked a lot of things he did, as most of them took him away from spending any time with her and the kids.

She'd never really understood his need to overcome the fear of failure. Ironically, it was the year of travelling with her in 1990 that had given him that confidence. But that was a long time and two kids ago. So it wasn't really a surprise when he came home early from a meeting and found her bent over the kitchen table with Ben from across the road. 'Her loss' he thought, 'Even if she did get the house. A small price to pay for the reduction in ear ache'.

The blood had started flowing round his ankle again, but it wasn't helping. If anything, it was making it worse. So much so that he stopped again, about fifty yards from the main road. It was still at least two miles to home. 'Don't think about it. Block it out, you wuss' barracked his logical side. This time there was no argument from his tangential side as it had got lost thinking about Fast Show clips.

Just as Jesse Farmer had told him that 'this week I have been mostly eating Taramasalata', a Black Cab pulled up at the side of the road.

"Don't you dare" he said out loud as the logical side took over the mouth area. He steeled himself and started to jog again. He got halfway to the Taxi. He could swear that he could feel the blood sloshing around inside his ankle joint now. "Oh bugger it, I'll get a Taxi home and do two miles on the treadmill. Give it a chance to rest".

He got in the back of the cab.

"The Quay please, drive", he huffed, still smarting from his lack of will power. He thought it was unusual when the locks engaged, but maybe it was some ridiculous new safety feature. PC gone mad, as usual, he thought.

"Nice area for a place, guv," said the driver, admiringly, "must have cost a packet".

"A bit, yeah," replied Mark quizzically, surprised at the cabbie's familiarity, "Why?"

"Just making conversation", replied the driver. Mark could see the driver's eyes staring at him in the rear-view mirror. He was shocked at how green the driver's eyes were. They almost glowed.

"Got an injury, did you?"

"Went over on my ankle," mark said as he shifted forward onto the edge of the seat, "look, shouldn't you be watching the road?!"

"Not like you, giving up like that" said the driver, still staring. "You normally just power through everything, don't you Mark?"

"Excuse me? How do you know my name?" he asked, panicking that this was either a kidnapping attempt (he was minted, after all) or Michelle's lawyers still tracking his movements.

"In fact, you've never really given up on anything except your marriage, have you?"

"How dare you!" shouted Mark. He'd been so transfixed with the driver's eyes, that he hadn't noticed that the Taxi was fast approaching the edge of Earth's atmosphere, "Where the hell are you taking me?"

"We've been watching you for a while Mark," said the driver, turning around to look at him, "I work for an organisation called Universal Corrections. You're exactly what we are looking for as a Galactic Defender and I'm afraid you don't have a choice in it".

Mark's panic subsided as his ego had just got the biggest stroking since he won Devon Businessman of the Year 2005. He subconsciously sat up in the seat and puffed his chest out,

"I knew it" he said through a newly-steeled jaw, as there was a bright yellow flash. The view of Earth out of the left window of the Taxi was suddenly replaced with that of a huge, wheel shaped Space Station...

CHAPTER 6
DÉJÀ VU, ALL OVER AGAIN

UNIVERSAL CORRECTIONS COMPOUND, UNKNOWN LOCATION, EARTH YEAR 2018

Agent Rigsan woke with a start as his alarm sounded that it was 6am.

"Wake up, you stinking maggot" commanded SARDOC, in his Deep Southern US accent, "If you are not out of that bed by the time I count to ten, it will be electrified!"

Rigsan swept his legs out over the side of the bed, knocking Colin the Cat onto the floor and waking him up in the process.

Colin shook his head rapidly and did the usual 'I meant to land like that' thing that Cats do, before waltzing off nonchalantly towards the kitchen area.

Rigsan sat for a second, before standing up in the way they show you how to stand up on a health and safety video. His body was a temple and he wasn't about to start putting cracks in it with shoddy routines.

"Now get down and give me Twenty, you pond scum!" shouted SARDOC, as *Runaway* by *Bon Jovi* began to blare out over the multipoint house speakers. He had managed to remember most his 'Run Fat Boy' exercise playlist from Earth and downloaded it to SARDOC.

Rigsan knelt on the cold hardwood floor, laid out flat on his stomach and started the push-ups. He liked his morning exercise routine. Particularly on mornings when he'd been dreaming of home, as it took his mind off it. He didn't want to miss home, as that showed weakness. And weakness could lead to failure, which wasn't an option. He was the universe's last line of defence against the Wardz. That wasn't his only enemy, but it had definitely started to feel like the main one. Everyone was expecting him to succeed and he was too good at what he did to let everyone down.

"Can you *HUFF* get my *HUFF* protein shake ready *HUFF* please, Sarge?" asked Rigsan in between reps, the first beads of sweat appearing on his forehead and upper lip as he neared the end.

"There's plenty of time for that solider, after you've proved you're worth it!" shouted SARDOC dismissively, "now give me a hundred sit-ups!"

Rigsan changed position and complied. He had asked for 'American Drill Sergeant' when given the options for SARDOC's personality implant at Orientation. He reasoned it would push him to be very best he could. And he did. He just wished he could turn his volume down a bit first thing in the morning.

'At least I didn't have the other dream again', he thought to himself as he neared 40 reps, 'I don't like the morgue one. What the hell does it mean?!'

He thought for a second of the woman who was always standing above him in the dream. He didn't particularly want to, as once he started thinking about her, those bright red glasses could stay with him for the rest of the day. As would the body storage door with his name on it. No matter what intergalactic, planet-hopping mission he was sent on, there were the glasses, lingering around at the back of his mind like a unwanted wasp at a BBQ. He hated himself those days for his lack of focus on the mission. At least, he hated the tangential side of his mind that his logical side couldn't control.

"Are you counting, Sarge, because I'm not"

"Of course I'm counting, maggot!" shouted SARDOC, "I can't trust you to do anything, can I?! 98…99…100 Now running on the spot for five minutes in 3…2…1 GO!"

Again, he complied, although he had arrived at the daily point when both sides of his mind agreed that they wanted SARDOC to blow a circuit. He knew he was about to. There was no doubt about it, he definitely favoured the half hour of Yoga that came after these bloody exercises.

-

The five minutes of stationary running felt like it took three times that. But it still came and went as all things do, and Rigsan was glad to move to the living area for Yoga. SARDOC dutifully changed the music to *Sad but True* by *Metallica*. That was about as relaxing as this playlist got.

"Can you hologise my protein shake now please, Sarge?" asked Rigsan, rubbing the sweat off his face with a towel. He was hoping that SARDOC's 'Morning Thunder' settings had finished, and he was back to his slightly-less-intense normal mode.

"Here you go, maggot!" SARDOC replied as a tall, white glass started to materialise on the table in front of him. The double set of golden rings looped their way up the glass, as it solidified beneath them. Whenever he thought to watch the process, he thought about the wet sock he would sometimes get before the double transmitter was invented.

"I'll have my Flarg Nuts after Yoga," he said, as he picked up the glass. It was now full of a foaming, thick green fluid, with what can only be described as dead flies floating in it.

He took a big gulp and choked a little bit, "10% less flies next time please Sarge". he croaked as he licked his lips to gather up the errant dried insect that has stuck there mid-spurt.

"Sir Yes Sir", complied SARDOC, "I will adjust the Hologiser settings straight away!" It wasn't that simple of course. The Hologiser and SARDOC didn't always see optical sensor to optical sensor. SARDOC usually accompanied any request now with some virtual flowers and a large bar of complimentary data.

Rigsan downed the rest of the viscous Fly smoothie and moved to the Yoga mat. Yoga helped to keep him supple. It helped with the strange noises that his knees were starting to make (that of course weren't happening, even though they were) and the pain in his back (that also wasn't there, even though it was). But most importantly, it seemed to deal with the errant farts that might need to come out that day. He had learnt very early on in this job that trumping in your Nano Byte suit was not a good idea. Especially if your diet (like his) contains a lot of vegetables. It had got to the point that even the Nano Bytes that formed the Faecal Recycling Systems had threatened to go on strike unless Rigsan found a way to minimise their exposure to the noxious fumes. They had even demonstrated during one mission by abandoning the area. This had left Rigsan looking like he was attempting to catch his target wearing butt-less Chaps.

"Engage the display wall, Sarge," Rigsan commanded, as he entered a Standing Forward Fold, "Let's see what's going on in the universe".

"Sir yes sir!" obeyed SARDOC, the wall starting to flicker. It looked as if the wall was full of fire flies, all waking up and shimmering their illuminated tails. After a few seconds, they began to turn either red, green or blue and started to close in on themselves, until they formed the familiar 3D images of Ichi and Ghukan Gav. The Gavs were the Thatovian husband and wife team who fronted Hello Infinity, the number one news show in the universe. Thatovians were a curious bunch. Only four feet in height, they have four arms (two on the front and two on the back) and five eyes (one at equidistant points on the front, left, rear and right and an additional one on the top of their head). Unbeknownst to Rigsan, a Thatovian invented the 3DVR video camera using a pair of their quintoculars. Her idea had subsequently been stolen by the being now known as Mark Zuckerberg on his journey to Earth.

They are also a matriarchy, with husbands being grown to the wives' exact specifications. If the female is not happy with the result, she has fourteen days to return him for a full refund. It does not affect her statutory rights.

"Later on, Silod 357 will be here to give us a sneak peek at what everyone will be wearing in the Brotath Nebula during stellar birthing season", reported Ghukan, happily. His crimson neck fold cover was particularly bright today. "And we've got Ollie Jaymiver here to show us how make a lovely Flermtwat Casserole for less than five Zondarian Dollars".

'Ugh, not Ollie Jaymiver' thought Rigsan, as he sunk into a Warrior One pose, 'why do all cooks in the universe have to pretend to be down with the kids? That restaurant he started on Qedox for young Straivats with only three birth mothers was a disaster!'

"But if you've just joined us, we have a developing situation on Yicorth 6," said Ichi, her throaty slurps being translated into Terran English by SARDOC, albeit with an American accent, "there are reports of warehouses disappearing around the outskirts of the capital city, Mrm. At this time, it is not known why"

"Sounds like we're needed, Sarge," said Rigsan, from out of his Downward Facing Dog. Colin wrapped himself around one of Rigsan's legs and meowed hungrily, "have you fed Colin yet Sarge?"

"Sir yes sir!" said SARDOC, "your Feline companion was administered sustenance at 0500 hours, 0600 hours and again at 0700 hours"

"Colin!" said a shocked Rigsan, peering at him through his tensely straight legs. Colin pretended not to notice, mainly by not noticing, "who's a naughty fat boy?! Maybe I'll leave my custom playlist playing for you!"

Colin cleaned his paw dismissively.

"Ready the suit, Sarge," said Rigsan, slowly coming to an upright position, with his hands on his hips, "Yicorth 6 needs its saviour!"

Rigsan couldn't see it of course, but if Colin had eyebrows he would have raised them sarcastically. Instead, he licked his arsehole and hoped his Human would get the metaphor.

Rigsan stood for a few seconds to complete the pose sequence properly and then strode off towards the suit chute. As he paced across the living area, he stopped only to straighten up the pens on his desk. Then the display tablet. Then the pens again. 'Everything in its right place' he thought, as he regarded the desk proudly. He carried on to a large tube in the corner of the living area, which opened with a *WHOOSH* as he approached. He turned around in front of it and backed in. It was just big enough for him to for his 6'1" body in and as soon as he was completely inside, the tube closed with another *whoosh*. The platform descended for a few seconds, until it opened into the equipment area of his compound (or the 'Rig Brig' as he called it, after Batman's Bat Cave in his favourite DC Comics).

He walked across the room to large cylinder, filled with a pulsating, metallic cloud. It always looked like a giant grey version of those luminous green spits one would hack up during a bout of Tonsillitis, Rigsan thought. Not that he could remember the last time he had been ill, of course. Even when he'd been stung in the eye by a wasp, he'd kept working. Much to his wife's annoyance. A glass panel opened in the side of the tube and Rigsan stepped in. The shape reacted to his presence, first by pulling away and then by beginning to join with it. Soon it was covering his hands and working its way down the tube. Pretty soon, it had engulfed his arms and was spreading across his chest and back. Rigsan loved this bit and admired himself in the strategically-placed mirror directly opposite the tube. He watched the Nano Bytes cover the remainder of his body and work their way up over his head.

He maintained eye contact with himself until the view went golden yellow and HUD popped up inside the helmet. He was complete again and ready to kick some Anti-matter ass.

"Have you called me a cab, Sarge?" he asked.

"Sir the TTAXI is incoming Sir," confirmed SARDOC, now in his ear, "T-minus 13 seconds until touchdown".

He stood admiring himself in the mirror until he heard the familiar *POP* of the TTAXI appearing outside the Garage door. It also opened automatically as he approached.

"Let's go waste some Wardz!" he shouted confidently as he climbed into the back seat.

-

'Who the hell wears one item of Denim, let alone two?' thought Rigsan, staring at the back of the driver's shirt. The clashing outfit assaulted his peripheral vision from between the gap in the front seats, 'what a complete tool! I mean, he's probably not minted like I was, but you can still look in a mirror before you come out, surely?!'

"Aren't you a bit hot in that?" he asked, shaking his head in disbelief, "Ever thought of mixing it up a bit? A Hawaiian shirt maybe? Chinos?"

"Nah, I love me Denim," replied the driver obliviously. The light of the little pocket button on his jeans glinting in the starlight as they left the atmosphere, "hardest wearing fabric in the universe, denim. Never bettered. You don't even have to wash it!"

If the driver had looked in the rear view mirror at that moment, he would have seen a face of disgust. The sort of face a person makes when they open the office fridge on a Monday morning and that idiot Greg from Accounts has left a half-eaten, unwrapped Tuna Sub in there since Friday lunchtime. But fortunately for everyone, the driver didn't and so his fashion sensibilities remained as untarnished as Greg's Sub had remained uneaten. Both however, belonged in the trash.

"Sir we have arrived sir!" said SARDOC. Rigsan was so fully obsessed with the driver's dress sense, that he had completely missed the trip. He finally managed to look out of the window and saw the familiar swirling plasma party that accompanied atmospheric entry.

"I don't think we've ever been to Yicorth, have we Sarge?" asked Rigsan, sitting up and waiting for his HUD to clear, "What are the locals like?"

"Well, they are some of the meanest sons of bitches in these here parts. They are clever enough to have gone into space but will blow their own Granny's britches off if she looked at 'em sideways. And don't get them started on joining the Galactic Alliance – they're too busy trying to 'Make Yicorth Great Again'"

"They still need saving, Sarge," said Rigsan, trying to do his best superhero voice, "So let's get down there and save em"

Rigsan hung his head out of the window so that his HUD could pinpoint any Anti-matter readings. Their last mission in the Xoyama system had been the biggest Wardz incursion so far. 'Their shielding must be getting better', he thought, scanning the ground far below as they approached the outskirts of Mrm. The city was like nothing Rigsan had ever seen before. Half of it was ground based, like a normal city and the other half was upside down and directly above it.

"It's like a city folder in half, Sarge" remarked Rigsan, agape.

"Sir it's like a Calzone sir!" exclaimed SARDOC, without a hint of humour.

As they circled the city, Rigsan could pick up a residual pattern. He could see that there were Wardz signatures all around the outskirts of both halves of the city, in a sort of vertical wheel pattern. There was still a gap in the virtual wheel, but the familiar red signature was growing in there too.

"Head for that gap there, driver". Rigsan opened the back door on the driver's side and leaned out, so that he was level with the driver's windows, on the outside. It took all his mouth control to not call the driver Denim. He pointed to a large grey warehouse to the front and left.

"Do you want stealth mode engaged, skip?" asked the Driver.

"Nah, we'll be fine up here," shouted Rigsan through the window, "According to Sarge, they've got space travel, but not air travel. They only invented space travel to win a bet. They don't trust each other enough to let anyone be above them. Engage it once we get a bit lower!"

They passed over a massive, confusing network of highways that connected the top and bottom bits of the city. If anyone had bothered to look down from the TTAXI at this moment, they'd have seen the Yicorthite Police Shooting Range. This was where young Yicorthite Police recruits would cut their three rows of razor-sharp teeth and practice shooting dummies in the face. This was before graduating and shooting real criminals in the face as fully qualified Officers. As the oblivious TTAXI sped across the clear, purple sky, the sunlight bounced off it and landed smack-bang in the orange eye of one of the Police recruits, Zlerg. Zlerg wasn't an average student. Sure, he was good at shooting things in the face, but then who wasn't. It was the Yicorthite national pastime, after all. No, Zlerg wanted to be famous. Zlerg had an idea that no one else had seemingly thought of until now. Zlerg wanted to start shooting criminals *in the back of the head,* or 'back face' as he adoringly called it. But before he could revolutionise Yicorthite Police work, he would need to make a name for himself – and in that moment, he decided that shooting down this Alien craft was just how he was going to go about it. So, very quietly, he went over to the weapons cabinet, picked out the biggest plasma cannon he could find, unlocked the safety catch and looked up.

By now, the TTAXI had come to a halt directly above the potential Wardz site, so that Rigsan could complete his area scan. Rigsan climbed onto the top of the TTAXI to get a better look and held up his right hand to the temple area of his helmet. His logical side liked to tell itself that it was because it helped him to focus. His tangential *knew* it was because he had seen a superhero do it in a movie once and he thought it looked cool.

"The readings are increasing, I bet they'll be through at any second!" shouted Rigsan.

"You sure you don't want stealth mode on now, skip?" shouted the worried driver, furtively looking at the ground below them.

He laid down on the roof and hung his head over the side, to look in the passenger window. He had to shout to be heard above the wind and the noise of the TTAXI's hover jets.

"Nah, they'll be too busy shooting each other down there to worry about us," said Rigsan flippantly, "As soon as the Wardz are through, we can cloak, descend to a safe jumping distance and then me and the Sarge will take care of the rest".

"T-minus 12 seconds to incursion, Sir!" interjected SARDOC.

"No problem boss!" shouted the driver, his hands tightening in anticipation on the steering wheel, "I'm ready when you are!"

The last syllable of his answer had only just escaped Denim's mouth, when the cab lit up from below with a blinding yellow light and a deafening crackling noise. The yellow plasma carried on up through the roof of the TTAXI and into the sky, narrowing missing Rigsan's leg by inches. Along the way, it popped the top of the driver's head off like he was a tube of toothpaste that had been squeezed too hard. Rigsan recoiled as brain matter was dispersed and instantly incinerated by the plasma bolt. As the light diminished, the driver's lifeless body slumped forward onto the half-disintegrated steering column and the TTAXI plunged violently forward.

"T-minus six seconds to incursion, Sir!" shouted SARDOC, as more plasma bolts fizzed through the cab, one narrowly missing Rigsan, who was now clinging onto the passenger side of the TTAXI as it plummeted to the ground below.

"I'll never get back inside in time in time, Sarge. Can you take control?"

"It will take 15 seconds for my systems to handshake with the TTAXI, sir," replied SARDOC, "and I reckon we will hit the ground in 7. We are going down!!"

Rigsan, now running on instinct, suddenly had an idea. He brought his legs up to his chest and placed his feet flat on the side of the TTAXI. He could see the Wormhole opening below him. The Wardz would be out any second, and he would have a surprise for them. A big surprise. A surprise that would turn out to be one as much for him as it would be to them.

"Engage Scalpel boost, Sarge!" he shouted. Nano Bytes flooded to his hands as his foot boosters fired, catapulting him away from the TTAXI and he thudded into the side of the neighbouring warehouse, with a noise that sounded like someone whacking two six-foot saucepans together. He was still a hundred feet from the ground when he began his fall towards the ground. He jabbed the sharp trident formed by his left hand through the thick, metallic wall of the warehouse. It was a desperate bid to slow himself down, but it seemed to be working to a point. He began to be showered in a mixture of sparks and dead Nano Bytes as his left hand cleaved down through the metal. SARDOC, knowing what Rigsan was trying to achieve, which was not dying, began to divert Nano Bytes from less essential areas of the suit to maintain the trident's integrity. More and more tiny robots rushing to the area to replace their expired comrades. He still hit the ground with enough force to knock him out for a few seconds.

Had he been conscious, he would have seen the hilarious sight of a raiding party of Wardz exiting a portal, looking up and disappearing below a nuclear-powered, time-travelling Black Cab. Which is a great shame, as it's exactly the sort of thing that would have made Rigsan's day. As it was, he missed the whole thing, including the explosion which picked him up and threw him against the side of the warehouse he'd just Nano-surfed down.

Rigsan finally came round to the sound of burning Cabs, crackling electrics and Yicorthites shouting gleefully in the middle distance. He looked curiously in the direction of the cheering and could see a young Yicorthite appearing and disappearing above a fence as they were carried around on the shoulders of their colleagues. As his mind began to clear, he looked up at the side of the warehouse. He had managed to gouge a slice out of the wall from top to bottom. It looked like King Kong had tried to open the building with a massive tin opener.

While his concussed brain attempted to imagine the amount of bubble wrap that would be needed to package up a kitchen utensil that big, something caught his eye at the crash site.

Apart from the burning carcass of the TTAXI and several fully-mattered Wardz, there was something happening *inside* the fire. As he staggered towards it in what was left of his suit, he could see what looked like a ten-foot high, glittering zipper. It glimmered, but not from the sunlight – this was making *its own* light. He kept shuffling towards it, open mouthed. When he got within twenty feet of it, the zipper opened. Through the hole created, he could see a humanoid. 'Definitely not Yicorthite', he thought, 'not enough teeth and he hasn't shot me yet'.

The humanoid seemed to be glowing like Rigsan was. His suit was also damaged. 'Hang on', thought Rigsan as his head cleared a bit more, 'That's MY suit!'

As his gaze got up to the mysterious humanoid's head, he thought something even more incredible. 'And that's MY face! Fatter, balder and greyer, but that's MY face?!'

They stared at each other in disbelief. Finally, Rigsan thought he had better say something.

"Who the hell is that?" shouted Rigsan, so SARDOC would hear him from wherever he was in the suit. To his amazement and confusion, the humanoid's suit answered, just after Sarge.

"That is Agent Abel" replied Sarge.

"That is Agent Rigsan" replied the humanoid's suit, in a posh English accent.

Rigsan blinked his eyes in disbelief. Before he could get his thoughts together and arrest the man for illegal possession of a Nano Byte suit, the zipper zipped back up with a snap. The blast threw him back into the side of the warehouse.

'I wish I had that bubble wrap' he sighed to himself before passing out again.

CHAPTER 7
QUESTION TIME

Agent Abel woke up back in his bed in the bungalow. He had the largest, most throbbing headache he could ever remember. It wasn't this bad after the Betamaj excursion when the whole mission was underground, and he kept hitting his head on the roof of the cave. It was even worse than the night he'd tried Sake for the first and only time. That night he'd slept in the garden and missed his mate running and down the street naked. One of those headaches where you hear the blood rushing through your ears, on its way to beat your frontal lobe with lump hammers. The memories of how he got into bed were very fuzzy. Fuzzier than a Kimakran Monbat after it had straightened its fur and then got caught in a rainstorm.

He struggled to remember events of the mission that had led to his current state of pain-soaked repose. As he lay there completely still, images of the previous day began to filter through his mind, like the tail lights of the car in front of you on the motorway in a fog. The Wardz readings, bigger than ever before, the newly-coordinated nature of them, the chase across the highway, the crash…then the thought that blazed like that one idiot that's left his fog light on because he doesn't know how to turn it off – the other agent. It was this thought that made Abel speak for the first time that day.

"SARDOC?" said Abel, into the air, "You there?"

"Of course sir," replied SARDOC, helpfully, "As always".

"How did I get home?" he asked, as Colin jumped up onto the bed, looking surprisingly content.

"I took the liberty of calling an emergency transit team, sir," replied SARDOC, as Colin nuzzled Abel's outstretched hand, turned around several times, and settled down in a lump of Cat between Abel's side and his right arm.

"Good thinking, S," said Abel, "it was quite hairy there for a minute or two".

"I did not detect any hair growth above normal levels during the accident sir," replied SARDOC, "Perhaps I should check the Nano Suit's sensors?"

"No, it's a…" Abel stopped his explanation midway through, as he realised it wouldn't help, "What I mean is that it was all a bit…last minute".

"Indeed sir, I believe I calculated a 0.83% chance of success at the point of the driver's death. I would never have thought of resolving the situation by exploding the TTAXI on top of the enemy. That is probably why Control persist with having a sentient being in the suit, sir".

"You sound disappointed with that fact, S," said Abel, sniggering.

"Not at all sir" replied SARDOC, unconvincingly, "We are here to serve".

"Indeed you are S," said Abel mimicking SARDOC's upper-class accent as he raised an eyebrow, "So with that in mind, are you programmed to tell me the truth?"

"I am programmed to protect you and help you in any way that will assure our ongoing success sir". replied SARDOC. If Abel didn't know SARDOC better, he would swear his digital butler was being evasive. That sounded like an answer a politician would give in a Breakfast TV interview.

"SARDOC?"

"Yes sir?"

"I was told at my Orientation that I was the only Agent. Is that true?" There was a pause before SARDOC's reply. A pause that Abel couldn't ever remember his assistant ever taking before, unless he had powered down some of his circuits for maintenance. You could have parked a metaphorical bus in the gap between question and answer. Finally, SARDOC answered.

"Sir, you are the only Agent defending this universe". He replied, in a classic example of an answer that generates more questions.

"So who was the Agent I saw through the portal?!" asked Abel, raising his head off the pillow for the first time that day. The pain that coursed through his brain at that moment convinced him to lay it down again.

"That was Agent Rigsan sir". replied SARDOC, who sounded like he thought he was helping.

"Well, if I'm the only defender of this universe, then who the bloody hell is Agent Rigsan?!" Abel really wanted to shout in frustration, but the myriad animals having the pain party in his head wouldn't let him, "because he was me!"

"Agent Rigsan most definitely is NOT you, sir" replied, "Due to the fact that only you are you".

"Are you making fun of me?" asked Abel, sharply.

"It is not within my programming to make fun of you sir, unless you specifically ask for the Sarcasm subroutines to be unlocked".

This was not something that Abel was ever planning to do, as he thought SARDOC had quite enough sass already. This job was hard enough already, without your suit telling you you're an idiot on top of it.

"So, is he a clone of me then? He looked exactly the same as me! You even answered him, so he's got the same voice as well?!"

"I am programmed to recognise and respond to your voice patterns. He doesn't look exactly like you though sir. He weighs 14 kilograms less than you and has 45912 more hair follicles". Replied SARDOC.

"Hey, what are you trying to do here S?" Abel cried, lifting his head again and pointing his finger at the ceiling, "I'm feeling bad enough already!"

"I'm afraid those are the major differences between you, sir"

"I could see that S, I'm not blind. Still…cheap shot"

"I'm afraid I have no more information than that, sir. You would need to speak to the Head of Control for more information".

"Well then, let's get 'em on the phone!" said Abel, sarcastically waving his hand in front of him in a sweeping motion.

He had never realised there was a *Head* of Control. He'd always assumed that the Cromulite scientists who had given him the suit and his TTAXI were in charge. In fact, when he thought about it, all he had ever seen of the UC Compound were the Orientation Station and this bungalow. He'd been so busy assassinating traitors and cracking open Wardz to really think about it. But now, since he had seen a buff, tanned version of him through that whatever-it-was, he'd realised he had a lot of questions. Judging by the conversation he'd just had, he wasn't going to get them from SARDOC. One of the main ones being – if you were going to clone me, why make it a much better version?! That's just rubbing his nose in it.

He resolved to wait, carry on as normal and await an opportunity to find out more. He would start by doing what every right-minded Human male would do when he had thinking to do – he would go to the toilet. He hoped the fast-asleep Colin at his side would understand.

He gently put his hands on either side of Colin's belly and slid him from one side of his stomach to the other. Colin gave a half-hearted 'meow' of admonishment as he slid across Abel's belly, but was soon comfortable where he had now been placed. He kept his head up just long enough to see Abel struggle to the edge of the bed, before plonking his chin back down between his tail and back paw.

Abel did his usual 'psyching himself up' before straining to a standing position, with all the usual accompanying noises. And by normal, it meant sounding like someone eating Doritos whilst being punched in the stomach. He hobbled out of the bedroom and along the hall to the toilet. His favourite graphic novel, Watchmen, was waiting for him in the magazine caddy by the side of the bowl.

He sat there for a several minutes, thinking on things that had happened. He briefly wondered, as he always did when reading *Watchmen*, whether he'd look good in a blotchy mask and a trench coat like *Rorschach*. He finished the chapter he was on (you can't stop halfway through a chapter of *Watchmen*, whether you've finished your ablutions or not) and placed the book back in the caddy. His mind was still alive with questions. Perhaps some intergalactic TV would help take his mind off them while he awaited his opportunity?

"Engage the display wall, please S" Abel asked, as he walked to the Living Area, "And get me a cup of tea and some Ibuprofen".

"Very good, sir" obeyed SARDOC, as the sound of the hologiser could be heard from the living area. Abel slumped down onto the sofa and put his feet up on the table. He realised just in time that he'd put them right in the space where his tea and tablets would appear and moved them quickly to the right.

The display wall began forming the 3D images. The Bungalow could receive 125 channels, most of which were produced and transmitted by CBS, the Cosmic Broadcasting Service, from their headquarters on Qedox. Their patented 'Qcast' (or Quantum Broadcast) technology meant their signal could be picked up anywhere in the known universe, if the recipient had a CBS Qivo box. Abel had found out on a mission to Qedox, that CBS had sent sales teams to Earth several years before. They had gone to Area 51 which they had assumed from the name was a shopping mall, a perfect place to generate interest in their product. When worrying reports came back to Qedox that the sales reps had been experimented on and their tech stolen, the Sol expansion project was abandoned until the Terrans had stopped being so aggressive. They are still waiting.

The 3D images came together just as an advert for Paintless came on.

"Why not join Gurble and Shurble Flurble, the double trouble brothers at 5 o'clock GST for another episode of the hit quiz show Paintless, where contestants attempt to answer general knowledge questions while the brothers fire paintballs at them".

Abel guffawed at the advert, as images of contestants getting hit by football-sized Paintballs as they try to name the biggest stars in the Milky way. It was just what he needed. Part of him hated himself for liking such low-brow entertainment. The part that thought he was cool because his favourite stand-up comedian was Bill Hicks. But this was a very small part. This part was currently sat in the corner of the mental party not talking to anyone, while all the other personality traits were having a good laugh.

The adverts ended and the rolling news channel resumed its reports. "Incredible news is reaching us from Zondar that the GMF (the Galactic Monetary Fund) is being rocked by a bribery scandal". Said the news reader, his fake shock almost palpable, "CBS has gained exclusive access to a former employee turned whistle blower, who tells us that there are still some higher-ranking officials within the GMF who are NOT currently susceptible to bribes. The full story on this unbelievable revelation in our main news at 10".

"It's certainly hard to believe", said the other news reader, as he wiped the slobber off his fifth eye, with one of his three tongues.

'A few years ago I'd have found a lot of things about this situation hard to believe,' thought Abel, looking around his bungalow in space as he blew on his hologised tea, 'but Galactic bankers who don't take kickbacks would still be the most impossible thing I've heard'.

He took a little swig to check it was cool enough to swig. It was right on the line between swigging and consonant-burning, so Abel decided to wait thirty seconds before picking up his tablets.

"Better get me two Co-codamols as well, S" he said quietly, almost guiltily.

"They will not help your current medical condition, sir," replied SARDOC, seemingly oblivious to his admonishing tone.

"Probably not, S" said Abel, leaning forward in his seat, "but they will damn sure make me feel better".

"Very well, sir" replied SARDOC, his Home Counties accent inflecting a sarcasm that Abel was never sure was intended or not.

He'd decided a long time ago that SARDOC was indeed oblivious to his sarcastic tone. SARDOC had decided at around the same time that Abel was indeed oblivious to his intended sarcasm.

The small, bullet shaped caplets appeared on the table next to the already-materialised Ibuprofens. Abel paused for a moment and looked at them. There was always a moment before he took them that he thought he probably shouldn't. To be honest, he'd been taking them so long, there was usually a moment a few hours after he'd taken them that he felt like he shouldn't.

But like he said to SARDOC, there was usually an hour where they made him feel great. And there was always something else to do that stopped him from considering withdrawing from them. Then a familiar thought decided the matter for him,

'Oh sod it,'

He picked up the four tablets, threw them in his mouth, took a big swig of Tea and swallowed them. He always had a little chuckle to himself, as he remembered he hadn't been able to take even one tablet until he was an adult. He imagined what it would be like at 46, having his tablets crushed up and added to a spoonful of Jam.

He sat back in his seat and waited for the tablets to take effect. The Ibuprofen would take care of his headache. The Co-codamols would take care of the mind inside.

"In other news," continued the second news reader as his name, 'Proog Whitzar', appeared on the ticker along the bottom of the screen, "Ordrot officials have continued their talks about their departure from the Galactic Alliance. Viewers may remember that 52% of Ordrots voted to leave the Galactic Alliance two standard years ago in a hastily-prepared and bitterly-fought referendum. Both sides have repeatedly accused the other of lying about the viability of a planet leaving the Galaxy that it resides in. And indeed, it is on this very subject that talks appear to have broken down today. Here is Taume Gonkriss with a report from outside the GA negotiation centre".

"Thanks Proog," the reporter appeared on the monitor behind the news reader. He was stood in front of a large stone building, with Roman columns stretching off into the distance. Between Taume and the gigantic building, about fifty Ordrots could be seen demonstrating, holding placards that read 'Strength and Stability' and 'Make Qukra Great Again',

"Yes another day of stalemate here at GAHQ on Ulepip, as the Ordrots have again refused to believe that a planet cannot leave the Galaxy it is in. They say they are developing sub-light

91

planet-sized engines capable of moving the planet into the Great Void, the area of the Galaxy currently not covered by the Alliance. It says that from there, they will be able to negotiate trade deals with other Galaxies.

Failing the invention of the engines, they have apparently listed 'Positive thinking' as their second option".

"But won't those Galaxies be too far away, Taume?" asked Proog, holding up a pencil to his mouth to try and look intelligent.

"One would have thought so, Proog", continued Taume, "But the ruling Ordrots are insistent. Of course, the irony here Proog is that the Ordrots only occupied Qukra because they had ruined the neighbouring planet, Vime. Now they appear to be on the verge on ruining another one".

"I'm sure we'll find out soon, with Quxit Day fast approaching," said Proog, turning away from the monitor, "Thanks Taume".

As Abel shook his head in disbelief, it was strangely comforting to him that being a stubborn idiot was not a character trait that was peculiar to the Human Race.

"Seems like my ratio is still holding strong S" he said, with a wry grin.

"So it appears, sir" replied SARDOC. Surprisingly, Agent Abel's contention that 3 in every 10 sentient beings are what would be generally regarded as 'idiots' seemed to hold true in SARDOC's estimations.

Of course, it depended on your definition of an idiot. Abel wasn't referring to those beings with mental issues or learning disabilities when he used the term. No, he was referring to those in society that drive in the middle lane of life. Those who take up the whole aisle in a supermarket by gormlessly zig zagging with their trolley. The ones who

have idiot children that climb up the slide in the park and ruin it for everyone else. The real idiots. However, as it was an average, some places would see a dearth of idiots and some would see a conglomeration of them. And when that happened, like it seemed was happening on Qukra, you're in trouble.

As Abel sat there, trying to think of a way to find out more about this 'Agent Rigsan' character, the tablets started to take effect. He felt the Ibuprofens start to lessen his headache and the felt the Co-Codamols give him a big, warm, squishy mental cuddle. He visibly relaxed in his seat and lolled his head on the top of the back until he was staring at the ceiling. He watched the Gleamtron anti-gravity floor cleaner silently glide around the ceiling for at least a few minutes, while he thought about what to do. Then it came to him. The TTAXIs he used must come from somewhere, he reasoned. There was more than one driver and indeed more than one TTAXI. He'd noticed some chewing gum left on the side column of the back door in one before, which had disappeared and reappeared a few times. He'd always assumed that it had been left there by the cleaning crew in a show of defiance. But maybe it was this 'Agent Rigsan' bloke that had left it there. He had only seen this mysterious person for their toy seconds, but he had seemed like a Gum chewer. 'That settles it, he *must* be a clone', thought Abel. 'They must be using him for missions when I'm already busy. Maybe they're making a film about me on Yicorth 6 and that was the clone who's playing me?'

He decided he would rest up for a few days, emergency missions permitting, commandeer the first adhoc TTAXI he was in and force the driver to take him back to wherever he had come from. Surely, there would be more answers there.

CHAPTER 8
I'M THE DANDY HIGHWAYMAN

Abel awoke at the usual time. The usual time being Colin deciding he was hungry, of course. As his eyes opened properly and started to focus, he realised that for the first time in three days, he didn't have a headache. Sure, he felt a bit dehydrated, but that was normal after his traditional 'sweating like a escaped convict in a corn field' method of sleeping that seemed to be the default setting nowadays. He also realised that he'd had the morgue dream again for the first time since the crash. So even his subconscious was repairing itself, back to its angst-ridden, chamber of horrors- style norm.

Then another thought followed hot on the heels of these – today's the day. Today's the day I get some answers. Or least, get more questions from another area of Universal Corrections. And possibly the sack from the job of Cosmic Defender. Whatever happened, today was not going to go the way of every other day since he had been here.

He got out of bed and headed for the loo. As previously mentioned, it was where he found he did his best thinking.

"Good morning S," said Abel, in his best 'everything's normal, move along' voice.

"Good morning sir," replied SARDOC, "The usual for breakfast, is it?"

"Indeed, Tea and Flarg Nuts, the cornerstone of any nutritious diet!"

SARDOC's silence spoke volumes. One of the most advanced Artificial Intelligence programs in the known universe, but sadly lacking in picking up Pulp Fiction references.

Abel made sure that he followed his normal routine for the next hour – breakfast, TV, twenty half-hearted sit ups and quietly secreting a Nano cannon down his pyjama bottoms. Okay, so that last one wasn't part of the normal routine, but SARDOC didn't see it. He was biding his time. Finally, he saw the right opportunity to call an adhoc TTAXI.

"Next on CBS News, we go over to the Tulgik system and our daily Quxit update from GAHQ" said the news reader, as Proog's all-too-familiar face appear on the monitor behind him.

'This is it', thought Abel, drawing his hand surreptitiously against the hidden gun in his pyjama pocket.

"S, call me an adhoc TTAXI please," he commanded, struggling up off the floor, "I'm going to take a trip to Ulepip".

"Really sir?" queried SARDOC, "I haven't received any reports of any high value target or Anti-matter occurrences in that system?"

"No, I know, just thought they might need a hand with…" he paused, weighing up the smorgasbord of potential lies in his head, "…crowd control".

"Seems a little below your skills, sir" pressed SARDOC. It was the first time Abel could remember that his digital assistant had questioned an order from him. His pulse started to quicken – did he suspect something? Had he been watching him more closely since the crash? Had he seen his steal the Nano cannon after all?

"Oh, you know me S" said Abel, trying to hide the quiver in his voice, "Always out to help the common man. Or whatever the police are on Ulepip?"

"Umakoam sir, and they do seem to be struggling to keep control of the influx of Ordrot protestors, judging by the latest news reports. Their pressure suits limit their movement".

"Well, there you are then!" replied Abel, jutting out his arm in agreement and trying to pretend it wasn't lightly shaking.

"Very well, sir," obliged SARDOC, "the TTAXI will be here in two minutes".

"Excellent, well done S" said Abel, wincing. He'd never complimented SARDOC before. Damn you Adrenaline! "I'll go and wait outside for him".

"Shall I prepare the suit, sir?" asked SARDOC, making Abel freeze in the doorway. 'Don't make it look too obvious, you idiot', he thought. He relaxed his shoulder and turned his body around slowly.

"Ha ha, yes of course S, what am I thinking?" he said, as light heartedly as he could manage, "You get the suit ready and I'll go outside for a bit. I just need to talk to the driver about something".

He walked towards the front door with all the relaxation of a death row inmate on his final walk to the electric chair.

"Something, sir?" questioned SARDOC.

"Yes…" Abel took another look at his plausible-lie buffet table, "…fashion tips".

Abel could hear the Nano Byte tube powering up in the bedroom as he walked out of the front door. No sooner had he reached the end of the bottom of the driveway, than the TTAXI materialised right in front of him with its customary *POP*.

"Tulgik system, isn't it mate?" asked the driver, his crisp denim shirt glowing with residual Tachyons as the window rolled down.

"Yeah, something like that," replied Abel as he got in the back seat. He could hear SARDOCs voice emanating from the house, "Sir? Sir? You seem to have forgotten your suit, sir?""

"Nice system, that" said the driver, entering the coordinates on the guidance computer. Abel heard the door locks engage.

"Yes, I'm sure it is," he replied as he produced the Nano Cannon from his pyjama pocket. He pushed it through the window between the front and back seats and pressed it against the driver's temple, "but that's not where we're going".

"Oh, bloody hell, oh, okay," stuttered the driver, raising his hands off the steering wheel, "don't shoot me mate, I've never been any good with this bloody guidance computer. Takes me long enough to send a text. I'll take you wherever you like mate!"

"Yes you will," said Abel, in his best threatening voice, "now take me back to wherever you came from!"

"Dagenham?!" asked the surprised driver.

"No, you fashion catastrophe, wherever you've just driven here from. Take me back to Control".

The driver slowly moved his right hand and started changing the coordinates on the guidance computer. As he did, he turned his eyes while keeping his head as still as he could. The Nano cannon pressed firmly into his flabby temple, "Are you sure, mate. I've seen things there mate. Things…that a man like you aren't supposed to see. And that's just from the cab rank to the habitation centre. Are you really sure?"

"Course I'm sure," said Abel, resolutely, "I've got questions!"

"Careful, mate," warned the driver, as the countdown timer wound down, "You might not like the answers".

Abel pulled the Nano Cannon back through the window as the timer hit zero. The TTAXI popped and flashed, but this time the flash was red, not yellow. The TTAXI windows cleared and Abel was greeted with a sight that he wasn't sure what to make of. It looked like an airport. Heathrow, to be precise. Above the main building, he could see two gigantic signs – 'Arrivals' at the closest end to them and 'Departures' at the other, far off in the distance.

The terminal building had a cab rank in front of it that seemed to stretch on even further than the building and was continually moving. As one TTAXI joined the end where they were, another one seemed to disappear out of eye-line at the front of the queue. It was like those moving walkways inside airports, only this one was for TTAXIs.

"How many TTAXIs are there?!" Abel was aghast, smushing his face against the window as the cab slowed and joined the end of the queue.

"Infinity minus 1" replied the driver, flicking switches on the dashboard.

"But that's still infinity!" corrected Abel, trying to keep his voice from breaking like a teenager.

"Is it? Oh, I don't know, I only heard one of the other drivers talking about it. I guess that's why I'm a cab driver and not a Maths teacher"

He could see the terminal building in the distance, crawling towards them. Under the 'Arrivals' section of the building, he could see what looked like security officers checking the vehicles as they crept past them. They then waved in what looked like cleaning teams, who did their thing (whatever that was, he couldn't see) and exited again before the vehicle left his eyesight.

It was still a fair way to the terminal. There had to be a place to get out and stay undetected. He kept a watch on the buildings in between, for a side door or some other secluded entrance. Finally, about five hundred yards before the TTAXI was to be inspected, he saw a small blue door in a recess of the building, with a "Cleaners Only" sign above it. This was his opportunity. "Thanks for your help," said Abel, as he opened the door, "Sorry about the whole gun-against-your-head thing"

"Ah don't worry about it, mate" the driver waved his hand as if batting away the apology, "That's nothing, one time I had… "Bye!" Abel was out the door before he had to pick up the name the driver was about to drop. The driver stopped mid-sentence and turned forward. "Nice bloke," he said to no one, "For a Cosmic assassin". Abel did his best commando roll from the TTAXI to the recess of the building. Which, without the Nano Bytes helping him, was about as graceful as a Buffalo attempting Rhythmic Gymnastics.

He ended up in a pile in front of the blue door. He turned the door handle slowly and quietly,

in case there was someone inside. There wasn't. What *was* inside was the key to getting any further into the compound. The room looked like it must be a cleaner's cupboard. There were three colours of buckets around the floor, all with small Maglev pads instead of wheels. Mops in colours matching the buckets they were in, were sticking out of each one. The buckets had little signs imprinted on the side – Yellow said "Matter", "Black said "Anti-Matter" and Red said "Toilets". A box full of triangular signs was on the bottom of a metal shelf on the other side of the room. The signs were yellow with red writing that stated "Caution – Anti-Matter – Cellular entropy likely!" and a picture of a creature with six legs looking like it was falling over. Above it on a higher shelf was a selection of folded up uniforms in a unit of pigeon holes, sorted by species. Luckily, there was one available in the hole marked "Terran". He grabbed it urgently and started to put it on. It was tighter around the midriff than he'd have liked, but at least the arms and legs were approximately the right length.

"Bet Rigsan could fit in this uniform, even with his 45912 more hair follicles" Abel said to himself sarcastically, turning his nose up. He said it out loud, expecting an answer from SARDOC, who for the first time in six years wasn't there.

He finished fastening the poppers on the front of the uniform, put on the matching baseball cap and looked around. He needed appropriate footwear, or else he'd be the first Universal Corrections Cleaner to be discovered wearing Granddad slippers. He searched everywhere, but there was no footwear to be found. What he did find, however, was a couple of coloured carrier bags, which he proceeded to tie around his feet as pretend shoe covers.

'Who says I need SARDOC to think on my feet?' he thought, pleased with himself as his bagged feet rustled on the floor with every step.

He took an access card from the pile on the shelf above the uniforms and a caddy of cleaning chemicals. He turned to leave and realised that not only had the door shut behind him when he walked in, but there was no handle to get out. Helpfully, there was a computerised sign on the door saying 'DO NOT LET THIS DOOR SHUT BEHIND YOU' in a variety of constantly rotating languages.

"Well that's just fabulous!" exclaimed Abel, again talking to himself, "They can afford a multi-lingual sign but not a double bloody door handle!"

He reasoned that he had two possible choices – he could find another way out or he could wait for a real cleaner to let him out. The former would probably involve a lot of climbing. The latter would involve trying to understand an Alien cleaner without a universal translator, making for a very awkward conversation. He quickly concluded that the less of them he had today the better and started looking around. Above the shelving unit, there seemed to be an air vent, which looked like it might work. He clambered up the shelves, hoping they were fixed to the wall. If they weren't, he would be suffering his second crash landing of the past week, only this time he wouldn't be protected by his state-of-the-universe Nano Byte suit. This time, only his fat arse could save him.

The shelves held firm and he managed to prise the side of the grill off with a scraper from his cleaning caddy. The hole it covered was about three feet by two feet –just big enough for him to crawl down, like a giant maggot. He climbed inside and set off to find a way out again.

He squirmed through the pipe as quietly as he could. Which, given that it was metal pipe and his suit-less body had all the mobility of a potato with limbs, wasn't very quietly. The pipe had branches off it every few hundred yards, interspersed with small grills that fed into different rooms or followed the corridors within the compound. Through these small openings, he could keep on track thanks to multi-lingual signs like the one in the cleaner's cupboard, until he found a way to a grill in another small room that was big enough to get out of.

He checked that the door had an inside handle before pushing off the grate. He was most thankful that the pipe-crawling section of his day was over with – to be honest, it had been over for him about five signs ago. This room looked like a stationary cupboard and as his knackered frame slid out of the pipe, he landed on the boxes of paper with a thud and rolled over violently, sending the empty folders on the bottom shelf flying. He managed to stay with the roll and landed on his feet with his arms out, like he was indulging in a spot of stapler-surfing. He shrugged his shoulder to correct the hang of his uniform and picked up the baseball cap that had flown from his head somewhere in the manoeuvre. He finished picking up the cleaning products he had brought with him, put them all back in the caddy and turned the door handle as slowly as he could. He opened the door by just a eye width and peered into the corridor. 'There doesn't seem to be anyone around', he thought to himself. 'Alright, Tiffany!' thought the overactive part of his brain that dealt with pop culture references, 'Really?! Now?!' thought the rest of his mind. He opened the door of the stationary cupboard fully and walked out into the corridor, doing his best cleaner impression. He made his way towards the next sign, polishing door knobs, dusting noticeboards and taking a sneaky look in each door window as he was pretending to clean it.

He was actually getting quite into it when he reached the T-junction at the end. He was almost disappointed that the next hallway only had two doors in it. As he was dusting his way down towards the next T-junction, he noticed the next sign read "Parallel Nexus", which sounded ominous, very important and exactly the sort of thing he was looking for. As he was looking at the sign, two alien workmen walked past him, chatting. They were a race Abel had never seen before. Humanoid, biped, but definitely not Human. If he had to describe them to people, he'd have used the term 'clammy'. They didn't pay the slightest bit of attention to the most-overzealous cleaner Universal Corrections had ever employed. They turned in the direction of the Nexus and Abel sped up his cleaning to the T junction so he could follow their journey.

He got to the sign and casually glanced in the direction of the Nexus room, just as the workmen got there – there was a set of large double doors, protected by a large creature. Each door had four sensor panels on the outside of the frame – four on the right of the right door and four on the left of the other one. Each door had a large window in it and Abel could see all sorts of activity going on inside. He couldn't make out anything specific, but the room was very brightly lit, with a variety of coloured flashes going off every so often. The door guardian was at least ten feet high as well as round, and all head. Apart from the eight arms protruding from the sides of the head, four on each side. Abel was sure it looked like something from his childhood.

'Oh! That's me!' said his pop culture reference lobe, leaping off its chair, putting down the *Micronauts* comic it had been reading and rubbing its metaphorical hands together, 'now's my chance to do something useful!' The lobe danced its hand across a bookcase full of shopping catalogues that had appeared in front of it. Abel's mind's eye waited for an answer, frustratedly looking at its watch and puffing.

'Zoggs…no…that's board wax… Zoids… no… Poggs… no… ah!" the lobe pulled 'Argos Autumn-Winter 1986' from the bookshelf and started to flick through it feverishly, 'Here we go…Boglins! Only two arms, but close enough!'

'Yes, that's it…a Boglin with eight arms. Well done, PCRL', thought Abel, His pop culture reference lobe didn't answer, now firmly entranced by the Transformers on page 564.

The eight-armed Boglin checked over the Workmen's paperwork closely, casting a suspicious eye over them. He glared at them, then back at the papers, then back at them. He finally shoved the documents back at the workmen and snorted. It spun on the spot and pressed all eight sensors simultaneously on what were clearly palm readers, or what passed for palms on an eight-limbed head monster.

As the doors opened and the Octo-Boglin moved to the side to let the aliens past, more of the room was revealed. Before the doors shut behind the workmen, Abel could make out what looked like a large table in the middle of the room, projecting a hologram of a region of space above it. Surrounding the hologram, were a few humanoid shapes milling about. The difference between the brightness of the corridor and the darkness for the room made their species impossible to ascertain.

Before he could make out any more details, or indeed make sense of what he had already seen, the doors automatically closed. The Octo-Boglin turned around and noticed that Abel was staring. He gave an angry grunt in Abel's direction, which snapped him out of his gormless gawping. Abel spun on his heels and tried to walk back down the corridor he had just come down. He stopped midway to make sure the beast wasn't following him. He was extremely relieved to see that it wasn't.

He suddenly realised he hadn't breathed for a while and let out a big puff of air, relaxing his shoulders as he did so.

How the hell was he going to get into a room that needed eight identical palm prints scanned at the same time?! He stroked his chin thoughtfully as he began to follow the signs for 'departures'. He'd seen people in movies do it and it always seemed to work for them. So he was beyond shocked when it actually did.

'Two heads are better than one,' Suggested his ideas lobe, 'and four palms are a lot closer to eight than two.'

"But where do I get another…" his mouth stopped and gasped,

"Rigsan!"

CHAPTER 9
YOU GOTTA HAVE FRIENDS

Abel decided he needed to find a way to contact Agent Rigsan, face to face if possible. He had to not only convince his clone of his plan, but to help get two more helpers as well.

'I'm sure something will turn up' he thought, as he walked down what felt like the same long corridor for what felt like the tenth time, 'If there's two of us looking, we've only got to get one each and we're there!'

He was following the signs for 'Departures', which he thought was probably the best bet – either he would find a way to get to Rigsan, or he would find his way home.

At the end of this corridor, he saw a slightly different sign, which gave him hope he was getting somewhere. This sign didn't just say 'Departures', but 'Departures Control Room' pointing to a door.

'Finally!' he thought, trying to up his pace without looking like he was rushing.

'Just a casual cleaner on his way to a spillage' he kept thinking. He was more correct than he could have realised, as he walked around the corner and bumped straight into a technician coming out of the door.

Despite the shock of the collision, Abel quickly realised this was a Cromulite, the race he hadn't seen since Orientation. A Cromulite whose brilliant white gown and red sash were now covered in a hot, green liquid. A hot, green liquid that Abel had just clumsily knocked all over the alien by smushing into his arm.

Abel and the Cromulite shared a moment of awkward silence, as both of them stood less than two feet apart. In unison, as if two sides of very strange mirror, they both looked down at the stain, then back up, then down at the floor.

The Cromulite was clearly very angry. Unknown to Abel, the technician's gown had been clean on today and Zepularian Coffee was a bugger to get out of whites. Even in the most advanced civilisation in the known universe, washing whites was still a problem. He would have to go back to his quarters and change.

'ZEBUDE A LAGO, DUMGOT!' exclaimed the alien, shaking his gown with his free hand. Abel didn't need any translation to realise how miffed this alien was as he continued his frustrated tirade, "SIGFOL, SIGFOL!"

Abel didn't know what to say. He just stood there, mouth agape and hoping that his brain would think of something to do next. Quite frankly, his brain had come to rely on SARDOC for technical decisions of this nature and was usually more preoccupied with thinking of how much it missed memes.

'Well, you need to think of something,' his brain shouted to his mouth, 'you're normally pretty good at this sort of thing'.

His brain was wrong.

"I am very sorry," Abel's mouth said, in an over-the-top, 70s-sitcom style, Eastern European accent, "I will clean at once".

If Abel's brain had had its own set of hands, it would have thrown them up over his head at this point and if it had had its own set of legs, turned and walked away in disgust.

He reached into his caddy and produced a cloth. He started to paw amateurishly at the growing stain on the Cromulite's gown, which was now dribbling its way towards the floor. He thought it was making the shape of a Buffalo with really thin legs, but he figured the alien probably wouldn't want to know this, even if the translators were working.

The Cromulite swiped Abel's hand away dismissively and stared at him for a moment.

"DUMGOT BABHET!" the alien said, breaking the second awkward silence in as many minutes. He barged past Abel and started off down the corridor, swearing in Cromuleese under his breath and continuing to shake his gown. As Abel turned away from the alien, he noticed that whole sorry incident had produced an unexpected benefit. The door to the control room had remained open, as the alien had been stood in it the whole time. Luckily, he managed to sidle his way through before it closed.

Inside, he could see at least ten more Cromulite technicians, each wearing the same red sashes that surely signified their job role within the Departures department. 'They must be the ones controlling where the TTAXIs go', he thought.

The room was a large semi-circle, with the flat side completely made of glass and facing the TTAXI rank. The ever-changing row of TTAXIs could be seen outside, the front one disappearing into a hole in space every minute or so. He looked around the room and could see what looked like computer workstations, each one with a monitor, a keyboard and a Cromulite. Each technician could be seen watching a video feed on their monitor, each one of a different scene. One showed a first-person view of someone fighting a Wardz incursion. Another displayed a human sat in a chair watching TV on his display wall. Both feeds felt eerily familiar to him. But these screens all had 'live feed' written in the top left hand corner of the screen and so they *couldn't be* him.

'What is going on?' he puzzled, trying not to become overwhelmed by it all. This became even harder as he looked above the monitors to the middle of the glass wall. Here, there was a large video screen, about ten-feet square, that looked like the boards you would find at an airport to see which gate your plane was leaving from. Except on this board there were ten names, each one with a code to the right of it. They were clearly the list of the next ten TTAXIs to depart, as he watched the name at the top disappear at the same time as a TTAXI did, with another name being added to the bottom of the list.

'Oh my god,' he thought, trying not to stare at the board in the same way you try not to stare at an accident on the other side of the motorway, 'how many clones of me are there?!'

He noticed one of the terminals was free and was still signed in. The video feed showed a humanoid who looked remarkably like Abel, feeding his cat and talking to himself. This must have been the terminal left behind by the technician he'd collided with in the doorway. He started to make his way towards the terminal, which was at the other end of the long semi-circular table he was right next to.

There was only one alien between him and empty terminal.

"Very sorry, I clean now," he said in the same dodgy, Eastern-European accent as before. He returned to his caddy and this time came out with a duster. He lightly flicked the yellow cloth against the table as he walked sideways along it.

"Sorry for mess" he said to the Cromulite as he dangled the duster onto the keyboard between the alien's svelte fingers. The alien gave a little cough as a tiny plume of dust rose up from the duster, "Oh my, keyboard is very dirty, no?" Abel commented, as the alien gave him what passed for stink eye when you have no eyelids. The Cromulite wafted him away and Abel carried on with the dusting charade all the way to the other end of the table. He gave a furtive look up above the level of the monitors to make sure no one was looking and touched a key on the keyboard. As he did so, the keys, which had previously been in what was presumably Cromuleese, seemed to change to English lettering.

'Now that's a good idea' thought Abel, as the key morphing spread out from the key he had touched, until the whole keyboard showed English lettering, 'If you had this on Twitter, the whole Galaxy could troll Piers Morgan'.

He typed in R I G S A N and pressed [ACCEPT]. The code at the top of the screen changed to 'RIG457' and the video feed changed on the monitor and showed Rigsan in his home base. It didn't look like Abel's. It was more modern, more angular, more...like an IKEA showroom. It was more aesthetically pleasing, more well-groomed, much like Rigsan was to him. But it was also cold and unwelcoming, like the sort of place you'd be afraid to put your cup of tea down without a coaster. Abel felt sure that Rigsan would be the sort to make you take your shoes off at the front door as well.

But surprisingly, he also had a black and white cat, that he could see curled up in a red basket by the side of the sofa.

'Well, he doesn't look that busy' Abel thought, 'maybe I'll pay him a visit soon. But first, I need to go back and get SARDOC. I won't be able to get much further without his help'.

He typed A B E L into the keyboard, the code changed to ABE111 and up came his video feed, which was of course empty, apart from Colin quietly cleaning himself whilst sat on the sofa. His cat didn't have a basket, he could sleep wherever he wanted. He pressed on the touchscreen on the button that read "Send Adhoc unit?" and confirmed the "Are you sure? Y/N" message that followed. When he now looked at the board, "ABE111 ADHOC" had appeared at the bottom of it. It was time to get outside.

He passed the alien he had bumped into coming back in as he left the room. His new gown was glowing white, so much so that Abel almost stopped him and asked what washing powder he used. But there was no time for that now. He turned right out of the door and headed for the end of the corridor. At the end, he could see another large glass wall, with a glass door in the centre of it. He could see the TTAXI rank on the other side of it. He nervously walked down to the ID card reader by the side of the door and pressed his stolen ID card against the panel. The card was on a bungee attached to the belt loops on his overalls, and it stretched just enough to allow him to scan it without removing it. A few tense seconds passed while a green line moved down the panel, under the card and back up again. After a few more tense seconds, the panel was filled with a green 'thumbs up' icon and a gave off a friendly beep. The door opened with a *WHOOSH* that original *Star Trek* would have been proud of. He was soon outside.

The front of the line was five TTAXIs away and as he turned right to head to the cab he had called, which was by now fifth in the queue. He looked left, back at the line of TTAXIs behind him. In the distance he could just about see the end of the line, at least fifty TTAXIs away. He could see the cleaner's cupboard in the distance where he had crept his way into the building and figured he'd probably be in there again before the day was over.

Each of the TTAXIs had their corresponding destination code in a little oblong readout on the back of the roof-mounted TAXI sign. He had never noticed this before, for some reason. Maybe he'd had no reason to until now. Maybe he had subconsciously noticed it and assumed it was the model number of the TTAXI – and you know what they say about assumption, don't you? The driver was already in his TTAXI when he got to it and got in.

"Excuse me mate," said the driver as Abel sat down, "This cab's already on a fare. You'll have to get out!"

"Emergency clean, comrade!" declared Abel, really going for broke with the Dracula accent now, "I clean Mister Abel's house for him. It Bob a Job week"

"Okay, fair enough," replied the driver after a few seconds of thought, "I've given up questioning the unusual around here. Ever since I became a Glomp's head. Stays with you, that does". The driver thoughtfully raised a denimed arm to his temple as the TTAXI pulled away from the rank and into space, "Right in here" whispered the traumatised cabbie.

The countdown hit zero and they were instantly transported to Abel's bungalow, with the customary flash.

"Thank you comrade," said Abel as he got out, "You wait here now for me to complete bob a job, yes?"

"Yeah, no worries", replied the driver, visibly relaxing and powering down the reactor, "I'll sit here and listen to some of me tunes".

As Abel walked towards the bungalow, he heard the driver flick on the cab stereo. The surrounding area was filled with *Margherita Time* by *Status Quo*. He chuckled to himself as he entered the front door.

"You there, S?" he shouted, as he closed the front door behind him.

"Is that you, sir?" asked SARDOC, sounding a little bit frantic, "Oh sir, I was most perturbed that you had gone off in a TTAXI without the appropriate protection. Where did you go? Are you unharmed?"

"Yes I'm perfectly fine, S" Abel replied, "I need to ask you some more questions before I can tell you where I've been".

He entered the living room and sat on the sofa, facing the display wall. Colin came into the room and told Abel off in the loudest way he could, before jumping on the sofa for an apology cuddle.

"You can ask me anything, sir" said SARDOC, the little red light blinking on the nearest interface terminal at the right-hand side of the display wall, "I am here to help you in any way I can".

"That's just what I needed to hear S", Abel replied, stroking Colin's head and continuing to be constantly amazed at how soft it was, "If a mission's success relied on you being operational but disconnected from Control, how would we go about that?"

"Why would I need to be disconnected from Control?" asked SARDOC.

"Doesn't matter. Hypothetically speaking. Say, there's a virus in the Control mainframe and we needed to be protected from it to complete our mission".

"I am not currently reading any problems with Control's mainframe, sir" SARDOC offered.

"I know, but it's always best to be prepared," Abel replied, trying to keep his voice hypothetical and not 'I'm about to do something naughty again'.

"So, hypothetically, how would I do it?"

"Well, you would have to give me the command to engage Emergency Autonomy mode, code 641253". Said SARDOC.

"...And Control can't override it if they detect you've gone offline?"

"No sir, they would have to either synthesise your voice pattern and override it in person or get you to do it yourself".

"...And you would retain all your normal functionality? Like, over the suit and everything?"

"Indeed, sir. My functionality would remain exactly as before. However, my knowledge base would be frozen at the point that EA mode was engaged.

So for example, if we journeyed to a planet we had never been to before, I would not be able to alter your suit to blend in, unless the race involved was already in the database".

"Well, that'll have to do I suppose," shrugged Abel, "SARDOC…"

"Yes sir?"

"Engage Emergency Autonomy mode, code 641253"

There was a series of clicks, whirs and electronic noises, that sounded like an internet router from the 1990s. Finally, SARDOC's voice filled the speakers once more.

"Emergency Autonomy mode engaged, sir" his digital assistant said, "I am functioning completely independently of the mainframe, including the suspension of all video feeds to and from this base and your stealth suit. Now, would sir mind informing me as to why this is happening?"

"I've been to Control S" said Abel, tickling Colin's chin to the feline's glowing approval, "I've seen the TTAXI rank. I've seen how many there are. I've seen the video feeds of others like me, but *not like me*". Abel's voice started to break a bit as the enormity of what he was saying was only just hitting him as he was saying it out loud.

"I see, sir," said SARDOC, stoically, "Well then, you have seen more than me".

"How can you not know there are so many others?!" exclaimed Abel, "You knew who Agent Rigsan was, didn't you?"

"I know of Agent Rigsan, just as I know of many other Agents," revealed SARDOC matter-of-factly, "It is not in my programming to ask who they are or where they are from.

116

I simply hold a list of all currently active Agents working for Universal Corrections".

"Well, I've also found out how to get to where Agent Rigsan is," said Abel, standing up, "And you're going to help me get to him".

"Very well, sir, always happy to help. Shall I prepare the suit?"

"Indeed, S", replied Abel, mimicking his assistant's posh accent again, "One shall be right there, as soon as one has completed a deeply satisfying poo".

Abel headed for the loo, as he could hear the suit being prepared in the bedroom area.

-

Abel read another chapter of *Watchmen* to calm his nerves and relax his colon. His poo was mildly rather than deeply satisfying. Once he had finished, he made his way into the bedroom, took off the cleaner overalls and stepped into the Nano Byte tube.

'It'll be much easier to blend in at Control in this' he thought, as the Nano Bytes followed their familiar path around his body, 'I just hope having SARDOC in Aeroplane Mode won't be too much of a hindrance.'

There was of course, only one way to find out. He waited for the suit to completely cover him as he thought out how to approach his return to Control.

"Before we leave the house, you need to make me look like I did when I walked in, S" he said, as the Nano Bytes began to cover his head, "The driver out there is expecting the cleaner to return".

"Very well sir," complied SARDOC, as the suit began to shift in both fit and appearance, into an exact replica of the cleaners uniform he had just taken off, "Will you need me to synthesise your accent, or are you going to persist with your...efforts?"

If Abel didn't know better, he could have sworn that SARDOC paused near the end of that question for comedic effect.

"No it's okay, S" said Abel, looking sternly at one of the interface panels, "I'll be fine talking on my own. Its got me this far!"

"Very well, sir," complied SARDOC, flatly, "Shall I leave your face open and just synthesise the hat?"

"Sounds like a good idea," agreed Abel, beginning to make for the door. He picked up the hand caddy as he did so, "I never think the suit does human faces very well anyway".

He didn't realise it, but the Nano Bytes heard what he'd said and were actually quite offended. They resolved to delay commencement of the Faecal Recycling Systems by 0.125 seconds the next time Abel needed them. To the Nano Bytes, waiting this long to start a subsystem was akin to sticking two fingers up to the suit wearer. That would teach him.

He walked back outside and made for the TTAXI, which could now be heard playing *This Ole House* by *Shakin' Stevens*.

'Jesus, even his music is drowning in denim' he thought, in a poorly-considered Eastern European accent for some reason.

"You ready to go back now mate?" asked the driver, sitting up straight and grabbing the steering wheel, "Done what you needed to do?"

"Uh, yes I clean good for Agent," replied Abel, as he put the hand caddy on the seat and slid it over as he got in, "Very good. We go back to Control now".

"No problem," said the driver, as he inputted the coordinates into the flight computer, "Do you mind if I leave the radio on?"

"No no, very good, very good," said Abel, holding up one hand and shaking his head, "I like the Steven Shaky very much".

"Very kind of you, guv, very kind," said the driver, appreciatively, "You obviously have good taste in music. Not like those blooming Agents, most of them are miserable buggers!"

The TTAXI reactor gave off the customary noises as they warmed up their Tachyons Collectors.

"Oh yes? How many Agents you drive for?" asked Abel, trying to lean forward and remain casual at the same time.

"Oh loads, let me see…" he tapped his right hand on his chin, thoughtfully, "More than fifty different ones I reckon. It's hard to tell which ones you've had before to be honest. Some of them look very similar and their bases look the same. Maybe more than fifty? Sometimes you can tell they're a new one if you've not heard the accent before".

Upon hearing this titbit of information, Abel gave in with the whole 'don't lean forward and appear too interested' and instead went with 'nearly stick your head through the glass with interest'.

"Different accent?!" asked Abel, his own spurious accent slipping a bit, "How many different accent can I…I mean, we…I mean they have?"

"Well, let's see, I've had a Scottish one, an Italian one, a Greek one, an Irish one, a Spanish one, a few German ones…yeah, quite a few German ones actually". The driver got lost in thought as his brain attempted to calculate an approximate ratio of German accents to the rest.

Abel slumped back into the seat, his arms flopping down by his side and resting on the leather. He couldn't quite believe what he was hearing. If these other Agents were indeed all clones of him, why would some of them have different accents? He could understand a physical variation like Rigsan, but not a geographical one. He was lost in thought himself now, but before he could get any more lost, the driver threw him a conversational life jacket.

"Here you go, guv, back at base," said the driver, as the TTAXI joined the end of the rank.

Abel blinked a few times and shook his head lightly, as if trying to shake the myriad of conflicting thoughts he was having out of his ears. He composed himself and picked up the caddy.

"Thank you, my friend," he said as he opened the door nearest the buildings, "I make very good comments for you".

"Oh, er, much obliged guv," replied the driver, a little bit confused. There wasn't a review system in place for the TTAXIs as far as he knew. But he'd take the compliment, nonetheless.

Abel decided against using the cleaner's cupboard this time and decided to make straight for the Departures control room. As he walked the sizeable distance to his target, he walked passed another large room that looked almost the same as Departures.

"That must be Arrivals," he quietly said to SARDOC as he tried to look in without looking, 'I suppose they control the cleanup operations".

"Yes and no doubt deal with the casualties". SARDOC replied coldly. Abel decided to let all the worrying connotations of SARDOCs answer go, as he was already dealing with enough life-changing revelations for one day.

He was soon in front of the entrance door for the Departures area. As he neared the door, he pulled the stolen ID card he had used previously out of his caddy and fastened it to his belt. Or rather, fastened it to the Nano Bytes belt department.

"Shall I override the entrance protocols, sir?" asked SARDOC in his ear, quietly, "I still have that functionality".

"No, that might raise the alarm S," whispered Abel, out of the corner of his mouth, "besides, I've got an ID card".

As he got to the door, he saw an access panel where he would have to scan the stolen card, just as he done on the other side. Abel's second go at scanning a panel was significantly more relaxed than the first one. He could have strutted happily through the now-open doors, if he wasn't keeping in character.

He was now back in the same large, brightly lit corridor as he had been a few hours ago. The Control Room door was accessed with a palm reader, meaning his stolen ID card would be no good here.

"I don't suppose you could rustle up a Cromulite palm print while you're disconnected from the mainframe?" Asked Abel, hopefully.

"Unfortunately not sir," replied SARDOC, "Even if I could, it would not necessarily be the right palm print. I would need the palm of an active member of the DCR team, in order to replicate the required print, sir".

"That's what I thought". He would have to bide his time and wait for the opportunity to 'persuade' a technician to help him.

He cleaned his way around the corridor whilst he waited for just such an opportunity. After a few minutes of light-dusting, a technician walked out of the Departures Control Room door, turned right and headed off down the corridor and into the compound.

'Perfect,' thought Abel, upping the pace of his duster wafting in order to keep track of his Cromulite target.

"I will begin the morphic calculations now", instructed SARDOC, "once you have access to the palm print, I can replicate it straight away".

"Hmm, leave that to me, S" said Abel, speeding up.

He got level with the technician, matching her walking speed and waited for his opportunity. He began looking in his caddy as casually as he could. The alien was oblivious to his presence, instead watching its tablet intently, which seemed to be showing a video on black holes. She briefly looked up at Abel, realising that now he was also intently watching her tablet. Abel sniggered nervously, looked up and down the corridor to check the coast was clear and roughly walked into her. He opened the side door they were level with and shoved her through it all in one motion.

The surprised Cromulite couldn't get her balance quick enough to stop him and collapsed on the floor of the maintenance room in a heap. One quick stun blast from Abel's "Atten-stun" finger blaster and a working palm print was his for the taking.

He looked around the room and found a oil-soaked cloth. He ripped it into strips and proceeded to tie the Cromulite's slender hands behind her back, her feet together and had just enough left to wrap a gag around her lip-free mouth. That should hold her long enough for him to get in and out of the Departures Control Room and onto wherever Rigsan was. He rolled his captive over and pressed the palm of his hand against hers.

"One working palm print, S".

"Indeed, sir," confirmed SARDOC, as Abel could feel the Nano Bytes rearranging themselves under his fingers.

It took no more than ten seconds for his suit to match the alien's palm print. The whole process was finished with a rather comical *BING*, a noise that made him think his Macaroni Cheese ready meal was cooked. It was such a vivid memory that the noise brought back, that he felt positively famished as he stood up and let the rest of his suit morph into the shape of a Cromulite technician, complete with flowing, ultra-bright white gown and red sash.

He left the captive behind on the floor of the side room and made his way back into the corridor. He closed the door gently behind him and made off down the corridor towards the Departures Control Room.

"What if someone talks to us S?" said Abel, with the tone of voice of someone who'd just remembered he'd left the gas on, "Is your universal translator working?"

"Don't worry sir," SARDOC replied, "Cromuleese is the language I was programmed in. In your parlance, it is my 'native tongue'. In fact, if my universal translator had stopped working when you engaged my EA Mode, you wouldn't be able to understand me at all!"

"Well, that's something you could have told me before I did it!" exclaimed Abel.

'Imagine if that had actually happened?!' he thought, 'It would be like when you accidentally set your DVD menus to Chinese and then have no idea how to get them back again!'

It was only forty paces or so and he was stood at the door to the Control Room. He placed his palm on the access panel and waited while the panel scanned the purloined print. The Nano Bytes on his hand giggled silently as the scanning beam tickled their Quantum molecules twice – once on the way down and once on the way up. The panel returned another green thumbs up and a much less hunger-inducing *BEEP*, although he was still thinking about the ready meal from the last one.

The door opened with another Original *Trek* *WHOOSH*. He half-expected a red-shirted Ensign to run out of the room, unknowingly on their way to their last mission.

He took a deep breath and casually walked into the room. As casually as his additional foot in height would allow, as he was still getting used to being this far off the ground inside the suit. It felt like he imagined hovering to feel. He scanned the room for an empty terminal, stopping when he saw one in the middle of the second semi-circular row from the front. He politely smiled at a few of the other technicians that looked up from their video screens to make eye contact as he walked towards the workstation. The smile was replicated by the Cromulite face the suit had made.

124

This gave Abel the impression that he was watching really dodgy CGI, as none of the Cromulite's eye lines matched up with his. He held his hand on the scanning panel next to the vacant keyboard as he sat down in a tall-backed red chair. The panel accepted his handprint and the display screen sprang into life, showing nothing but a small green data box in the centre, with alien lettering above it.

"Clear my hand temporarily, S" whispered Abel, as he held his hands over the keyboard, "I need to be able the touch the keyboard with my skin to change the lettering".

"Well now, that is most ingenious system, sir," admired SARDOC, as the Nano Bytes shrunk back from Abel's fingertips, revealing just enough of his own fingers to do the job, "A tactile universal translating interface. I must say, my creators never cease to amaze me".

Abel touched the keyboard with his uncovered fingers and just as before, the keys and the writing on the screen changed to English.

"Incredible," SARDOC said as Abel watched the transformation happening. Abel felt that if his digital assistant had a head, he be shaking it in awed appreciation at this moment.

Once the conversion had completed, Abel typed R I G S A N into the system and once again, the Agent's live video feed filled the screen. This time however, he seemed to be halfway through an exercise routine, with one leg up on the coffee table and one leg on the sofa. His cat could be seen sitting in its basket and watching the whole thing. Abel waited a few seconds for the "Send ADHOC Unit?" data box to appear and when it did, he confirmed it. The message, as before, changed to "Unit Confirmed. Added to Queue".

He looked up at the Departures Board and waited for the Adhoc TTAXI for Rigsan to appear. He only had to wait a few seconds and it blinked into fifth place on the board. 'Ideal, that gives me time to get outside' he thought, as he stood up and started back towards the door, 'now I've just got to go back and change into a driver'.

-

He decided to go back to the room which still held his Cromulite captive. He untied her this time, as now there was no danger of them both being caught in the same room at the same time. It would have been even more awkward than two people wearing the same thing to a party.

"Okay, S, now change me into a driver," he instructed, standing as still as he could, "and give me a grey mullet".

He looked down as the Nano Bytes went about their business, busily making Denim.

'Like 8-year olds in a sweat shop' he thought to himself, chuckling.

In no time at all, his new outfit was finished, right down to the faded brown cowboy boots, with their ornate patterns on the top of each foot. He examined the three St Christopher rings on his right hand and the two Sovereigns on his left, as he left the side room and headed for the exit to the TTAXI rank.

As he got outside, he could see a driver heading for Rigsan's TTAXI. Abel sped up and intercepted him just as he reached the bonnet of the vehicle.

"Alright, er, mate" greeted Abel, in his best 'Apples and Pears' style Cockney accent, "You got a minute?"

"Not really, got an adhoc fare to get to," replied the driver, continuing to move around the front of the TTAXI.

"You won't believe what's going on in the Control Room, old fella me lad!" said Abel, excitedly pointing over his shoulder at the door he'd just come out of.

"What's that then?" he asked, stopping in his tracks. If there was one thing all cab drivers liked, Abel thought, it was gossip.

"Matey boy's giving away Neil Diamond tickets in there!" Abel exclaimed, trying to sound like an extra on *EastEnders*, "It's gonna be right old knees up!"

Abel internally cringed, fearing he'd overcooked the cockneyness.

The driver looked at Abel. Then at the Control room. Then back at Abel, biting his lip in consternation.

"Ere, cover for me, will ya?" he asked finally, starting to move back towards Abel.

"With pleasure me old mate!" Abel said cheerfully, "You go. Fill yer boots!"

The driver nodded appreciatively and ran off towards the Control room. Abel waited for them to cross paths and then made his way quickly around the front of the cab. He got in and began the warm up sequence he had seen the last driver do, when he had returned to his base to get SARDOC. That was the first time he'd ever paid attention to this start-up sequence, so he hoped it was as easy as it had looked.

"Flip that there…press that…that lever goes up…" Abel was muttering under his breath, as he waited for the familiar noises to come from the engine compartment. He was most relieved when they did. He inputted the code for Rigsan home base into the computer and the 30 second timer started, just as the cab moved to the front of the queue.

As the countdown timer wound its way towards launch, he could see the driver out of the window. He was now being held by two security guards, who were stopping him from entering the complex. He relaxed and stepped back a few steps, only to try forcing his way past again a few seconds later. The three of them repeated this dance three times before the driver gave up. Abel could see him start talking to the Guards and pointing in the TTAXIs direction. The Guards nodded at the driver and started moving in Abel's direction, their hands visibly tensing on their holsters as they did so. But it was too late. The countdown timer hit zero and the TTAXI was instantaneously transported outside what looked like a parking garage.

CHAPTER 10
MEET AND GREET

As soon as Abel arrived at Rigsan's base, the first thing he noticed was how much posher it was than his. The building looked like a modern double-parking garage and a modern bungalow had been bolted together, one on top the other, with the one-storey house on top.

"Blimey, S!" exclaimed Abel, unlatching the driver door and beginning to get out of the TTAXI, "This place is well nice. Why didn't I get something like this for my base?"

"I can't say for sure, sir," replied SARDOC, "but if I had to guess, I would suspect it was because you didn't ask for it".

"I wasn't asked at all, I don't think!" Abel protested as he shut the TTAXI door behind him, his mouth still agape at how much nicer this was than his bungalow, "Another question for whoever's running this show, I suppose!"

Abel would have to hold onto that thought and store it for later, as the silver garage door began to open in front of him. Once it had reached the top of its opening arc, there he was – Rigsan was striding towards him, with his stealth suit rapidly trying to form around him, like he had been startled by a fire alarm and was having to evacuate the building. He did not look happy.

"What the hell are you doing here?!" shouted Rigsan as he approached the TTAXI, the shimmering Nano Bytes frantically making their way up and over his head until he was fully enclosed and protected. As he didn't need to change appearance at this moment, it looked like his suit was in default protection mode, which meant Rigsan looked like he was walking towards Abel in a very form-fitting bubble of golden wee. Abel had never seen someone else wearing a complete suit before and he now realised how ridiculous he must look when approaching someone unstealthed.

"Be ready to uncover my mouth, S," whispered Abel as he spun around slowly 360 degrees, before Rigsan was close enough to hear, "The code to do so will be 'Avocado'. Mute your microphones for ten seconds immediately afterwards as well".

"Very well, sir", SARDOC whispered back. Even though there was no way that Rigsan would hear him what with him being in Abel's earpiece, he thought he would get into the clandestine spirit.

"Can you understand why, S?" asked Abel, seemingly very proud of what he was about to do.

"I have an inkling, sir" agreed SARDOC. He was capable of playing two million games of Chess simultaneously whilst repairing a coffee machine, so he was more than capable of foreshadowing his Agent's 'Barely above Simian' level of thinking.

"I didn't call a TTAXI! What is the meaning of this? Is there an emergency mission?" shouted Rigsan as he reached the TTAXI and stood about four feet from Abel, "This is most irregular!"

"Alright mate. TTAXI for Agent Rigsan," said Abel in his best EastEnders accent, happily extending his hand, "I've been given a very special mission for you".

Rigsan stared at Abel's disguised face, then down to his outstretched hand, then back up to his face. Abel gingerly placed his hand back down by his side.

"What special mission, why isn't my SARDOC aware of this?"

"Aw, it's top secret, guv!" replied Abel, "Even the SARDOCs aren't being told about it!"

"SARDOCs?" Rigsan asked, his face contorting in his urine bubble.

"What?" said Abel, blinking nervously.

"What?" asked Rigsan, becoming increasingly frustrated.

"Pardon, sir…er…guv?" asked Abel.

"You said SARDOCs!" confirmed Rigsan, pointing his finger at Abel, "As in more than one SARDOC. How can you mean SARDOCs, plural, when I know for a fact that I have the only one in existence?"

There was an awkward silence, akin to if someone's phone had gone off at a funeral. As his Faecal Recycling Systems went in amber alert, he decided to go for broke before he explained any further.

"Avocado!" he shouted, so loudly and suddenly that Rigsan was visibly shocked and took a step back. The suit reacted and instantly removed itself from the lower front quadrant of his face, uncovering his mouth. SARDOC dutifully muted his microphones at the same time.

"Pardon?" asked Rigsan, subconsciously worrying he was about to be suicide bombed by the 'Vegetables Have Feelings Too' pressure group. He'd always had his doubts about them.

"SARDOC, engage Emergency Autonomy Mode Code 641253!" Abel followed up in his own voice. He suddenly thought that he hadn't stopped to think if each SARDOC might not have had different coding system built into them. Luckily, the Cromulites who had invented SARDOC hadn't stopped to think of this either, so Rigsan's SARDOC made the same 'old internet' noises as Abel's had at this moment in the process.

Rigsan stumbled a few steps backwards, patting his right ear with his hand like he was trying to push something out the other side. He had obviously been surprised by the noises coming from SARDOC and his digital assistant was attempting to adjust to being unexpectedly cut off from the mainframe by what he thought was his human.

"What did you do to SARDOC?!" exclaimed Rigsan, re-establishing his balance and walking back to confront Abel.

"I've engaged your SARDOC's Emergency Autonomy Mode," replied Abel, as calmly as he could while stepping back towards the TTAXI, "It cuts him off from the mainframe and allows us to talk freely without being spied on".

"Spied on?!" Rigsan looked dubious but stopped walking towards Abel, much to his relief, "How did you know how to do that?"

"Because I'm you, you bell end," replied Abel, sarcastically, "Remove the rest of my face plate, please S".

There was another awkward silence as Abel realised that ten seconds was a lot longer than it sounded.

"S?"

"S?"

"...SARDOC!"

"Yes sir?" asked SARDOC, who had been as blissfully unaware of his Agent's commands, like a partner in the booth on *Mr & Mrs*.

Abel took a deep breath and composed himself.

"Remove...my...face...plate...please" he reiterated, slower and through gritted teeth this time, like a rubbish ventriloquist.

"Indeed, sir".

Abel's false face retreated back into the body of his suit. As it did so, a look of realisation spread across Rigsan's yellow-tinged expression. He visibly relaxed, stood up straight and his mouth dropped open.

"Abel?" he muttered, frozen to the spot as if he'd just been confronted with a reality that he'd thought had been a dream.

"Hello 'Agent Rigsan'" said Abel, making air quotes with his fingers as he said this mystery character's name, "How does it feel to be a clone?"

"A what?" asked Rigsan, shaking his head and blinking his eyes to attention.

"A clone," said Abel, shrugging his shoulders,

"You're me. A physically fitter, hairier me. But still me. But you *can't* be me, as I'm still me. So you must be a copy of me, get it?"

Rigsan thought for a moment, staring at Abel with a mixture of fury and bewilderment.

"Wait a minute, maybe you're the clone? You ever thought of that?" said Rigsan defensively, "I'll agree we look very similar. But I'm in much better nick than you. Maybe they cloned me to make you and didn't get it…quite right".

Now it was Abel's turn to think for a moment. To be honest, the thought that *he* might be the copy had never occurred to him. Now that *would* be something, wouldn't it? He decided that maybe they needed to discuss this in more depth and there was only one suggestion to make.

"It's an interesting thought," replied Abel, nodding his head thoughtfully, "Maybe we need to discuss this over a cup of tea?"

Abel motioned towards the garage, his conciliatory tone surprising his fellow Agent.

"Shall we?"

-

Rigsan had agreed that a cup of tea, herbal in Rigsan's case, was probably the best starting point to unravel this mystery and invited Abel into his base. As they began to walk towards Rigsan's base, Abel's Nano Byte suit reverted to it default settings. They joined Rigsan's suit in encasing their wearer in a form-fitted bag of wee. The only difference between their suits now was that Rigsan looked like an Olympic Swimmer in his and Abel looked like a baked potato with pencils sticking out of it.

They both made their way into the garage and the large silver door automatically closed behind them. Abel couldn't believe how much like James Bond's equipment room this place was.

"This place is amazing!" said Abel, resisting the urge to run his fingers across the perfectly positioned weapons hung on a pre-cut display unit on the wall, "My suit is in my bedroom!"

"You gotta think big if the you're the universe's last line of defence against evil!" replied Rigsan without turning around.

"Except you're not". Corrected Abel.

"Pardon?" asked Rigsan, trying not to sound offended.

"Well, you might have *thought* you were," continued Abel, "the last line of defence, I mean. But now we know we are both here, kinda makes us both the penultimate line, doesn't it?"

Rigsan decided to ignore his fat clone's truth bomb and carried on showing off his garage.

"Yes, this is energy weapons wall," Rigsan continued, motioning towards the display they had just walked past.

"Over there is the ballistics wall," he pointed to the opposite wall, covered with even bigger weapons. They stopped in front of a person-sized metal tube in the back corner of the garage, "And here is what I like to call the 'Suit Chute'. Would you like go up my chute, Abel?".

As Rigsan finally turned around, he was wearing the biggest smug grin Abel could remember. It was all Abel could do to stop himself from cracking up.

"Mhm," agreed Abel, nodding and answering without opening his mouth. He wrestled with, and eventually gained control over, the corners of his mouth before being able to answer without laughing, "Yes that sounds fun".

Rigsan's grin started to dissipate as his brain tried to work out if Abel was making fun of him or not.

"Okay, well, you watch me and follow behind," Rigsan said, suspiciously, "You just press this, wait for the door to open, step in and the chute will do the rest. Got it?"

"Oh I think so," replied Abel, as Rigsan followed the steps he'd just laid out for him. As the door closed, Abel breathed out and added, "I can't believe I'm such a douche!"

Abel waited for the chute to return and followed Rigsan's instructions.

"Got that?" He mouthed, sarcastically mimicking Rigsan's patronising tone as he stepped into the tube.

He was soon travelling upstairs in the plush, blue-leather covered single person elevator.

The door opened on the living area of Rigsan's base. He had to admit it was just as impressive as it was from the outside. It wasn't massive, but it was decorated smartly (and expensively, by the look of it). The kitchen, dining area and lounge were all one open plan area, with everything appointed in black and white. The sloped roof on two sides made Abel feel like he was inside a giant, hollowed-out Toblerone. Next to the kitchen, glass double doors led out onto a balcony that looked like it ran the width of the base. Above the kitchen units, there were large square windows, through which you could see the blackness of space beyond the protective atmosphere bubble, just as you could from Abel's living area bay window.

"You'll have to excuse the mess, I don't normally have anyone back here," apologised Rigsan, walking towards the kitchen area.

Abel looked around as he walked towards the double doors. This place was immaculate. There wasn't even any dust on anything, let alone any rubbish anywhere. In fact, the only thing remotely out of place was on his desk, where one of the five pens lined up was not quite parallel to the other four.

"Oh don't worry, it'll do!" replied Abel, raising his eyebrows. He stopped at the double doors, "does the artificial atmosphere extend out to the edge of the balcony?"

"It does," confirmed Rigsan, proudly, "I don't go out there much though. Reminds me how much unfinished business there is to do out there".

"Oh…uh…yeah, I'd be the same," Abel nodded in agreement, putting his hands on his hips and backing away from his dream balcony, "It's all about the work for me, too. That's why I didn't ask for one," he lied.

"So, it seems like we have a lot to talk about," said Rigsan, moving over to the stool chairs that lined the black-topped breakfast bar, "Take a seat".

Abel thought he'd never ask. He'd eyed up the corner sofa the minute he walked out of the chute and this was finally his chance. He slumped down into the corner of the L-shaped sofa and let out a grateful "Ahhhhh". He leaned back, placed his arms on the top of the cushions and closed his eyes. 'I think I could get to like this clone' he thought, until he opened his eyes. He was greeted with the sight of Rigsan, sat at the breakfast bar, staring judgingly at him. Without a word, Abel got up and made his way to one of the other stools, in the same sort of way that Colin would walk away when he fell off the sofa whilst fast asleep.

"Sarge, make us two cups of tea, please" said Rigsan as Abel sauntered over to the next stool. Rigsan pointed at him as he sat down, "You a Green Tea man like me?"

"Oh...uh..." Abel wondered how much more judging he would get from a honest answer. He decided his give-a-toss-o-meter was probably already at maximum, "No, normal for me".

They both paused as they independently wrestled with the fact that everyone's definition of 'normal', when referring to anything might have to change after today's events.

"Okay, did you hear that Sarge, one Green, one English Breakfast please".

"Sir yes sir!" replied Rigsan's SARDOC. Abel was taken aback by his tone, as this was the first time he'd heard Rigsan's digital companion speak since the rip.

"Is your SARDOC a..."

"American Drill Sergeant? Yeah," Rigsan cut him off, "The boffins decided that it was the best personality type to keep me focused I suppose. What's yours?"

"English Butler," replied Abel, as two differing cups of steaming hot Tea materialised in front of them on the bar, "I'm not sure what that says about my personality! Maybe you've seen the movie *Arthur* with *Dudley Moore*?"

Abel sniggered at his own embarrassment, as Rigsan nodded knowingly.

"Blimey, I have a strong memory of watching that film at my Nan and Grandad's house. Maybe during the…"

"…Summer Holidays," interrupted Abel, picking up his tea and nodding, "I used to spend ages at my Nan and Grandads house during the summer holidays".

"Yeah, me too, always in the shed, building…" continued Rigsan, reminiscing suspiciously.

"…model boats…" agreed Abel, looking at his tea-drinking clone,

"…which would never float…" they both said together, in the exact same voice. Rigsan's eyes slowly met Abel's as they started to think there might be more going on here than even they had wondered.

"How have they copied my memories?" Abel wondered aloud, before taking a swig of tea,

"Your memories?!" protested Rigsan, "They're my memories – you're the one nicking them!"

"Look, I know what I remember!" said Abel, trying to stay calm.

"Well, so do I!" replied Rigsan, "What was my Nan's favourite record?"

"She was my Nan and Mario Lanza. How many showers did my Grandad have a week?" Questioned Abel, slamming the tea down on the bar,

"He was my Grandad and it was one, Sunday evenings, listening to Sing Something Simple!" fired back Rigsan, slamming his tea down as well, "Which of their cars was my favourite?"

"He was MY Granddad and it a was red and white Triumph Herald!" shouted Abel. They were nose to nose before they both realised. They breathed heavily in each other's faces before silently relaxing back into their chairs, all without breaking angry eye contact. Colin broke the tension by jumping on the counter in between them and meowing in confusion at the two similar beings he was presented with. They both took a minute to recompose themselves and looked back the cat.

"Why is Colin here?!" asked Abel, after a deep breath.

"Colin lives here, that's why!" replied Rigsan, holding out his hands picking his feline friend up, "And he knows he's not allowed on the worktops, don't you Colin?"

Rigsan could see Abel's anger turn back into confusion as he returned Colin to the floor.

"Don't tell me, you've got a cat called Colin as well?"

Abel didn't tell him, as instructed. He just nodded.

"This is stupid, we are not going to get any answers doing this," said Abel, breaking the silence after drinking what little of his tea wasn't all over the counter, "But I know where there might be some".

"Oh really, and where the hell would that be?" asked Rigsan, all his bravado melted away by Colin's relaxing 'fur and purr' routine.

"Look, I've been to the head office of Universal Corrections. I've seen inside the compound. There are hundreds of TTAXIs. Thousands maybe. Thousands of agents too. If the notice board I saw is to be believed, you and I are just two cogs in a very large wheel. It's set up like an airport terminal and there are TTAXIs coming and going constantly. It looked like a massive operation, more than just something that would service the two of us".

Rigsan opened his mouth to say something, but it looked like his brain couldn't think of anything, so it shut again. He tried this three more times before Abel continued.

"I managed to infiltrate the compound disguised as a cleaner. I used the ventilation tunnels to get right to the door of what seems to be the main control room. It's called 'the Parallel Nexus'. But there's an eight-armed bouncer guarding it and I think we need help to get past it.

Rigsan thought for a moment. Abel sympathised, "Look, It's a lot to digest, I know. It's not every day you find out there's a 50/50 chance that you're a clone…"

"I am not a bloody clone!" snapped Rigsan, angrily.

"I can show you if you don't trust me! I managed to get all the way in without my suit or my SARDOC the first time. With two of us fully equipped, it should be no problem at all. What do you say?"

Rigsan sat and stared out of the window at the vastness of space. Abel could see his colleague's eyebrows moving up and down as his brain attempted to process all of the last hour's revelations. He finally drank the last of his Green Tea, placed the mug down on the counter and turned to look at Abel.

"Let's go get some answers!" he agreed.

-

"Right, so I'm thinking I'll be the driver for the trip over and you be you". Said Abel, as the Garage door closed behind them and they walked towards the TTAXI.

"Won't that look a bit obvious?" asked Rigsan, "What did you do the first time you were there, when you didn't have your suit?"

"I had to be me until I could get a cleaner's overalls to dress up in," replied Abel, opening the door and getting in the driver's seat.

"Can't I just get Sarge to disguise me as a cleaner?" Rigsan asked as he got in the back seat.

"Not at the moment, as you're disconnected from the mainframe. So until you see what the cleaner's overalls look like in person, your suit won't be able to reproduce them".

"Oh," said Rigsan, pursing his lips sardonically and turning his head away, "How very 20th century!"

"Well, it's either that or you reconnect to the mainframe and they find out exactly what we're doing!" snapped Abel, beginning the start-up sequence, "Don't worry, I've got a secret way in. It'll be fine!"

'It'll be fine' thought Rigsan, mockingly. 'Things are very rarely fine when people say that. Things are normally made up as they go along when people who say that are in charge.'

"As soon as Sarge sees an example of each employee at the compound, you can ditch the overalls". Said Abel, as he inputted the coordinates for the TTAXI Rank.

They had agreed to call their SARDOCs different names, to avoid any overlapping commands like they had during the Rip. Luckily, Rigsan always called his SARDOC Sarge anyway and Abel would stick to calling his S. Also luckily, the Emergency Autonomy mode that both suits were currently in meant they couldn't communicate with *each other*. God alone knows what each digital companion would make of their alternate versions. Abel suspected it would be just as much of a clash of personalities as his and Rigsan's. They were similar, but different – that seemed like a common theme over today.

"Sarge, can't you just copy Abel's look once he's disguised himself as whatever we need?"

"Sir no sir," replied Sarge, apologetically, "When Agent Abel's suit is in stealth mode, all I can see is the Nano-varmints underneath, sir".

"Wonderful. So, what's the plan once we've infiltrated the compound then, Abel?" asked Rigsan, as he saw the countdown timer begin to tick on the dashboard.

"Well, once we've got you a disguise, we'll slip past the guards at the Departures door with our ID badges," replied Abel, assuredly, "Then I can show you the door and get your thoughts on it. Once we've done that, we'll go to Departures disguised as drivers and take a TTAXI each. Then we just have to convince two more of us to help".

"That actually sounds like a pretty good plan," said Rigsan, nodding his head in mild appreciation, "…for a clone…"

"Don't start," Abel replied, trying not let this version of himself get to him. It was like his sarcastic conscience from his dreams had been made flesh and was sitting behind him, "Don't worry Rigsan, we'll have you back in plenty of time to give your next lecture at Arsehole College".

143

Abel said the burn so matter-of-factly, that all Rigsan could do was let out an absent-minded "Thanks".

Before he realised the slight, the countdown timer had hit zero and they were rapidly coming up on the TTAXI rank at the compound. For once, he wished the Tachyons hadn't done their job so efficiently and he would've gotten some time to think of a decent come back.

"Right, watch for the cleaner's equipment room coming up on the right," said Abel, as the TTAXI joined the back of the constantly moving line.

"Well, it isn't going to be coming up on the left, is it?! That would put it in the middle of space!" Rigsan hoped that his snarky reply would count as a retort to Abel's last comment with whoever was keeping score, much to the tangential side of his brain's disgust.

They could both see the recess coming up on the right, as the cleaner's door slowly showed itself.

"Right, follow me," said Abel, as he opened the driver's door and started to get out.

Rigsan dutifully followed, which was something he really wasn't very good at doing, even *before* he became the Universe's 'Last Line of Defence'. They both looked around to make sure the guards further down the rank at the Arrivals door hadn't seen them. Abel opened the cleaner's room door and slipped inside, closely followed by Rigsan.

"Right the equipm...DON'T LET THE DOOR SHU..." Abel spun around as he could see the light from outside disappearing, but it was too late, "T!" Came the end of his sentence.

"What the…?!" exclaimed Rigsan, looking as confused as a Cat watching Snooker, "What's your problem?"

Abel engaged his hand torch and shone it at the door, right where a handle should be.

"There's no handle on the inside of the door," he said, through gritted teeth, "Look!"

"Well that should be…" started Rigsan.

"…on a sign, yes" interjected Abel acidly, moving the torch quickly upwards so it illuminated the sign, "it is".

There was a moment of silence, before Rigsan started again, quietly,

"Well, that should really be…"

"…on the outside, yes!" finished Abel, nodding and smiling in fake agreement.

Abel found the light switch and turned to look for a disguise. Rigsan took a few steps behind him, with his arms out, apologetically.

"It's okay, you've done the route through the ducts before," said Rigsan, as positively as he could muster, "We'll just follow the same path you did before!"

"Er…yes…good idea," replied Abel, not looking around so that Rigsan couldn't see his face, which currently looked like he was doing an impression of Wallace from Wallace and Gromit.

He realised that S hadn't been there to record his route the last time he did it. 'It'll be fine' thought the same deluded, positive thinking part of his brain as before. 'Have you met our memory?!' replied the logic centres, blinking in amazement,

'That confused old DNA thief can't remember what we had for breakfast!'

But Abel knew that was the only way out, so he would have to ask his memory to step up on this occasion, which probably terrified him more than anything else that happened today, a day when he'd become aware that there were potentially thousands of clones of him running around the universe.

"Here's one," he said, picking a cleaner's uniform our of a box on the bottom shelf, just behind the red bucket., "Here you go, try it on".

Rigsan still wasn't sure about all this and Abel could see it. He started to step into the right leg of the overalls and suddenly stopped.

"Hang on," Rigsan had clearly had a thought, "I've got an idea. Why don't *you* put on the uniform and I'll get Sarge to scan you?"

"Hmm, that's actually a good idea!" agreed Abel, wondering to himself why *he* didn't think of it. But then he reasoned *he* did, if he thought about it.

Abel complied and struggled into the overalls. Rigsan engaged his Nano suit while he did so. Abel then stood there, arms down by his side while Sarge scanned him for measurements and colours. After a few short minutes, Abel had disrobed again and both men were disguised as cleaners.

"Don't forget this," said Abel, handing Rigsan an ID card from the top shelf, "And this". He handed him a hand caddy and kept one for himself. Rigsan went to push it away.

"I don't clean," said Rigsan smugly, "I have always had people for that!"

Abel pushed the caddy back at him, sternly.

"You do here, mate" replied Abel, forcing the caddy into Rigsan's hand and starting to climb up the shelving towards the duct.

"Well I'll carry it, just for the character," said Rigsan, like a schoolboy that had just been told off, "But I'm not dusting anything".

-

Abel was surprised how much of the route he remembered. He resolved to give his memory a metaphorical pat on the back once this was all over. Before too long, they were almost at the exit into the same stationary cupboard as he had climbed down in before. Luckily, this time he had S to help him glide through the pipes with a lot more ease than last time, meaning that he managed to climb down into the room this time, rather than plopping out the tube like a pat from a cow's bottom.

Rigsan followed his colleague into the room, glad that his days of sliding through a tube looking at his clone's fat arse were behind him.

"Okay, it's out this door, left down to the T-junction, left and then follow me to the next T-junction and look right. But don't make it obvious! Do as I do and let me do the talking, I've got the accent down and everything!" instructed Abel.

'Who does he think he is?' thought Rigsan, his fake nose well and truly getting out of joint, 'I mean, I know he's been here before, but this is not the first stealth mission I've been…hang on, he still thinks *I'm* the clone!'

However, he didn't have time to pursue that line of thinking any further, as Abel was already opening the cupboard door and disappearing into the corridor.

Abel started enthusiastically dusting his way down the corridor, just as he had before. Rigsan smiled to himself at how ridiculous he looked, until he saw two guards appear at the T-junction they were heading towards and start walking towards them. What followed was the most half-hearted cleaning Abel had ever seen – and he'd worked in a supermarket.

"What's that?" whispered Abel, barely hiding his frustration, "What are you doing?"

"I'm cleaning!" Rigsan whispered back aggressively, "What do you think I'm doing?"

"Your cloth isn't even touching the surface!" Whispered Abel, switching glances between Rigsan's face, his cloth and the approaching guards, "It's not a cloth vacuum, you actually have to place the cloth on the surface and rub it!"

Abel placed his hand on top of Rigsan's and pushed the cloth onto the door frame. Rigsan snatched it away.

"I'm in character!" defended Rigsan, "I'm a lazy cleaner who *pretends* to clean".

Abel motioned towards the guards, who were less than twenty feet away now, "You're going to get us found out!"

"You there, cleaning team!" shouted one of the guards, pointing at Abel, "Are you here for the emergency clean up call around the corner?"

They both froze. Abel took the chance to chance to stare at Rigsan while he still had his back to the guards, in a classic 'I told you so' way.

"Let me do the talking" he mouthed to Rigsan, slowly as he turned around.

"Yes comrade," Abel said in his now-standard-and-definitely-not-racist Eastern European voice, "I clean for you round corner, yes?"

"Well what's keeping you?" asked the guard, pointing to the end of the T-junction, "The plasma dust is everywhere round there. Fallapdax really made a mess of those workmen".

The guard looked at his mate and sniggered.

"You know what he's like if you've got the wrong paperwork," he joked, as his fellow guard smiled and nodded.

"Maybe he needs to get laid?" said the other guard as they both laughed. He turned back to Abel.

"You'd better take your friend as well".

"Yes, is good idea," Abel agreed, motioning to Rigsan to follow him as he began to walk between the guards.

"Yes mon!" exclaimed Rigsan, in a Jamaican accent so bad that even the non-Human guards looked taken aback with, "Dis is a jab dat will earn ma rice and pea tonight!"

Rigsan smiled and tipped his fellow Agent a confident 'I got this' type of wink. He wondered why everyone was staring at him.

Abel couldn't quite believe what he had heard but decided there really wasn't time to explain to Rigsan where he was going wrong. He just grabbed his accent-confused colleague by the arm and pulled him down the corridor. Rigsan remained quite impressed with himself as they rushed towards the T-junction.

"See, not my first stealth mission," he said proudly.

"Oh, I can see that!" agreed Abel, wondering how this copy could possibly have been fashioned from his DNA, "How many White Jamaican Cleaners have you been in contact with exactly?!"

"They clearly weren't from Earth, so I thought I'd have a little fun" replied Rigsan, chortling. But Abel wasn't chortling, he was too busy worrying that his partner's arrogance was going to get them dusted by the big Octo-Boglin.

The big Octo-Boglin that Rigsan had just noticed.

"What the hell is that?!" Rigsan whispered loudly, if that's even possible, "Its like an eight-armed…um, of what was that big-headed toy called from the 80s?"

"A Boglin, yes already been there," replied Abel, as they got to the dust piles.

"Yes, that's it," confirmed Rigsan, giving himself a thumbs up, "A Boglin, ha," he began to snigger, "Maybe it should be called an Oc…"

"Octo-Boglin," finished Abel, "yes, been there as well".

'Maybe we are the same in some ways,' worried Abel to himself. They both bent down and started sweeping up the piles with the portable vacuum cleaners they found in their caddies, the Dysmension 43.

Abel and Rigsan probably weren't aware, but they held in their hands the cutting edge in dust removal technology. Dyron Jes had patented his Dysmension cleaning system on his home planet of Sweeren 2, when he invented a tiny stable wormhole generator that would fit in the palm of your hand. As the other side of the wormhole was in space, the difference in pressure meant that it produced the most powerful suction force ever seen in the field. 'There's no vacuum like the one of space' was the advert that quickly made Dyron Jes a very rich man. It wasn't until several standard years and hundreds of off-world planetary expansions later, that a terrible fact was discovered. No matter where in the galaxy a Dysmension cleaner was turned on, the other end of the wormhole was always in orbit around Dyron's neighbouring planet, Sweeren 3. It's flora and protoplasmic fauna were quickly killed off, as a universe's worth of dust, dead skin cells, lost buttons and paper clips encircled the planet. Luckily for Dyron, by the time this was public knowledge, he was one of the richest men in history and was able to buy the affected planet so that he could ironically sweep the whole thing under a metaphorical carpet.

As they sucked up what was left of the workmen, they kept sneaking quick glances of Fallapdax and the door behind him. The big Octo-Boglin looked like he was having a quick nap, the double murder seeming to have taken it out of him.

"So that's where we are trying to get into, is it?" asked Rigsan, as part of the workmen's cheek flew up the vacuum tube.

151

"Yep, by my reckoning we need eight matching palm prints the same to get past the door. That's after we've distracted his lordship, of course!"

"I think you might be right," concurred Rigsan, as Sarge zoomed in momentarily on one of the windows in the double doors, "Certainly looks like that's the place to get our answers. Let's get these piles cleaned up and go get more help".

"I thought you didn't clean?" poked Abel, a sly grin appearing in the corner of his face, which the Nano Bytes embarrassingly replicated on the outside of his suit.

"I told you, this is not my first stealth mission," replied Rigsan, ignoring the sarcasm and standing up, "I do whatever it takes!"

'Oh please,' thought Abel, mentally rolling his eyes so that the suit didn't replicate it this time, 'They really turned up the arsehole levels with this clone!'

Abel was also finished with his pile, so he joined Rigsan in an upright position. They placed their tools back in the caddies and Abel led them off to find Departures. Meanwhile, the workmen took up their new residence in orbit around Sweeren 3.

-

"So that's the room where the Departures are controlled from," said Abel, pointing to his right as they turned the corner, "Just hang on here a second".

Abel disappeared into a door to his left before Rigsan had a chance to look around. He spun around on the spot, sort of taking all the various information he was being bombarded with at this moment – to his right, the Departures Room door, to his left the door into which Abel had disappeared and straight ahead, a door marked "TTAXI Rank" straight in front of him at the end of the corridor, protected by an ID card panel. Two guards were on the outside of the doors, armed with Gutsalizers from what he could make out.

"Where have you gone n…" he started to say, before the door to his left stopped closing and started opening again, "Abel?"

"Alright me old mate!" greeted the chirpy driver who appeared out of the door, winking at Rigsan to make sure he knew the fix was in.

"Blimey," exclaimed Rigsan, starting to chuckle, "The Nano Bytes really capture that double Denim look, don't they?"

"Blooming right they do, guv" Abel replied, maintaining the thick Cockney accent with a little too much enthusiasm for Rigsan's liking, "It's your turn now!"

Rigsan sighed as he realised Abel was right. He already knew what the drivers looked like, so there was no need to delay. He was about to commit a gross clothing crime upon his person and his Nano Bytes. It was the fashion version of self-harming.

He disappeared into the side door and reappeared in his own version of a driver costume, complete with a grey mullet, just as Abel had done. They stood and stared at each other, until Abel's face was the first to crack and they both burst out laughing. Even Rigsan had to admit that this was not a situation he had envisaged when he woke up this morning.

They took a few seconds to compose themselves before they decided to move onto the exit door. Before they did, Abel could see that his partner was fidgeting about uncomfortably.

"What's wrong with you?" asked Abel, looking him up and down.

"These bloody Cowboy boots!" exclaimed Rigsan, trying to wiggle his foot about as if to get a better fit, "I've never worn them before".

"What are you talking about?" Abel looked confused, "I used to wear them all the time in my early 20s! Always wore them out to clubs. They were one of the main reasons I never pulled, remember?"

"Why would anyone wear this rubbish in their early 20s?!" questioned Rigsan, jiggling the other foot now, "My university running mates would have roasted me!"

"Your uni…?" Abel was even more confused now. He hadn't been to university for more than a year, certainly not into his early 20s. He was already working in the supermarket then. And even when he was at university, he certainly didn't have any running mates. Not unless they were late for the bus, anyway. How had the Cromulites managed to clone him, implant memories, but then add different memories? 'Add another question to the list' thought his logic centres, eager to get on with the mission in front of them.

"Get your ID card ready," whispered Abel, rummaging around in his caddy and grabbing his card. He looked up at Rigsan, who was already holding his card in his hand. Not for the first time and probably not for the last if Abel was right, a smug grin bathed Rigsan's face.

Abel ambled up to the security panel and placed his card on it. It did its usual uppy-downy-scanny thing and one green light later, the doors opened. Rigsan did the same and they were both now out on the TTAXI rank.

Just as before, the drivers were gathered in a small hut between the Arrivals and Departures areas. It was a hut that was far too small for the number of drivers needed for the amount of TTAXIs, so god knows what was going on in there. Abel imagined the stench of well-worn Denim that must be prevalent inside that room, along with the glint of cheap gold jewellery. There was a group of five of them congregating outside the hut, who sounded like they were discussing the merits of Greyhound Racing as the Agents walked past. They saw their opportunity and quickly jumped the queue and quickened their pace toward the next two free TTAXIs.

"You take that one, Rigsan," Abel said, pointing at the third TTAXI from the front, marked with DOF976 on its sign, "I'll take the one behind, KIN437. We'll meet back in the cleaner's cupboard in two hours".

"Roger, start the timer, Sarge" said Rigsan, quietly as he walked towards the TTAXI.

"Sir yes sir!" exclaimed Sarge "7200...7199....7198..."

"To yourself, Sarge" said Rigsan, tutting. The counting stopped abruptly.

"Rigsan!" Abel shouted after him.

"What?"

"Good luck".

"Roger that!" Rigsan got in his cab.

"Good luck to you too, Abel me old mate" said Abel under his breath, raising his eyebrows as he got in his TTAXI, "Honestly, some people".

CHAPTER 11
GRAB YOUR TIN FOIL HAT

PLYMOUTH, TERRA, SOL SYSTEM, MILKY WAY, EARTH YEAR 2012

"I saw a Bee do a Poo yesterday Mary" said Mark, as he grabbed the *Point Break* DVD out of the cardboard box in front of him, "He was just there, hovering next to me and then *PLOP* out came the poo, just falling out of the back of him".

He looked at the row of DVDs on the shelf and desperately tried to find where it went in the alphabetical order of the ones that had already been donated. Some of them had been there for years – Who the hell was going to want *The Darling Buds of May* box set, even if it was 50p? He found a gap between *Papillon* and *Pot Black: Virgo's Trick Shot Bonanza* and slid the case in.

"Are you sure it wasn't just some pollen it dropped?" asked Mary, who was used to Mark's hallucinations after volunteering with him in the charity shop for the past five years.

"Well, I thought that as well," replied Mark, excitedly grabbing *Timecop* out of the box, "but it didn't look like it had dropped it. What I mean is, it didn't look like it went 'oh bugger!' and swooped down to get it, like I would if I dropped this DVD. No, it just let it drop and then flew off, large as life. It was definitely poo Mary".

"Well I don't know," said Mary, shaking her head in amazement.

"Then I started wondering if Honey is really Bee Poo," he continued, resting his hands absent-mindedly on the shelf in front of him, "imagine if it is, Mary. Maybe that's why they get so riled up when you take their Honey? They're not trying to defend it, but instead they're shouting 'what are you doing? Stop! That's my poo you're eating! That's disgusting!'

"isn't nature wonderful?" Asked Mary, unfolding a pink blouse and pushing a hanger through the neck hole.

"They're getting smarter, Mary, it's not wonderful at all!" admonished Mark, turning around, "Up until now, a bee pooping has been an intrinsically private affair. But now they're doing it in public. Right next to a human. What's next, I ask you?"

"Oh Mark," sighed Mary, slumping her shoulders as she hung the blouse on the clothes rack by the side of her, "what will you think of next? It's all that wacky baccy you keep smoking – you know it makes you see things. A couple of months ago, you were convinced you saw a dog on the phone!"

"He WAS on the phone, Mary!" replied Mark, still looking for a gap for *Timecop*. T was a very popular section since he'd decided to include '*The*' in the alphabetical title of the DVD.

He was regretting that decision if truth be told, but he was too proud to admit it and too lazy to change it back again, "I mean, him and his owner went through this whole charade of 'Ooo I've dropped me phone' and 'Ooo the dog's trying to eat it', but I saw what was going on. I saw the dog pushing the numbers on the keypad"

Mark nodded his head knowingly to himself just as vigorously as Mary was shaking hers.

As if the mention of a phone was all it needed to spring into action, his mobile suddenly started ringing in his pocket. They both jumped, as it was quite a bit louder than the radio.

"This could be him, Mary" he said jokingly, maintaining eye contact with his elderly co-volunteer as he slid his Nokia 3310 out of his pocket.

'Ten years and still going strong' he thought to himself, proudly regarding his battered old phone, 'You can keep your smartphones with their traceability and GPS'.

"Woof woof?" he said as he answered it, still looking at Mary as she laughed along with him.

"Oh…hi Dad…yeah, not too bad…in the shop, why?" Mark produced a plastic timer out of his cardigan pocket, its display already set to 90 seconds and pressed the 'start' button. On the reverse was message written in Dymo labels – 'Mark's timer. Do not touch!'

Mary went back to folding the clothes on the counter in front of her, breaking eye contact with Mark. It was always awkward for Mark when his parents called, and she wanted to pretend to not be there if at all possible. She had an idea and rapidly made the international sign for 'cup of tea?' at him.

He gave her the thumbs up signal and she disappeared round the back of the shop to the kitchen area.

"No, I can talk...not for very long though, remember?" he continued, subconsciously drifting towards the tightest corner of the shop, behind the DVD rack, "You know why...what do you want?"

70 seconds.

Mark fidgeted as he listened to his Dad's query.

"Well, you just have to...I know, it's confusing...have you got your email password there...the pass...for the TalkTalk account, yeah"

He nervously played with the corner of the rack, where the plastic was coming away from the metal frame, the bare area of the silver evidence of how many times he had worried it before.

50 seconds.

"It's in your password book, isn't it...no, that's your account login...no, your phone account, not your email account...yes, it is confusing, I know..."

He waited as he could hear pages turning in his Dad's Staedtler notebook.

30 seconds.

"It's definitely there, I remember writing it in the last time I was...got it? Under the other...yeah, that's right...944, yeah that's the one. Good...how's mum?"

10 seconds.

He half listened to the answer as his focus drifted more to the stopwatch with each passing second.

"Okay, well…"

5 seconds.

"Tell her I said hello…"

3 seconds.

"Yeah, I'll try. Gotta go, bye Dad!"

He hit the red button on the Nokia and the 'Stop' button together with the thumbs on either hand.

1 second.

"That was close, Mary, 1 second," he shouted to the back, so Mary could hear him over the kettle, "They almost got a trace that time!"

"Of course they did, dear," shouted Mary, as the kettle clicked, "How was your Dad?"

"Oh, you know, okay…I think" Mark replied as he moved back to the box of DVDs, "Didn't get a lot of time to talk really".

He wasn't about to break the '90 second rule' and risk detection by the government just to ask his Dad about his knees. Someone had messaged him a year ago through the *Greyhammer.com* conspiracy website that he ran and told him about the amount of time it takes for the MI5 to trace a call. Ever since then, he'd stuck to it fastidiously.

"Well than maybe it's time to go and see them again, dear" Mary said as she appeared through the doorway with two steaming mugs. Mary's was always the one with blue Irises on it, Mark's the *Star Trek* one.

"Yeah, maybe it is…but they're so far away!" Mark nodded, as he grabbed his mug from off the tray.

"They're in Plympton, Mark!" laughed Mary, her face doing the 'aw bless him' expression it did quite regularly where her co-volunteer was concerned, "It's hardly the Moon!"

"It takes all my courage and willpower to get here, Mary!" Mark cried, laughing ruefully, "I don't think you understand how much effort it is for me to leave my flat at all!"

"I know, dear" agreed Mary.

"I'm not sure you do, Mary," Mark sighed, dropping his head to one side and staring past her as he remembered seeing the backs of his friends running off, twenty-five years ago, "When you're fragile mentally and then your best friends leave you to get beaten up, it changes you. It changed me, anyway. I haven't really trusted anyone since then. Some days its physically impossible to get out of bed. My bladder gets me up more often than my willpower does".

He took a sip of Tea, his lips unknowingly kissing Captain Kirk on the top of his head. If there was one thing he *could* trust, it was Mary's Tea-making ability.

"It's why I lost my job at the Supermarket; it's why I've never been able to do anything with my life; sometimes I go for weeks without leaving the house or talking to anyone in person. If it wasn't for you and my YouTube subscribers, I wouldn't talk to anyone most days!"

Mary rested a bony hand on his forearm and did the face again. It was warm from holding her mug, in contrast to usual.

"You're doing a good thing here, dear," she said, trying to comfort him, "We like having you around, even if you do run out the back every time someone comes in. The media section has never been so organised. It's fine. You're just not a people person".

"Huh, you can say that again," Mark laughed, a smile returning to his lips, "I don't mind helping people, just as long as there's a… barrier between me and them".

"Well, you keep sorting the DVDs and books and I'll keep talking to the customers".

Mark snorted and placed his hand gently on top of Mary's.

"Deal".

The nice moment was broken by the bell on the door ringing, signalling that someone was coming in the front. Which was Mark's cue to scuttle out the back.

-

"Are you here tomorrow, dear?" asked Mary, as she waited for Mark to bring the shutter down on the shop front.

"Oh you know me, Mary, who knows?" Replied Mark, pushing the shutter all the way down so it touched the pavement, "I hope so. Your tea always makes me feel better".

"I hope so too, dear," said Mary, as she locked the shutter in place, "You do make me laugh. And besides, you can lift the shutter a lot easier than I can!"

"I'm glad I have my uses Mary," he laughed, playfully pushing her shoulder, "I'll try, I'll try. Night Mary". he nodded as assertively as he could.

"Goodnight dear," she replied. She could see Mark was looking over her shoulder at someone. She turned her head and saw a dodgy looking gentleman walking towards them. He was familiar to her, as he was who supplied Mark with his Marijuana. She turned back to offer her advice before the man arrived.

"I wish you would cut down on the wacky baccy, dear". She said to him, her face a mask of concern.

"I wish a lot of things, Mary" he replied as the man got nearer, "I wish I'd never gone out that night. I wish I didn't panic every time strangers talk to me. I wish I could have convinced Michelle how much I loved her before she took out the restraining order."

He smiled timidly at her, before pushing past her to talk to the dealer. He hopped from one foot to the other, as Mary walked away in the opposite direction. She looked back every few steps like a worried mother Duck watching her ducklings' first trip onto the pond without her.

Mark already had the money in this right hand when the conversation began. The dealer had the baggy in his. They shook hands and in complete silence, the deal was done. They nodded at each other and walked their separate ways, with Mark walking to the pedestrian crossing to begin his half hour walk home.

As he waited for the lights to change, he could feel the expectation of lighting up his first joint of the evening begin to fill his mind. He could almost feel the relaxation washing over him already, just knowing he was 45 minutes away from it. He bit his lip in anticipation. That feeling of your whole body being still, but your mind moving more than it ever possibly could in the physical realm. Life had become a series of unrelated events that happened between joints. He pretty much lived for it these days. That and trying to uncover the truth for his website and YouTube followers. The 'truth behind the great lie' as he liked to term it on his online channels. He went under the pseudonym *thegreyhammer* in the online world, which was another way of separating himself from the pain of the physical one. He knew, scratch that, he was convinced that there was more out there than the 'normal' world was showing us. If there wasn't, the alternative was too depressing for even him to think about. He often felt his life force was being drained away, like a tea bag expunging its remaining contents uselessly onto a serviette. All that energy must be going somewhere.

He crossed over the pedestrian crossing and into Houndiscombe Road, which would eventually come out on North Road East. He took a slightly different route every day, so the 'powers that be' couldn't predict his route. Today he was in a particular hurry to get home, for obvious reasons, so he had decided on pretty much the quickest route possible.

The road took a long bend to the right and as it started to flatten out, he could see a group of youths standing at the bus stop. A group of unsavoury looking youths. 'All tracksuits and baseball caps' he thought to himself, as he relived that night 25 years ago in his mind for the umpteenth time.

He could still feel every kick, every punch, every wad of spit that had been projected onto him that night. Smoking the Skunk was the only time he couldn't feel it when he was still. The 45 minutes seemed to be getting further away. In reality, it was, as he had subconsciously stopped dead in his tracks and become frozen to the spot. The sweat had started beading from his forehead and soaking through the front of his grey beanie hat.

He thought about crossing over, but the double yellow lines both sides meant there was no cars to hide behind even if he did so. He thought about running back to Mutley Plain and finding Mary. He even thought about ringing his Dad and asking for a lift, but his pride stopped him.

He finally decided that he would have to double back and take a different route. But he had already planned this route in the shop like he always did and now the shop was closed for the night. The panic began to shake his hands and started to travel up each arm. The rapid, subconscious quivering that was as imperceptible to other people as it was impossible for him to control in these moments. Calling them 'panic attacks' was exactly the right description for them. They really did feel like your mind was waging a Cold War against your body. Sending rogue signals to your extremities to disrupt your movements. Dispatching muscle spasms to the throat to deprive the lungs of fuel. Heating up the skin and making it leak. It was a battle that he had become all too familiar with over the last 25 years.

The latest battle threatened to engulf him like it had so many times in the past, when his ears popped and a Black Cab drew up beside him.

He must have been more entranced by the group of youths than he thought, as he hadn't even heard the Taxi driving down the road behind him. Maybe this was a hallucination, another dirty trick in the Panic War? The driver, an old Cockney-looking gentleman leaned over and shouted through the open passenger window.

"You need a lift, mate?" asked the driver, his gold Sovereign rings reflecting in the street lights, "You look like you could use one".

"Er…I haven't got any money". Replied Mark, which he hoped the driver could see clearly wasn't a 'no'.

"That's okay, I'm between fares," the driver replied, looking out of the front window and then back at Mark, "where are you off to anyway?"

"Union Place," replied Mark, taking a step towards the cab window, but stopping himself from taking another one, "it's the other side of town".

"Oh, I know where Union Place is, guv'nor" the driver smiled, "I'm on my way to Union Street for my next fare anyway. Come on, I'll call it my good deed for the day".

Mark looked down the road at the gang again and the thought of boot connecting with the side of his head nearly knocked him back into the nearest garden. That decided it.

"Okay thanks, er…mate" said Mark, smiling nervously as he opened the door with his trembling hand and got in the back of the cab, "Rathbone House".

"No problem mate".

The Taxi set off and Mark couldn't help but stare at the gang of youths as they drove past them, "Friends of yours?"

"What them…no, definitely not!" Mark laughed, visibly relaxing as they got past them. The battle had subsided for the moment, "Too many bad memories".

"Yeah, terrible business what happened to you" said the Driver.

"Pardon?" Mark stopped looking at the youths and turned to face the front. He noticed the driver was looking at him in the rear-view mirror, as if to gauge his reaction, "I'm sorry?"

"Don't be sorry Mark," continued the driver, still staring into the rear-view mirror, "It's your friends who should be sorry".

The attack hadn't quite started again, but the panic soldiers were definitely loading their weapons and manning their positions.

"How do you know about that?" Mark asked, his hands starting to shake again in a pre-emptive strike.

"Fancy leaving you like that," the driver went on, shaking his head and tutting as he looked back at the road, "They could have helped you, but they ran away didn't they? No wonder you've got trust issues".

"I…you…how…" Mark stuttered, the attack reaching his throat and making it damn near impossible to speak. He would usually retreat to his bed for a week after an episode like this, but he was beginning to think that this wasn't going to be an option in this instance. He had not decided his route home until two hours ago. How had they intercepted him so easily? What were they going to do to him?

"You've never been able to relate to people since then, have you?" the driver looked back into the mirror, "Never allowed yourself to fulfil your potential".

"How…dare…you!" Mark managed to force out, the enemy Adrenaline starting to invade most of his body, "I've got a degree in Computer Science and I've got 50,000 subscribers on YouTube!"

The driver let go of the wheel and turned around to face him. He pulled back the screen and folded his arms on the back of the front seat.

"That's great Mark," confirmed the driver, "What about if you could be revered across the whole universe?"

"What…how…when?" The Adrenaline invasion was now making his voice tremble violently. He wasn't sure if it was because of the question or the fact the Taxi appeared to be driving itself.

"We've been watching you for a while, Mark. I work for an organisation called Universal Corrections. You're exactly what we are looking for. We think you have what it takes to be the last line of defence against the destruction of the universe. We can give you all the tools you'll need to fight the forces of evil. All you need to give us is yourself".

Mark slumped back into the cab seat. The trembling had subsided – he was too stunned to shake. His mouth started to form a start to his reply, only to shut again after the first syllable. His mind had stopped the panic attack now that it had a much bigger topic to think about.

"So…you're aliens?"

"No, I'm from Fincham," replied the driver, a playful smile dancing across his lips, as he turned back towards the front and flicked a selection of switches on the dashboard, "But I do work for Aliens".

"I knew it!" shouted Mark, far too loudly for such a little cab. He even scared himself a bit, "Um…the aliens bit, I mean. Not the 'me being the ideal choice for the defender of the universe' bit. Why me? Surely there must be someone braver?"

"C'mon Mark, you've read enough comics to know it's not always the strongest personalities that make the best heroes!" argued the driver.

"Oh, you wait until I tell Mary about this!" said Mark, laughing ruefully.

"Yeah, don't hold your breath about seeing Mary for a while," said the driver, as a large countdown timer started counting down from 30 seconds next to the steering wheel.

It was now that Mark looked out of the window, as it had suddenly got dark outside. He realised, as stars began to appear everywhere he looked, that it was because they were in space. In a Taxi. On his way to become an intergalactic superhero. And the most amazing thing he'd seen up to this point in his life was a bee doing a poo.

CHAPTER 12
HOX IS WHERE IT'S AT

**UNIVERSAL CORRECTIONS COMPOUND, UNKNOWN
LOCATION, EARTH YEAR 2018**

Agent Dofe awoke in his now customary sweaty mess. His eyes took a few seconds to focus, so it took him a little while to affirm to himself that he wasn't dead and that it had actually just been a dream.

'That bloody morgue' he thought to himself, as the room continued to come into focus around him, 'I hate that dream.'

He hadn't been having the dream for very long, but since he had had it the first time, it seemed to be an increasingly popular one. It was vying for top spot with the one where he was a professional gamer at the World Tetris Tournament only to realise he is completely naked.

As he got his bearings he realised that, as he wasn't as dead as previously thought, he could in fact move his limbs. Except, his left leg wasn't following the script. Good old Righty was fine, dancing about like he'd forgotten to take his nerve medication, but oh no,

Lefty was staying exactly where he was. In fact, Dofe was sure he couldn't feel his foot.

The panic began to wake up. However, it was quickly put back to sleep by the feeling that his leg was immobile because Colin had been, and in fact still was, asleep on his withered calf muscle. Dofe struggled to get his head off the pillow and leaned upwards to check if his suspicions were correct. Indeed they were, as the face of a very comfortable Colin stared back at him, woken from his graceful slumber now that his Human had had the temerity to move slightly.

"Oh for god's sake, Colin!" Dofe croaked, his voice box several places behind his eyes in the waking up Olympics, "You nearly gave me a heart attack!"

Colin was the only organic being in the universe that Dofe trusted. He was sure that Colin loved him and appreciated all the things he did for him. But Dofe was also acutely aware that, being a Cat, Colin would not hesitate to eat him if he dropped dead.

Colin seemed to sense Dofe internal monologue, as he rose from his position of vein blockage and walked up Dofe's side, positioning his head right above his owner's.

Dofe grabbed him gently and placed him next his stomach as he rolled over in the bed. This was for three main reasons: - 1) it was more comfortable to lay on his side; 2) it was easier to stroke Colin in this position and 3) Colin had the propensity to dribble when being stroked and Dofe didn't want an eyeful of Colin-spittle at any time of day, let alone first thing in the morning.

"Morning Dr S," Dofe called out, gently squeezing Colin's cheeks with one hand and squishing the top of his head with the other.

172

"Good morning my lovely, did you sleep well?" SARDOC's soft, feminine, soothing tones filled the room. Dofe found her half-English, half-Antipodean accent very attractive and very calming all at the same time. He always assumed that the crush he'd had on Pamela Stephenson since the 80s, was why the Cromulites had chosen it for him at Orientation.

"Not bad Dr S," Dofe replied, as Colin flopped down on his side to give Dofe a better angle for stomach smoothage, "considering I had the Morgue dream again".

"Oh sweetie, that pesky dream is putting you through the ringer isn't it?" said SARDOC, a concerned inflection in her voice, "Dreams of being dead are commonly interpreted to mean you see a new beginning or an end to your old ways. So I'm sure it's nothing to worry about".

"Nothing to worry about?!" exclaimed Dofe, "You know I hate new things! What new things could this job possibly bring, apart from bigger Wardz attacks and more danger?"

"Whatever happens, Sweetie, you know I'll be there to protect you," she replied comfortingly, "you've come so far since we were first paired together".

"Yeah I guess, Dr S", agreed Dofe, as he swung his legs out of the bed and he sat up, sending Colin jumping to the floor. His old, creaky joints made their usual protests as he struggled to stand up and he stood by the side of the bed for a few seconds to let the protests die down. Maybe the first toilet stop of the day and a chapter of *Watchmen* would make him feel better.

-

As suspected, he *did* feel better when he exited the toilet several minutes later.

"Do you want your usual for breakfast, sweetie?" SARDOC asked, already preparing the Vegan Flarg Nuts and Organic Decaf Coffee as she fully knew the answer in advance.

"Oh you read my mind, Dr S," replied Dofe, staying right on script and picking up the remote control for the display wall. He preferred using a remote for the display wall instead of letting SARDOC do it, "Let's see what's going on in the universe".

He plonked himself down on the sofa as the wall opposite him flickered into life. The image of a large egg with no hair and a big bushy beard appeared and Dofe recognised him straight away.

"Hey there universe, I'm Wene Dintros and you're watching...How the Hell Did They Happen?!" shouted the bearded man-egg, shaking his arms in front of him in his customary way.

"Ooo, I like HTHDTH, especially this time of the morning," said Dofe, wrapping the sofa blanket around his shivering, skeletal frame. If there was one thing he liked to see, it was confident people being brought down a peg or too until they were almost as physiologically damaged as he was.

"This is the show," continued Wene, who Dofe always thought looked like a drawing of Humpty Dumpty that a graffiti artist had drawn a beard on, "where we meet couples from across the four quadrants.

One of them is noticeably more attractive than the other. Could be him, could be her. We ask them a series of very personal questions. Finally, we ask the studio audience to vote on what they think is the reason that this unlikely pairing is together. The people who are right go onto the next couple and a chance to win prizes! Let's play…HTHDTH!!"

Wene motioned to the side of the stage and the first couple appeared from the side of the stage. The audience could be heard in fits of laughter before they'd even reached the host at centre stage. One of the creatures was a slim, almost elven beauty, six-foot-tall, with eyes like sapphires and a glowing white aura around them. The other creature could only be described as a giant Watermelon with legs. It didn't even have a head – its facial features looked like they were carved out of the side of its body, like a Pumpkin on Halloween.

"Oh, this is going to be a good one, Dr S!" said Dofe, shuffling in his seat expectantly and rubbing the creased skin on his forehead, "How the hell *did* these two get together?!"

"Of course, dear, here's your breakfast – be careful its very hot!" warned SARDOC, as the bowl and mug hologised onto the table in front of Dofe.

"So, couple number one here," continued Wene, as the Watermelon and the Elf stopped in front of him, "What's your names and where do you come from?"

"Hello Wene, my name's Aganax and I'm from Quimala IV," shouted the Watermelon in a high-pitched, piercing voice, "and this is my boyfriend, Gorgas from Vimevin V!"

Dofe was lucky his Decaf Coffee was still too hot to drink, or he'd have spit it all over the display wall. He wasn't sure whether the Watermelon's voice or the Elf's gender was the more shocking detail so far.

175

"Lovely stuff," said Wene, glancing up at them from his cue cards, "I'm not surprised by his name dear. I mean, he is Gorgas to look at!"

The crowd groaned and laughed in equal measures, as Wene mugged for the cameras. Dofe was ashamed of himself for laughing at the host's terrible joke, but he thought of something that could make this show even better.

"Hey Dr S hologise me a joint, would you?" he asked SARDOC, casually, "Just to help me with my Arthritis, you understand".

"Of course, Sweetie, it'll be there in two ticks". Confirmed SARDOC, as the Watermelon took her seat on an L-shaped sofa next to Wene, while the Elf climbed into a sound-proof booth and donned the eye mask, so he couldn't hear or see his partner's answers.

As the audience began to ask the personal questions, Mark thought back to his orientation. That feeling of suddenly realising that he was stood in a gigantic alien spacecraft with a baggie full of drugs in his pocket. In what he still considered to be one of the bravest things he'd ever done, he had asked to go to the toilet at that moment and swallowed the baggie in a cubicle. Four days later, as he always got bunged up when in stressful situations, he had washed the baggie off and hidden it in his bedside table. It was another two weeks before he plucked up the courage to ask SARDOC if she could hologise new foodstuffs from provided examples. She had confirmed that she could, and she'd been his supplier ever since. She didn't judge him or tell him off for it either, as she could see the benefits to his state of mind. Also, because she didn't reap any tax benefits from any other more addictive chemicals, she was able to treat the matter with no bias.

"Well, that's fascinating, time to swap the partners and see what Gorgas has to say!" said Wene, as the suddenly morose Watermelon and oblivious Elf swapped places. Aganax attempted to put on the blindfold three times, each time failing as the elastic string just rode up the oval head and formed a little crown on top. Finally, one of the floor managers came up with the idea of sticking large plasters over her eyes.

The joint had by now appeared on the table next to Dofe's breakfast. He reached out and picked it up with his left hand and the lighter with his right. He lit it and took the first drag like a professional that had done it thousands of times before. Which of course, he had. The effects of that first puff always felt like the first time though. He relaxed into the sofa and didn't even notice Colin jump up and sit next to him. It would take all of Gorgas' questions and the ensuing audience vote, for Dofe to be able to summon enough arm control to pick up his Decaf Coffee. He did manage to process the results of the couple though, which was that the Watermelon was rich, and the Elf was a gold-digger.

"What's on the agenda today then, Dr S?" asked Dofe finally, still exhibiting the relaxed, slow blink, "I'll be ready for the first mission once I've finished my breakfast".

"Well Sweetie, the first mission for us today is to the planet Hox, in the Theta Expanse," replied SARDOC, "A mainly water-based planet ruled from the oceans by the Chukulakans. They have recently joined the Galactic Alliance and have just started complaining of villages going missing".

"Sounds familiar, at least," said Dofe, "Okay, you call the TTAXI and I suppose I'll finish my Flarg Nuts and get the suit on. I need a bit longer at my age".

"That sounds like a great plan, my lovely," said SARDOC, reassuringly, "I'll get right on it!"

He stared at the old, pock-marked skin on his hand, as the joint burned down between his index and middle finger. It was an old hand. An elderly hand he still hadn't really got used to looking at. But the effects of the joint meant he *really* stared at it for what would be an unusual amount of time for an onlooker.

'Just my luck' he thought, for the hundredth time since the accident, 'the universe is still against me, even when I'm trying to save it.'

As he finished his Vegan Flarg Nuts, he had noticed that his spoon hand was shaking. Even without the panic, this was just what his limbs did now. Must be another side effect of ageing, he supposed. He downed the last of his Decaf Coffee and stood up, once again despite the protests of his body. At his age, sitting down was not only his greatest friend, but also his most vociferous enemy.

He could hear the Nano Bytes powering up in his observation room as he shuffled down the hallway. He stepped into the Nano Bytes tube once he got next to the window. While the Nano Bytes made their way down his body, he saw the TTAXI warp into being on the road below. He thought for a second that the landing didn't look as smooth as usual, but his attention was soon elsewhere. His eye was caught by a comet high above the base bubble. He shivered and thought about the accident again, as the comet started to produce a wondrous multi-coloured trail as it was caught by the gravity of one stellar body or another. Or it could be an alien ship on the way to abduct another poor unsuspecting victim. The paranoid jury was perpetually out on things like this.

He made his way back up the hallway and outside to meet the TTAXI. "Calm down sweetie, everything's going to be alright," SARDOC said, her soothing settings turned up to maximum, as she sensed Dofe's spike in heart rate and respiration, "remember to moderate your breathing. Remember the breathing exercises we learned".

'Easier said than done' thought Dofe, as he stepped towards the TTAXI, but he tried to follow SARDOC's suggestion. He took a deep breath in through his nose and a long, slow breath out through his gritted teeth. He kept doing it and it seemed to help, even if it did mist up the suit momentarily. In the four missions since the accident, his anxiety levels were through the roof whenever he was around these bloody machines. The driver quickly took a bit of his mind off his troubles.

"Aright me old mate, how's it cracking?" asked the driver, in what sounded like a mixture of Irish and Cockney, "Off to Hox are we? What's the situation?"

Dofe squinted inside his suit. He'd never met an Irish Cockney before. He didn't even know they existed, to be honest. This was not good for his stress levels. His palms decided to start sweating, just as a precaution.

"Er…yeah, sounds like it," Dofe answered, as he got in the back seat, "Another disappearance to look into".

"Ah, those pesky Wardz!" exclaimed the driver, now seemingly fully Irish. Dofe watched as the driver fumbled with the dashboard buttons in a way he hadn't seen before. The driver was clearly looking for the next switch in the launch sequence. Dofe gave him a few tries to find it himself, before he decided to help out.

"It's that blue one you want next…" he offered, gingerly pointing to a spot on the dashboard between a green lever and a red slider, "…I think, anyway. Sorry…"

179

"Ah, of course," said Driver O'Malley, throwing his hands up and shaking his head, "I'd forget my head if it weren't screwed on, so I would...er...apples and pears".

The countdown timer finally sprang into life and began its job. It's only job, mind. No one had ever asked the countdown timer what *it* had wanted to do with its life. But, ironically, we haven't got time to get into that now.

"Um...first trip?" asked Dofe, making a concerned face under his suit.

"Ah, no..." replied the driver, his cockney accent returning, "Err...heavy night on the beer last night...down the boozer, to be sure!"

"Oh, okay," Dofe said, turning away as the palm sweat returned.

'So, I get an Irish Cockney driver who's probably still drunk from the night before' he thought, laughing at his repetitive misfortune, 'great. Well, nothing's going to go wrong here, is it?!'

-

They crashed through the atmosphere in the customary ball of light and heat and came to a wobbly landing on a beach. Probably the biggest, longest beach Dofe had ever seen. It disappeared off into the distance and merged with the horizon to both the left and right. He would have thought they had landed in a desert, if it wasn't for the fact that the sea was less than a hundred metres in front of them.

The planet looked remarkably Earth-like, with the sky a mixture of reds, oranges and blues. It made for the type of sunset he remembered from home. Or at least, the sunsets he remembered looking at from the only window in his flat that wasn't covered with tin foil. In the distance behind them, he could see the beginning of a forest that seemed to be glowing as the sun went down. Bioluminescent trees were definitely NOT something he remembered from Earth.

He opened the TTAXI door, thankful once again that it had been a safe trip. The landing had turned the sand around the TTAXI into a circle of glass, on which the vehicle was now standing. It made it look like the TTAXI was an ornament of some kind, maybe for a 100-foot high car collector. He slipped slightly as he took the first step onto the glass, before the Nano Bytes corrected their grip settings to compensate. As he walked away from the TTAXI, he noticed that the driver was getting out too. Now things were getting *really* weird. The drivers NEVER get out during missions.

"Hang on, me old mate," the driver said in his confusing accent, "Could you be a dear and read this out loud for me?"

He handed Dofe what looked like a napkin. Where the hell did he get a napkin in space?! The napkin had a note written on it. He looked down at the napkin and quizzically looked back up at the driver.

"...It's just a little thing I like to do," said the driver, his face and hands contorting into a begging stance, "brings good luck".

"Okay..." complied Dofe, partially to get rid of this Irish Cockney as quickly as possible in the same way you Lucky Heather off a Gypsy even though its actually Heather. But mainly so he didn't get beaten up.

"Engage Emergency Autonomy Mode Code 641253".

Dofe suit made a series of noises like he remembered his first modem making when trying to connect to the internet, back in the days when his Conspiracy My Space page was his life. He felt every Nano Byte in his suit flinch, like they all shivered at once. It made him shiver too. It soon passed, but he could feel something had changed.

"EA Mode engaged, sweetie, "said SARDOC, in a way that made him feel like he should know what that meant, "you are now disconnected from the mainframe. Now, what's the problem, dearie?"

He looked at the driver, as he fought the urge to run away with every fibre of his being.

"What…what did you do to Dr S?" he asked as forcibly as he could muster, his voice cracking in the effort, "why have you disconnected her from the mainframe. And why didn't I know you could do that?!"

The driver's head suddenly started to pulsate and move around like someone was mixing it up with an invisible whisk. It gradually stretched and pulled back, as Dofe realised that this must be what his face must look like when his Nano suit's helmet was disengaging. The face that was left behind left him speechless. There was no other way to describe it – it was a better-looking replica of him. Or at least, how he *used* to look in his 40s. But this version of him had straight, white teeth, a full head of hair and a tan. So many conflicting thoughts attempted to get through his processing centres, they created a log jam that meant his idiot mouth took over.

"You're me! How are you me?" he said, like a child looking in a magic mirror that made you better looking, "and why are handsome?"

"Ha-ha! I'm Agent Rigsan," said the handsome man, "and I'm here to convince you to help me".

"Help you?" asked Dofe, as he commanded the Nano Bytes to vacate his head area, "I think you should be helping me!"

The Nano Bytes complied with their instructions and revealed Dofe's true appearance. Unbeknownst to Rigsan, Dofe's suit was now always replicating his appearance from how old he should, not how old he now was. His saggy jowls, his nebulous eyes, his milky-white hair that hung from halfway down his head to his shoulders.

"Wait…you're old!" Rigsan pointed, surprised, "How can you be old if you're us?"

"Because of one of those bloody things!" complained Dofe, pointing an angry, ancient finger at the TTAXI next to them, "I was on a mission a few months ago and we went through a comet's tail as we were about to come out of warp. It reset the protective time bubble inside the cab. So it disengaged 0.1 seconds too early and I aged 30 years instantly. So now the universe's last line of defence has to stop to have a wee every hour, even if he doesn't realise!"

"Well that's just great!" exclaimed Rigsan, holding his hands upon exasperation, "Just my luck to choose the clone that's an OAP Terry Nutkins lookalike!"

"What do you mean, clone?!" asked Dofe, angrily, "I'm not a clone, you must be the clone. Why would they make a clone of you and turn it into me?"

Dofe could see Rigsan's brain going through the same logjam as his just had. So they just stood there for a moment, thinking aggressively at each other. Rigsan finally broke the mental deadlock.

"Anyway," Rigsan said, trying to shake all the competing thoughts away, "Like I said, I'm here because I need your help. I've already met another version of us and I've seen things in the last day or so that suggest that there's a lot more of us out there. So what do I need to do to convince you that I'm on the level?"

"I'm not sure there's anything you can do to make me trust you," replied Dofe, sadly turning away and kicking the ground, "I haven't trusted anyone except for Colin in about 25 years".

"Who's Colin?" asked Rigsan, seeming like he already knew the answer based on today's events.

"My cat, back at base".

"Well, that's hilarious!" Rigsan laughed, sarcastically, "My Cat's called Colin too. And Abel's is".

"Abel?"

"The other version I said I'd met. It's a lot to process, I know. I'm still not sure I understand it myself, to be honest. But we've found a door that needs four of us to get past and we think our answers might be in there".

Rigsan extended his hand toward Dofe and knocked him gently on the elbow to get Dofe to turn and face him.

"Come on, let's do this mission together and then go find out what's going on".

Dofe thought for a second, did some breathing exercises and turned around. He grabbed Rigsan's hand and shook it meekly. A fleeting look of disgust danced across his face, reacting to Dofe's limp handshake. It was like trying to wrestle a Trout. But he caught himself and quickly covered it up.

"Let's go. So what's going on here, Sarge?" asked Rigsan, as he strode confidently onto the sand, his suit changing to its default settings from the Double Denim.

"Sir, this here is Hox, sir" boomed Sarge on speaker mode, so loud that Dofe adjusted course so that there was more distance between them, "There was a helluva war here until a few years ago. The land critters and the sea critters was tearing up the place. The sea critters won and now control the whole darn planet!"

They could both see hundreds, maybe thousands, of little mushy balls, dotting the beach in both directions. They ranged in size from 50 centimetres to a couple of metres in diameter. As they got closer to a few of them, they looked like dried, grey papier Mache.

"What the hell are these, Dr S?" asked Dofe. He tried to bend down to pick one up, but the pain made him decide against it. He was still getting used to his 80-year-old joints and sometimes he forgot to let the suit do the work. He extended his arm and let the Nano Bytes form an arm extension, which picked up one of the smaller balls and retracted back to his hand.

"Well sweetie, the war was between the sea-dwelling Chukulakans and the land-dwelling Mox. The Mox were losing and scanned the stars looking for ways to upgrade their weapons technology. One of their top scientists intercepted a transmission from a war-like planet that was entitled 'the strongest substance known to man'".

"Don't tell me, it was a YouTube video from Earth about Carbon Nanotubes!" said Dofe, examining the soggy sphere in his hand, "But this isn't Carbon".

185

"Very clever, my lovely," replied Dr S, "Unfortunately, the video predated the discovery of Carbon Nanotubes, so the Mox ended up building their whole armada out of corrugated cardboard, which up until then had the strongest power-to-weight ratio of any substance on Earth".

"Not when wet!" chirped Dofe, as if trying to warn the now long-dead Mox.

"Well, precisely, sweetie, but that bit wasn't on the video".

"Unbelievable," Dofe shook his head, "Those poor Mox".

"Sad? Bloody idiots more like!" said Rigsan, kicking one of the smaller balls as he walked past it to scan the ocean in front of him, "Who makes a tank out of cardboard?!"

Dofe was shocked at Rigsan's callousness. He was having trouble believing that this arrogant, strutting peacock was in any way the same as him. But physically, the similarities were too compelling to ignore.

"Oh, come on Rigsan, haven't you ever made a bad decision?" asked Dofe, dropping the salty ball back into the sand.

"Nope," replied Rigsan, placing his hands on his hips as the Nano Bytes crawled around his eyes and transformed into a set of binoculars to help him scan the ocean, "Well, until I started meeting you lot, anyway".

Dofe raised his eyes to the heavens in astonishment at the arrogance of his new colleague. But he thought he had better do a bit of scanning for himself. It was *his* mission, after all.

"The coordinates given in the mission briefing are 20km at mark 315 from here" said Dofe, as they both turned to the right in unison, to face the right direction, "nothing visible from the surface".

"Agreed. I'll use the suit boosters," instructed Rigsan, pointing back at the TTAXI as he marched towards the water, "you better use the TTAXI, or you'll be half dead by the time we get there".

Dofe didn't have much pride. Hardly any, in fact. But that little bit he did have was very offended by Rigsan's assumption.

"No its alright, suit boosters will be fine for me too," he said, walking towards the sea, trying to keep up with Rigsan, "Dr S, secure the TTAXI until we get back".

"Of course, sweetie, good idea," complied Dr S, "You'll be just fine in the suit for the journey. Don't even think about the mega-Sharks".

"The what?!" exclaimed Dofe, as the water rose above his head and the suit's engines took over. Before he knew it, he was flying through the water like a big, anxious torpedo.

-

As they approached the mission site, it was quite obvious where the problem was emanating from. The sea floor up to this point had been a patchwork of underwater villages, miles upon miles of bioluminescent coral reefs and sub-nautical forests. But from about halfway to the target, they could both see a large black area in amongst the plethora of life.

It was as if someone had left a black marker pen open in their shirt pocket and the colour had been leaking through the pattern. As they continued to get nearer, the black area grew larger and larger. They started to see how the water around the Wardz wormhole had formed a horizontal whirlpool, as the water pouring through it wasn't being replaced quick enough. It was so loud within a Kilometre of it, that both of them could *hear* the wormhole through the vibrations in the water, something neither of them had ever experienced before. They didn't realise it, but this was the first underwater attack either of the them had been a part of.

The flora and fauna around the wormhole were being sucked towards the Anti-matter wormhole while still fixed to the seas floor, creating a strange sight of an entire area leaning at the same 45-degree angle. The whole area was covered in Anti-matter signatures, according to both agent's HUDs. As he surveyed area, Dofe's HUD picked up three black spots in the middle distance, moving in the tell-tale, haphazard way that could only mean one thing.

"There they are! I scan three of them!" He shouted, before realising that the Emergency Autonomy modes meant that suit-to-suit communication was impossible at the moment. He looked towards Rigsan, held up three fingers, pointed them in the direction of the scanned signatures and nodded first at his fellow Agent and then in the direction of his fingers.

Rigsan gave a thumbs up, acknowledging that he had come to the same conclusion. He then proceeded to motion a series of tactical hand gestures that confused the hell of Dofe.

Dofe floated for a moment, trying to work out what the hell Rigsan had just asked him to do. It had looked like he was playing charades and had been given *The Unbearable Lightness of Being* by a particularly evil host.

And since he hated charades, or more to the point, other people, Dofe was rubbish at them. He decided a good, old fashioned shrug of the shoulders was the order of the day.

Dofe didn't need a universal translator or *SAS Hand Signals for Dummies* to tell that Rigsan was infuriated by this.

Rigsan started his hand gestures again, but this time much slower with much more aggressiveness. The same way an English tourist starts to shout slowly at a Spanish waiter that doesn't speak English. He pointed at himself, followed by a large semi-circle away from his body and to the right. He then jabbed his finger firmly into Dofe's chest three times, followed by a large semi-circle in the opposite direction. This was finished with the angriest thumbs up Dofe could ever remember being given for such a positive gesture.

Luckily, this time he understood Rigsan's plan. It looked like he wanted Dofe to position himself in above the wormhole and just a bit in front of it. Rigsan would then go around the front of the marauding creatures and stop them getting any further. If they tried to escape back through the wormhole, Dofe would be there to spear them. He hated to admit it, but it was actually a pretty good plan and a demonstration of how Rigsan's tactical brain adjusted much quicker, this being the first time either of them had worked in a pair. Dofe wondered if this might be a side effect of his drug habit. He resolved that helping with his constant physical pain and mental anguish probably outweighed any negative impact it might have on tactical speed.

He gave Rigsan as enthusiastic a double thumbs up as he could muster. Rigsan nodded his approval, tapped Dofe patronisingly on the top of the head and sped off to start his part of the plan. Dofe duly fizzed his boosters into life and headed for the top of the wormhole.

He got to his position, making sure he wasn't too close to the wormhole's vortex to avoid getting sucked in. He wasn't about to deal with that just yet.

"Just out of interest, Dr S," he said into his helmet, as his boosters fired on and off to keep him in position, "if I get caught in the vortex, how many seconds of full thrust can we manage to get me back out again?"

"Oh don't worry sweetie, you'll be fine," comforted Dr S, "I'll keep you right here where it's safe. We can spear the Wardz without going anywhere near the vortex if we need to. And we can hold position here for at least an hour. So, you concentrate on your breathing and the agents of chaos and I'll worry about the anti-matter".

Dr S always knew the right thing to say to help Dofe relax. That was her job of course, but she still did it very well. The Cromulites clearly knew what they were doing when they gave her to him. He managed to drag his gaze away from the swirling vortex of anti-matter that he was suspended 5 metres above and back towards Rigsan. He could see Rigsan's signature (a glowing green outline on his HUD) closing in on one of the black spots. It did not seem to be swimming away from him, meaning that it probably hadn't spotted its approaching death. Dofe's guess proved to be accurate, as Rigsan's outline expanded to show his scalpel mode being engaged and a second later, the black spot enlarged and then dissipated from view. This seemed to alert the other two Wardz, as the black spots stopped in their tracks. They held still for a few seconds and then started back in the direction of the wormhole, with Rigsan's signature in hot pursuit.

"He's not going to make it to them, is he Dr S?" asked Dofe, already knowing the answer just from experience. He started to tense before Dr S even answered.

"I don't think so dear," replied Dr S, with a concerned tinge to her voice, "Now remember, breathe, relax and get ready to engage scalpel mode. You can do this, sweetie, although you'll have to be quick to get both of them".

Dr S's positive reinforcement might not be enough this time, Dofe feared. He tried to control his breathing, but the rapidly growing black spots heading directly for him had other ideas.

In his mind's eye, he was back there on the floor of Union Street again, curled in a ball, waiting for the next kick.

The black spots still grew.

He tried to think of something else, like Michelle's smile when he would visit her for his appointment. He made up all sorts of rubbish to get back and see that smile every day. But the thoughts of fists connecting with his cheek bulldozed their way to the front, tearing down the positive memories like Barbarians destroying the Library of Alexandria.

The black spots still grew.

He tried to think of the feeling of that first drag of his morning joint. The feeling of complete relaxation and enhanced oneness with the energy of the world. But the image of a boot plunging into his stomach ripped it away.

The black spots still grew.

The first black spot was so close now, that Rigsan's outline disappeared behind it. It was close. In fact, it was so close that it was within range. The time was now.

"Engage scalpel mode!" he shouted, pointing his left arm in the direction of the closest black spot. The suit boosted down and towards the target, his left arm quickly becoming a trident and severing deep into the Wardz front. The momentum of the Wardz jerked Dofe towards the wormhole and he froze for a second instead of bringing up the matter cannon like he should have. The Wardz was now dragging him towards the dark matter portal. As he bounced along the ocean floor, he managed to bring his matter cannon arm into position and fired a shot deep into the fleeing beast's armour, and the foamy matter expanded through the hole. The creature instantly stopped moving and started to float towards the surface. He pulled at his arm, attempting to free the trident from the foam while trying to bring his breathing under control at the same time. He took too long. As he breathed in deeply, he turned around to repeat the process with the second demon. But it was right on top of him, meaning he didn't have a chance to bring his trident arm up into firing position before it clattered into him. It barged him out of the way and knocked him senseless for a second. The pain shot through his chest and back and radiated out to his extremities. His body felt every one of its 80 years in this moment, as he floated away. Luckily for him, the Wardz had barged him to the side in its desperation to return to the wormhole. If it had pushed him directly backwards, he would now be anti-matter soup.

Dofe watched as the creature disappeared into the wormhole, which immediately collapsed behind him. The vacuum created made the whirlpool bigger for a few seconds, before the weight of the ocean gradually brought everything back to normal. Dofe let himself get taken by the changing currents, as Rigsan arrived rapidly and stopped right where the wormhole had been. For the second time on this mission, Dofe didn't need to be able to hear what Rigsan was saying to understand his mood.

Rigsan floated in place, facing Dofe as he turned his head to look at him. Rigsan, shrugged both his shoulder while holding his arms out in the international gesture for 'what the hell?' Dofe shrugged back in the international gesture for 'what do you want from me, I'm a pensioner?'. Rigsan lowered his arms and shook his head. He stared for a few seconds and then sped off towards the TTAXI. Dofe floated for a few seconds on his own, waiting for the ringing in his ears to stop.

"Don't worry sweetie, you did your best," said Dr S, trying to make him feel better, "Anyone would have struggled to get two of them in that space of time".

"Thanks, Dr S, but I'm supposed to be the last line of defence for the entire universe," replied Dofe, solemnly, "Or at least I thought I was".

He turned over slowly and set off to meet up with Rigsan on the shoreline. He was not looking forward to it.

As Dofe, or rather the Nano Bytes, dragged the suit out of the water, he could see Rigsan waiting for him by the TTAXI. He had his arms crossed and was tapping his foot rapidly in frustration. He looked like a stereotypical 'angry housewives' that were always portrayed on 70s UK sitcoms. He may as well have been holding a rolling pin and had curlers in his hair. Rigsan gave him the luxury of trudging up the beach before laying into him.

"I can't believe you let one escape!" Rigsan shouted, angrily, "You were right there, and you just let him go!"

"There wasn't time to get both," Dofe defended himself, through troubled breaths, "by the time I'd killed the first one, the second one was right on top of me".

"You hesitated in between, I saw you!" shouted Rigsan, pointing out to sea, back to where they had just come from, "you can't afford to hesitate in this game!"

"This game?" Dofe looked at him in a disbelieving smile, "You're not selling second hand furniture! These are inter-dimensional killing machines".

"So are we!" said Rigsan, menacingly, then realising he'd probably gone too far, "Look…you won't be able to freeze like that in front of Fallapdax".

"Who the hell is Fallapdax?" asked Dofe, walking towards to the back of the TTAXI as the Nano Bytes engaged their heating systems to burn off the remaining sea water, "Is that who we're trying to see in the room thingy?"

"No, that's who's guarding the door". Replied Rigsan, waving his hand in front of his face to dissipate the steam Dofe was generating, "10-foot tall, octopus, all head". He held his hands up as far as they would stretch in case Dofe didn't know how big ten feet was.

"Oh great," sighed Dofe as he got in the back of the cab, "now there's an Octo-Boglin guarding the door!"

"Hey, that's what we called it". Said Rigsan happily, as he got in the front, "Great minds think alike, huh?"

"Heh…yeah, or fools never differ" agreed Dofe.

As they set off for Arrivals, Rigsan wondered how a clone of him could be such a coward.

Dofe wondered how a clone of him could be such an arrogant prick.

Arrivals warped into view and Dofe was as fascinated as Abel and Rigsan had been before him.

"So all of these…" Dofe pointed at the TTAXI rank.

"…are going to other versions of us, yes". Rigsan nodded sagely.

"Blimey, there's hundreds!" Dofe face was almost pressed up against the glass, like a child seeing the tops of the Disneyland Fairy Castle for the first time.

"At least," agreed Rigsan, pulling the TTAXI to a stop at the back of the queue, "now, here's the plan – in a minute, you'll see a recess coming up on the right. In the recess, there's a door to a cleaner's room. That's where we're meeting Abel and whoever he's managed to bring back with him. Sarge, how long have we got until the two hours is up?"

"Sir 17 minutes sir!" replied the Sarge.

"Thanks. Who knows, they might already be in there. Doubt it though. Can't imagine Abel is as efficient as me. Anyway, that's where we will get you your disguise as a cleaner and we can move on to the Nexus".

"Can't I just get Dr S to change me into a cleaner?" asked Dofe, turning away from the window.

"Well you can, but only if you want to reconnect to the mainframe and blow another mission. When you're disconnected from the mainframe, you can only replicate an outfit once you've seen someone wearing it in person".

Rigsan replied smugly, pretending like he hadn't asked the exact same question of Abel in the very recent past.

"Oh okay, I see," said Dofe, timidly, "I hadn't thought of that".

"It's fine," Rigsan replied magnanimously, "It's your first time here. Just listen to me, you'll be fine".

Dofe could see the recess coming up, just as Rigsan had said. He readied himself to get out, his hand tightening around the door handle.

The TTAXI trundled along the queue and was finally alongside the recess. Dofe could see the door within. Both his and Rigsan's doors opened at the same time and within a few seconds, they were out of the TTAXI and next to the door. Rigsan went back to the edge of the recess to make sure no guards had been alerted and then returned to Dofe. Rigsan pressed down on the door handle and confidently pirouetted in through the opening. Dofe took a last furtive look around and followed inside.

"Right, there should be a uni…DON'T LET THE DOOR SHUT!" Rigsan suddenly remembered the handle situation, but again it was too late. "Now we're stuck in here!" He sighed.

He flicked on the light switch, "There's no handle on the inside, look!"

"Oh…sorry," Dofe said, looking down at the floor, unaware that Rigsan was a previous initiate of the 'let the door shut' club, "They should put a sign on the door," he continued, almost whispering.

Without a word, Rigsan angrily pointed at the sign on the door, just as Abel had done when he was last in here.

"That should really be on the outside". Offered Dofe, pointing as if through the door, to where the handle was.

"AAARRRGGGHHH!!!" cried Rigsan, turning around and throwing a uniform at Dofe, "Get dressed!".

CHAPTER 13
FROM GERMANY WITH LOVE

WALLDORF, GERMANY, TERRA, SOL SYSTEM, MILKY WAY, EARTH YEAR 2012

(NOTE: FOR THE READER'S COMFORT, ALL GERMAN SPEECH IN THIS CHAPTER HAS BEEN UNIVERSALLY TRANSLATED INTO THE NATIVE LANGUAGE OF THE OTHER CHAPTERS OF THE BOOK - UNLESS OF COURSE, THE READER IS READING THE WHOLE BOOK IN GERMAN, IN WHICH CASE, FORGET WE SAID ANYTHING.)

"Christian, I'm open!" shouted Mark, loud enough to be heard above the constant squeaking of everyone's trainers. He could see his tall, German friend patting the handball expectantly as he scoured the court for the best passing option, "Left wing, I'm open!"

Mark was indeed open, and Christian found him with a customary almost-too-hard pass. You always needed two hands to catch one of Christian's passes, else you might end up with a sprained wrist or two.

He took two of the three allowed steps and stopped. He was less than 50cm away from the line that marked out the Goal Area. He knew that if he went inside, his team would lose the ball and with it, the match. They were 28-27 behind, with 14 seconds left on the clock. Sure, it was only a friendly match with the other amateur team that played out of the same Gym. But why play at all if it wasn't to win?

He quickly looked around to see if anyone was making a run towards the goal area, meaning they would have the momentum needed for a goal attempt. Out of the corner of his left eye, he saw Mattias start a run from the centre line. He bent his run to the left and then the right, arching his way between Christian, where the pass had just come from, and Marcus who was sidestepping to create a decoy.

Mark decided he would try the decoy plan too. He transferred the ball to his right and swung it back behind his head, as if to shoot. As he did so, he dropped his right shoulder to set the trap. The defender in front of him sprung it willingly. The central defender next to the one in front of Mark must of thought it looked quite nice inside the trap, as he moved to get in as well.

This left the oncoming Mattias with a clear view of goal. Now all he needed was the ball.

Mark didn't look at his teammate until the last possible second, leaving it until he was at the top of his fake shooting jump. When he did turn his head, his ball hand followed suit. The ball dutifully travelled straight into the left hand of Mattias, just as he was about to begin his shooting jump. And his jump wasn't in the least bit fake. In one smooth motion, Mattias caught the ball in his favoured left hand, drew the ball back behind his head and catapulted his arm forward.

He released the ball at just the right point for it to fly into the bottom left hand corner of the goal. It went just beyond the outstretched foot of the goalkeeper, who looked like he was trying to do a star jump without leaving the ground.

Christian and the other teammates threw their arms up and howled in celebration, as the buzzer sounded the end of the game. Mattias picked himself up off the court from where his momentum had carried him, two metres inside the goal area. There would be no victory this time. But coming back from five goals down to end with a tie felt like a win to them right now. They took a few seconds to notice that Mark was still on the ground.

"Hey, you okay old man?" asked Christian, laughing as he ran over to Mark. He grabbed his older friend's hand and pulled him into a standing position.

"Yeah, I'll be fine," Mark laughed, trying to mask how much his left knee was hurting, "I must have slipped on something when I landed".

But he hadn't slipped on anything at all. That wasn't what had *actually* happened. What had *actually* happened, was that his knee had buckled when he landed, and Mark knew it. He knew it because it had been happening more and more over the past year or so. So much so that he had visited the Doctor six months ago and been told it was early-onset Arthritis. He had been shocked at the diagnosis, so much so that he hadn't told anyone else yet. Sure, he'd expected it as both his Mum and his maternal Grandfather suffered with it, but not this soon. What he needed was some strong anti-inflammatories and at least a dozen Konigs Beers to take away the pain.

"And less of the old," Mark said, limping off the court using Christians shoulder for balance, "You're only three years younger than me!"

"Agh, it might as well be ten judging by your current state!" replied Christian sarcastically, as he helped his friend back to the changing room, "Look at the size of your knee already! You won't be able to get your trousers on in a minute!"

Mark looked down as he put his foot to the floor and felt the pain shoot up his leg and through his side. Christian was right, his knee had started swelling already and would soon be the size of child's head. And this wasn't a guess either, as Dietmar had took great delight that his head was the same size as Daddy's knee the last time this had happened.

He finally got to a bench in the changing room and plonked himself down. Christian could see how much pain his teammate was in and very kindly took his key from him and retrieved his clothes and sports bag from his locker. Mark sat still, with his head leaning back against the wall and an ice pack on his knee, as he watched his Samaritan's journey to and from the lockers.

"Thank you Christian, thank you for helping the elderly," he joked, as his friend dropped the bag on the bench next to him, "Now where are we going after this?"

"Must we go for a drink after *every Handball* session?" complained Christian, getting dressed, "You're only undoing the good work you've just done".

"Just a few drinks," defended Mark, struggling to pull his trouser leg on over his swollen knee, "what's the harm in a few drinks?"

They both knew it wouldn't just be a *few* drinks though. The difference between them was that Christian knew Mark had a problem and Mark hadn't admitted it to himself yet. Christian decided that he would relent in the hope that he could talk his friend into an early night for a change.

"All I'm saying is that an American Eagle is actually the perfect analogy for democracy," Mark shouted back to Christian as he fell out of the pub door and onto the pavement, "If you look at one from the side it's majestic. Like the concept of democracy. But if you look at one head on, it looks like a complete mess. Like democracy in practice!"

"I'll take your word for it Mark, as always," replied Christian, following steadily behind. He had succeeded in only having a 'few' drinks himself. But he'd once again summarily failed in his attempt to stop Mark from overdoing it, "Right, time the elderly were going home I think".

"You speak for yourself, youngling," Mark guffawed, stumbling into a lamppost and pretending like he meant to rest right there, "It's onward to the Metro-Bar!"

"Oh no, not on a work night, this is where I say goodnight, old friend," Christian walked a few steps back toward the direction of the Gym and stopped, "Come on, I'll give you a lift and you can get a Taxi to work in the morning".

"Nonsense, Christian!" said Mark, leaving the sanctuary of the lamppost and setting out on a epic journey to reach the road sign he could see a hundred metres in the direction of the Metro-Bar, "I will celebrate our glorious draw for the both of us! Goodnight, kind sir!"

Mark spun around to face his friend and began to bow deeply. The pain in his knee made him stop and swing bolt upright, where he stayed for a few seconds before spinning back in the direction of his next drinking venue.

"Mark," Christian's smile faded and was replaced with the features of a concerned friend, "I wish that you would know when to stop. Just once".

Mark stopped in his tracks, apart from the involuntary swaying of a man who should heed his friend's advice but wasn't going to. He answered without turning around.

"I wish a lot of things, my oldest friend. I wish I had pushed myself for a better job. I wish I had gone travelling before settling down. I wish…I wish I hadn't chosen home over Michelle. Who knows what I would be celebrating now?"

As Mark began to walk away again, Christian shook his head, defeated. He resolved that Mark was beyond help for the moment. It had cost him his wife and family and was costing him any hope of progressing any further in the SAP ranks. But he knew his current job so well and had been in it for so long, that he could do it in his sleep. Which, since the drinking had been a problem, he had most of the time.

"Goodnight, my oldest friend…safe trip". He said quietly, as he watched his former school friend shambling towards the Metro-Bar.

-

"Last orders please," said the barman, to the usual chorus of quiet boos from the regulars. Mark could certainly be classed as a Metro-Bar regular by now, as he spent at least four evenings a week in there. It made a nice change from getting drunk at home and falling asleep alone in front of the TV. It was costing him a fortune in Taxi fares though. Maybe he would have to up the ratio of home sessions and lessen the Metro-Bar trips? And why was his pocket vibrating?

He managed to somehow pull his phone delicately out of his pocket. He tried to focus on the screen enough to press the green answer icon. His finger did a few circles around the icon before landing on it and answering.

"Oh, hi Father...I've had a few beers, that's all, with the Handball team...we came back from five down to draw...well, it felt like a win". Said Mark, trying his best to wobble to the exit door, "I can talk, sure".

He turned and waved back at the barman with his free hand and blinked his appreciation for a job well done. The barman waved back at one of his best customers. Two metres of controlled falling and Mark was outside again.

"Well, you just have to...I know, it's confusing, I know...have you got your email password there...the pass...for the Vodafone account, yeah".

Mark was always the man 'who knows about computers' in his family, which meant that he had to provide forgotten email addresses for everyone even when he was plastered.

"It's in your password book, isn't it...no, that's your account login...no, your phone account, not your email account...yes, it is confusing, I know..."

As he stumbled towards the edge of the pavement, he knew his chance of driving home had been zero percent for the last three hours. He lurched between two parked cars at the kerb and looked slowly one way then the other for a cab to take him home.

As if by some mental command, a Taxi appeared in the road in front of him. He thrust his arm out to stop the Taxi, even though that to a sober person it was clear it was already stationary.

"It's definitely there, I remember writing it in the last time I was…got it? Under the other…yeah, that's right…944, yeah that's the one. Okay…byeeee!"

He shook his head in that way that only extremely drunk people can as he got into the back seat of the waiting cab. That way that looks like they're having an argument with themselves and they really don't agree with the points they're making.

"Evening sir," said the driver, as Mark fell across the seat, before forcing himself back upright, "celebrating something are we?"

"Yes, my friends and I drew our Handball game tonight!" Mark said, holding up a shaky index finger in the usual 'we're number one' type way.

"Blimey, if this is how you celebrate a draw, what do you do when you win?!" asked the driver, chuckling as he pulled away.

"It was a moral victory," instructed Mark, trying to do a serious face and failing miserably, "and I'll take a win any way I can get at the moment!"

"Oh really?" asked the driver, as the taxi stopped at the traffic lights, "Things not going too well at the moment?"

Mark shrugged ruefully and snorted his agreement. He looked out of the window for a few seconds, like he was reviewing the events of the last few years in his head.

"Well, if you must know," Mark said quietly, leaning forward as if to share some great secret, fearful of unseen prying ears, "My wife left me and took the kids. Said she couldn't cope with my 'excessive drinking'," he made air quotes with his fingers, "do I look like I drink excessively?"

There was an awkward silence as Mark and the driver pondered the irony of his statement, when weighed against current evidence. He closed his eyes and pursed his lips in the way that drunk people do to expunge the last thing they said and wipe it from history.

"I think we both know the answer to that, Mark," said the driver, as Mark heard the doors lock, "the more important question though, is how much more have you got to lose before you realise you have a problem?"

Mark's brain was too far gone to digest properly the gravity of what the driver had just said. Instead, his face decided to take over and register his lack of comprehension, while the information swam to Mark's processing centres through the river of beer.

"How do you know what I'm all about?" asked Mark, his body swaying with the lateral movements of the cab.

"Oh, I've seen plenty like you Mark, believe me," replied the driver, turning around as the cab stopped at a roundabout, "you are not my first drunk Mark".

Mark had what is traditionally known as a moment of clarity. He finally registered what the driver had said; he registered that the doors had locked; he registered that a black London cab had no place being in Germany; he even registered that the Taxi had started pulling away at the roundabout without the driver turning back around to face the front. The only thing he didn't register was the lack of a comma in the driver's last sentence, but that wouldn't become relevant for a long time. But you dear reader, know exactly what he means.

"What do you want with me?" Mark asked, grabbing for the door handles and missing, falling onto the seat horizontally, "and how is this Taxi driving itself?!"

The driver smiled at him for quite a few seconds before answering him. In that pause in the conversation, quite a lot happened. First, Mark noticed the road disappearing down below the level of the bonnet over the driver's shoulder. The cloudy night sky came into view. Through the clouds, Mark could see all sorts of stars. Within a few seconds more, the cloudy sky became just the sky as the Taxi sprinted its way above the cloud level. Red and yellow strands of pure heat began to emanate from the top of the bonnet, making their merry way across the sides of the vehicle. They quickly engulfed the whole cab, as Mark watched with an increasingly large gawp. He slowly turned to look out of the back window and could see his home rapidly disappearing below them, until he could see the whole of Germany, then the whole of Europe, then the…well, you get the idea.

He turned back around to face the driver, closing his mouth and licking his lips. All the gawping had made his mouth dry. He finally broke the silence.

"This…this is a space ship," he said, sobering up more hurriedly than if you get stopped by a policeman, "why did you pick me up in a space ship. I'm only going to Schriesheim!"

"Correction, you *were* only going to Schriesheim". replied the driver, finally turning back to face the front. Mark could see him flicking switches and pressing buttons, in a way that Mark could tell he had done a thousand times before. He noticed a countdown timer had started on the dashboard, counting down from 30 seconds

"Where you're going now sure isn't Schriesheim. I work for an organisation called Universal Corrections. We've been watching you for a while, Mark. We think you have what it takes to be this universe's last line of defence against the forces of chaos".

"Really?!" said Mark, "Why would you want me?"

"You're exactly what we've been looking for," confirmed the driver, "I can't explain here. Let me take you to headquarters, the scientists there will explain everything and show you your equipment. Don't worry, your family on Terra won't even know you've gone".

"Huh!" shrugged Mark, "I doubt they'd notice anyway! So how long is it to get to this space station of yours?"

Before the driver could answer, the countdown timer hit zero and there was a flash of white light. Mark turned around to look at Earth and it wasn't there anymore. It had been replaced with stars – millions of stars. The sort of amount of stars that you'd struggle to see even out in the middle of the Bavarian countryside, away from the light pollution of the cities. He turned back around and out of the right-hand window, there was suddenly a massive, wheel shaped space station that he didn't remember being there before.

The gawping had returned.

"No time at all". Replied the driver, as he banked to the right and headed for the centre of the wheel, which Mark could see was in the process of opening for them.

CHAPTER 14
'ALLO 'ALLO

UNIVERSAL CORRECTIONS COMPOUND, UNKNOWN LOCATION, EARTH YEAR 2018

"AAARRRGGGHHH!!!" Agent Kinmal sat up screaming, grabbing and pawing at his sweat-ridden sternum, at an imaginary incision that was just about to made in his dream. The bloody morgue dream again. It had been happening more and more often recently and frankly, he was tired of it. Partly because it took him ages to forget about it through the day. But mainly because waking up screaming is the single worst way to wake up when you're hungover – and Kinmal was *always* hungover.

He had got into a depressing pattern in this job – wake up, TV, yoga, liquid lunch, mission or two, holographic Handball in the Visigym, celebration drinks, bed. The only alteration that might come with the routine was if the grateful locals on the planet of whatever mission he was on wanted him to celebrate with them. In that case, he was only too happy to allow them to show their gratitude. Luckily, his Nano Byte suit was able to get him home through its self-locomotion systems and indeed it did on a very regular basis.

In fact, a good proportion of the time, it was the Nano Byte suit doing most of the locomotion on the way *to* the missions nowadays, with SARDOC picking up the strategic slack in the 'mental faculties' department.

SARDOC was well aware of the long-term dangers of this type of excessive alcohol intake, but had reasoned that with the increase in Wardz attacks, her Human could not afford to be out of action whilst recovering from withdrawal symptoms. So for the moment, they would have to carry on the way they were and make the best of it. Of course, SARDOC did not discuss any of this with her Human, as it was a very touchy subject.

"Bad dream again, sir? Was it the Leichenshauhaus, the Morgue again?" asked SARDOC in her light German accent, already knowing the answer.

"Yes it was, Unter," replied Mark, grabbing his head with the hand that wasn't still grabbing his fictitious wound. SARDOC had suggested that Kinmal call her 'Unterstutzen', which is German for 'support' or 'sponsor', in the hope that he would take the hint about his drinking. He ignored the subtext and just thought it sounded like quite a better name than SARDOC,

"Ugh, my head..."

"I've already hologised your wake-up items onto your nightstand," said SARDOC. Kinmal looked around and sure enough, there was a large glass of water and two Paracetamol tablets. Kinmal reached for the glass and started to drink deeply from it. As he did so, Colin appeared from the living room and jumped onto the bed, in his daily attempt to convince his Human that SARDOC hadn't already fed him.

"Agent Kinmal, you are well aware that you don't..."

Kinmal held up his hand in mid-air, attempting to stop SARDOC in mid-sentence, like you would with an annoying relative trying to give you life advice. SARDOC however, here to give you advice on the best methods of water intake efficiency, was not Auntie Flora.

SARDOC was the universe's foremost Artificial Intelligence program. And she wasn't about to put up with any of her Human's shenanigans.

"...get the benefit of the water by drinking it all in one mouthful," she continued, as Colin helped Kinmal to finish his drink by nuzzling the bottom of the glass and pushing it upwards, "I don't know why I bother!"

Agent Kinmal had been given a SARDOC who's personality profile was that of a highly efficient, female German scientist. She would keep him focused on the task at hand, limiting his Handball time and ensuring that he was as ready as he could be for each day. She reminded Kinmal far too much of Nicole, his ex-wife. But he had accepted her, for the good of the universe of course. He figured that the Aliens with universe-spanning technology and leading AI programs probably knew more about just about everything than him.

"Oh come on Unter, you know the routine," gasped Kinmal, as he finished the last of the water in the glass, placing it back down on the bedside table, "I down the first one and then you refill it for sipping!"

If SARDOC had the facility to roll her eyes playfully, Kinmal felt sure she would have at this point. The fact that the glass was already magically refilling meant that his digital companion had been expecting it. He smiled to himself and picked up the drink again once SARDOC had finished re-hologising its contents. This time, he picked up the drugs as well and downed them with the first sip of the new glass.

Kinmal sighed and relaxed back against the headboard of his bed. He closed his eyes, but the lingering image of the mysterious morgue technician in his mind's eye made him open them again. Those red glasses. They were always the last image to disappear during the day.

 He would remember them in every face, every advert, every TV show he would see throughout the day. But also, he wouldn't see them at all, not the same anyway. He was actually quite attracted to the lady in the glasses in his dreams, at least until she started cutting his chest open and shutting him in a cold store. That's enough to turn anyone off, unless they have a very specific fetish. And Kinmal didn't clearly, or he'd be waking up with more than just a stiff head.

He had a little shiver as he thought about the scalpel coming towards him and he absent-mindedly ran his fingers over his chest. Colin seemed to sense his master's sudden distress and playfully stuck his head under Kinmal's free hand, effectively stroking himself, the dirty devil. Kinmal had to admit, it did help. He tickled Colin under the chin and the Cat's familiar loud purr was enough to vibrate Kinmal's leg through the sheet. He decided a spot of Breakfast TV would be the best thing to help begin the forgetting process. But first, a chapter of *Watchmen*, his favourite graphic novel, would be devoured whilst sat on the toilet. He pursed his lips and nodded, congratulating himself on a very good idea.

-

Kinmal had finished his chapter (and his ablutions) and headed purposefully for the lounge area. His base had been modelled by the Cromulites on his flat on Earth, but with the key addition of a Visigym underneath it. A Visigym is a fully-fitted Gymnasium but can have any number of virtual people added to it. In Kinmal's instance, this meant that he could play Handball whenever he wanted, with whoever he wanted alive or dead. This was always Kinmal's high point of any day, even more than the liquid lunches or after-mission celebrating.

Just the other week, he had managed to play Handball with a team consisting of five members of the 1980 East German Olympic Handball team and, to spice things up, Abraham Lincoln. His chosen opponents that day had been the Soviet Union team from the same Olympics. They all had a whale of a time, particularly Abe, who insisted on keeping his stovepipe hat on for the whole game and even offering to wrestle the losers afterwards. Kinmal had never seen a better collection of facial hair, apart from when he played a game with the East German Women's Team. The Visigym was where he enjoyed this job the most. It was quite a lonely existence apart from that. He was fully aware that the other players were just virtual constructs of solidified photons, but they were the nearest thing to Human contact he had now. He couldn't remember the last time he had seen a real Human. Sure, he saw the drivers on every mission, but he was convinced that they were Androids, so they didn't really count in his eyes. He'd often considered asking them in for drink when they dropped him off anyway, when he was feeling particularly lonely.

The lounge area had a floor to ceiling window, showing off the view of the billions of stars outside the base bubble.

Next to the windows were a pair of French doors that led out to a small balcony, on which he would often sit, drink and think of home. He worried that the kids had worked out that his replacement was an automaton. If he was being honest with himself, he was more worried that they had discovered this ages ago and didn't mind because the automaton was more fun than their real Dad.

"Engage the display wall please, Unter". He said, pushing one of the two sofas back enough for his Yoga mat to go on the floor, "Let's see what the universe has in store for us today".

As he sat on the floor and began to stretch, the wall to the left of him began to fire into life, light from the projectors at each corner of the wall beginning to meet on the centre and form the three-dimensional image. It was the unmistakable cube-shaped head of Marv Blatworthy, CBS' number two anchor-man. Blatworthy was a member of the Remidian Prime race, which naturally produced perfect teeth and hair, making them the perfect choices to be TV hosts. They had managed this through thousands of years of selective breeding. Much like the parents of a supermodel both being ugly, it was found that matching the right ugly people together for breeding purposes made the ugly genes cancel themselves out. Every other generation of Remidians were therefore deemed 'Prime' and every other one 'Value'. Two 'Values' will always produce a 'Prime' and vice versa. To use an Earth-based analogy, the 'Prime' generation would be given the job of the front man, whereas the 'Value' generation would be the backup singers. Marv was definitely a front man.

"Drama on Zuli 4," boomed Marv, his bright green and purple tie shimmering below his unconscionably perfect teeth, "Disaster at the planet's biggest trade festival as one of the contestant's dances is misinterpreted, leading to many deaths".

Dance is very important to the Porr. In fact, it's their primary means of communication. They can talk - they evolved that skill aeons ago and use it to great effect when they choose to. But these foot-long, bee-like creatures, prefer to say what they've got to say through the medium of dance. This is mainly because they find it hilarious to see the confused looks on the faces of other species, as they desperately try to arrange a trade deal for Zuli's rich resources. The Porr have been known to conduct dance-offs lasting several days, in order to agree tariffs on their Honey, which is generally regarded as the best in the Galactic Alliance. The Porr also find other races' fascination with eating their Poop hilarious.

'For deaths to have been involved, something must have gone seriously wrong.' Thought Kinmal, as his Flarg Nuts and Café Hag began to materialise on the table in front of him. He would complete his set of poses first. Or his knees would be grumbling all day.

He always started with the Chair Pose, as it was one of the most helpful for strengthening his aforementioned troublesome leg elbows. He bent deeply into it and controlled his breathing, as Marv continued his report.

"According to eye witness reports from the scene, Lurlaas the Persuader, the head of the Aquarii trading delegation from the planet Hihina, was halfway through his initial dance sequence when things began to unravel. He was trying to communicate that they would not agree to a 10% sell-on fee for the Porr's Honey, but Lurlaas extended his right arm in a moon shape, rather than his left. The left moon shape is of course a reference to the Porr's Queen's parentage, which the routine was inadvertently now calling into question.

The head of the Porr delegation, Rogg Disselpoof, was understandably angry at this and conveyed his disbelief in a thirty-second head spin. Unfortunately, Lurlaas took this as a good sign and repeated the incorrect gesture twice more. So far, there have been thirty deaths from both sides. It's hoped that calmer heads will prevail. A Galactic Alliance peacekeeping force has arrived with large smoke machines to placate the Porr".

"Blimey and I thought Bees got angry on Earth!" laughed Kinmal, remembering the pain of getting stung by a Bee at the age of five. He had seen one fly into a tube that was only open at one end and thought it would be clever to hold his hand over it.

Of course, being a child and therefore an idiot, this was a bloody stupid thing to do and the angry Bee let him know as much by stinging him to get out. The Bee soon learned that he was just as stupid, as his insides fell out of the hole left behind by its now-missing sting. It is not well known to Humans, but Adult Bees do not talk about what happens to them if they sting something, instead informing their young that any Bees who do not return have just moved to other hives. They instead spend their time teaching their young to 'think before you sting' and Humans are weird creatures that eat Bee poop.

Kinmal thought that he'd like to take a trip to Zuli 4. He quite liked dancing once he'd had a few. Well, more than a few in reality, but the designation of 'a few' had become much more fluid over the years. He wondered how nice Porr Mead would be, made as it was with such high-quality Honey. His mouth watered as he transferred to the floor for his next stance, the Bridge Pose. He watched the rest of the news headlines on a sideways tilt, as he peacefully and slowly dry humped the ceiling.

–

"I have just received word from HQ that your first mission of the day is inbound," reported SARDOC, as Kinmal was finishing up the last round of his Eagle pose. This was much to Colin's disgust as it meant he no longer have anything to swipe at, "It is a mission to Torlup 6, in the Yorrall system. Possible Wardz activity sighted in one of their underground cities".

"I don't think we've visited the Yorrall system before, have we Unter?" asked Kinmal, standing up gradually as his virtual Yoga instructor had taught him in the early days. He no longer needed the instructor. His daily routine was so ingrained that he could probably instruct others now, given the opportunity. Maybe he would summon up Abe Lincoln in the Visigym one time soon and show him. For now, he needed a shower before entering the Nano Byte suit, so he guzzled down the now-tepid Café Hag and headed for the bathroom at the other end of the flat.

"Unter, can you make my Flarg Nuts into a smoothie please," he asked as he entered the bathroom, disrobing as he went, "I'll drink it before I go. And stick a double Vodka in it, for my nerves".

"Of course, Agent K," replied SARDOC obediently, as the bowl of cereals dematerialised from the living room.

Kinmal could hear the Stealth Suit tube powering up in the utility room next door to the bathroom as he showered. He always found it to be a strangely comforting noise. He always felt safer in the stealth suit, like it made him the best version of himself that he could be. The sound of the TTAXI arriving outside meant it was time for him to don his better half.

He walked into the adjacent room and could see the Nano Bytes already swirling around at the base of the tube. There was no need to dry himself off, as the heat of the Nano Bytes would do that for him once he was covered in it. Truth be told, the Nano Bytes had felt a bit weird about Kinmal wearing them without an under suit, or indeed under*pants*, but they had soon gotten used to it. If anything, it was easier for them, particularly for the Faecal Recycling department.

As he stepped towards the floor to ceiling tube, the glass panel at the front glided open with barely a sound. He stepped over the Nano Bytes, who were currently in a holding pattern, awaiting their host. They preferred the term 'host' to 'pilot' as the latter inferred that the Human had too much control, which couldn't be further from the truth, particularly in Kinmal's case.

He turned to face back the way he had entered, as the glass panel silently shut again. The Nano Bytes began their journey up Kinmal's body, squadrons of Nano Bytes breaking off from the group and attaching their selves to various parts of Kinmal's anatomy. As they landed, they began to spread out in their chosen areas, looking like grey, metallic flowers blooming all over him. As the blooms enlarged, they began joining up to form the suit. As they expanded, they gave off enough heat to dry their host, making the whole tube fill up with a light steam, accompanied by a low hissing sound. The warmth always felt astonishing, although Kinmal always wished the Nano Bytes had a 'Talcum Powder' function, especially for his nether regions.

The suit always chaffed a bit around around that area, especially since his 'old man balls' had started to appear. He still preferred nakedness over pants though.

The suit was soon covering his whole body, from his feet to his bald head and goatee beard. The tube panel pulled back once more and he stepped out, along with a plume of steam, that made him think momentarily of being a rock star entering the stage.

He made his way down the spiral staircase, past the Visigym (which was in darkness) and out onto the roadway, to the awaiting TTAXI. The driver had got out of the cab to meet him, which he thought was unusual, but probably just the misplaced enthusiasm of a new recruit. He removed the face portion of his mask as a gesture of friendliness and strode toward the cab, the door to his base closing automatically behind him.

As he walked towards the TTAXI, Kinmal could see the driver checking himself out in the mirror. He seemed to be attempting to move his face around. At first, he thought that was odd, but then he faced facts that it wasn't the oddest thing he had seen in the last six years since his recruitment. It wasn't even in the top 20, to be honest. The driver stopped adjusting his face and turned to face him.

"'Ello me old mate, how's you?" the driver asked, the spot on his face where he had been adjusting still wobbling and sparkling gently. But Kinmal didn't even notice this, as he was far more perturbed by the fact that the driver wasn't speaking in German, as every previous driver had.

"Sehr gut danke. Wohen gehen wir heute?" asked Kinmal suspiciously, which was German for 'Very well, thank you. Where are we going today?'

"Er…yeah, hang on there a minute mate". Said the driver, holding up a nervous finger. He quickly opened the driver's door of the TTAXI and scurried inside. Kinmal folded his arms and waited while he could see the driver sat inside, apparently talking to himself. If he didn't know better, he could have sworn he looked like he was talking his own SARDOC. But that was impossible wasn't it? The digital assistant was exclusive to him. He leaned in to attempt to listen through the TTAXI window.

Muffled voice of driver "…don't know, I didn't know he was going to be German, did I? *silence* Well why would the Cromulites make a clone of me and then make it German? *silence* Can you access German without contacting the mainframe? *silence* Well that'll have to do".

The driver gave a guilty cough as he opened the door and returned to standing in front of Kinmal.

"Guten Morgen, ich bin dein Fahrer," the driver said. Kinmal stared at him, noticing that the driver's lips weren't matching what the words he was saying. He cocked his head to one said like a curious dog and raised an eyebrow. Before he could question this strange character further, he spoke again.

"Notruf-Autonomie-Moduscode einschalten sechs vier eins zwei fünf drei!" he shouted, again his mouth shapes clearly not matching the words coming out of it. But that was the least of his worries at that moment in time. The driver's command had forced his suit into a body-wide spasm, accompanied by the noises an old modem would make if your Mum picked up the phone to call Grandma when you were busy trying to download a picture of Anna Kournikova in the late '90s. Kinmal faltered backwards by a step, almost dropping to one knee. He grabbed the side of the TTAXI to steady himself, as he could feel the spasm start to pass.

The previously warm Nano Bytes had suddenly gone cold, all at once. It felt as if they had all restarted at the same time. It was at least ten or twenty seconds until his SARDOC spoke and made some sense of what had gone on.

"It would appear that we have been cut off from the Mainframe, Agent K". she said. Kinmal thought he could hear hesitancy in her voice, but he wasn't sure if his current personal situation was causing him to infer emotions that weren't there.

In all the confusion, he had only just noticed that the driver's body was changing, and his head was in the process of joining it.

"What did you do to me?!" demanded Kinmal as he straightened up. He immediately lost his train of thought as the driver's head fell away in the unmistakable way that Nano Bytes do.

What was also unmistakable was the face that they left behind. It was his. A little more hair, crooked teeth, no beard and about 20kg more inflated. But definitely his face. The nose and the eyes were a giveaway. Just as Rigsan and Dofe had before him, Kinmal could do nothing but gawp and assume this was a clone of himself.

"Oh good, you speak English. I wondered what the hell was going on for a minute there!" exclaimed Abel, his Nano Byte suit now fully transformed back into its default setting of a shimmering gold Morph suit.

"That's because I *am* English, you fool!" replied Kinmal, angrily, "Now what have you done to my Unter...I mean my SARDOC?!"

"If you're English, what's with the German talking and the 'schmells goot!' accent?" asked Abel, affecting a comedic German accent.

"My parents moved to Germany when I was just 8 years-old," explained Kinmal, "Father took a job working on the British Army base in Bielefeld and we moved out there. Apart from four years at Bristol University, I have lived in Germany until the abduction".

It was Abel's turn to cock his head and raise an eyebrow. How could this be a clone with a completely different back story? The need to get past the Octo-Boglin and into the Nexus Room was becoming ever more pressing.

Speaking to oneself was usually a way to resolve problems, but all these conversations were doing was posing more questions. He resolved that the quicker they completed the mission at hand, the quicker they could get back to the rendezvous point. The deeper questions could wait.

"Agent Abel," he said, thrusting his hand out and encouraging Kinmal to shake it, "let's get on with your mission and I'll explain what's going on with this," he wiped his other hand in a circle in front of his face, "on the way".

Kinmal gingerly pushed his hand out and shook Abel's. Their matching grips surprised him further.

"Agent Kinmal". He said, making eye contact with Abel as his Nano Bytes removed themselves from his head. Kinmal had independently come to the same conclusion as Abel, that answers to this current predicament could only be learnt elsewhere. And more importantly in the short term, the beings of Torlup 6 needed his help. Their help. Someone's help. Maybe it would be good to have actual physical company for a change?

-

"So let me see if I have gotten this correct," said Kinmal from the back seat, as Torlup 6 loomed into existence out of the left-hand window, "There are thousands of clones of me…"

"Me…" corrected Abel.

"…us," corrected Kinmal, tactfully, "and they're all doing the same job that we've been told we're the only ones doing?"

"Yes that's about the size of it," nodded Abel, turning the wheel so that the planet was dead ahead, "and I've found a door that looks like it might contain answers to what is going on, but we need eight identical hand prints to get in.

Rigsan and I said we would go and get another one of us each and meet back at the terminal. We just have to work out a way to get past the monster guarding the door".

"Monster?" asked Kinmal.

"Yeah, it's about ten feet tall, all head, with arms coming out of the side of it".

"Like a Boglin!" Exclaimed Kinmal.

"Yes! Why can everyone think of that straight away except me?!" Abel said, shaking his head, "Anyway, it's got eight arms and is standing right in the way!"

Kinmal started chuckling to himself. So much so that he struggled to get his words out.

"Ha-ha! Maybe you should call it the Octo-Boglin, yes?" Kinmal said with a broad smile, his shoulders shaking. He was clearly very proud of his humorous suggestion. Abel didn't have the heart to tell him about his lack of originality.

"Hah!" Abel laughed, half-heartedly, but smiled as wide as he could, "I wish I'd thought of that!" Even though it wasn't a new joke today, Abel had to admit that it took on a new comedic twang when said in Kinmal's pidgin-English accent.

"Well, in a way Agent Abel, you did!" followed up Kinmal, letting out a loud belly laugh.

Abel had to admit that this was funny. Properly funny. All the tension of the day was, just for that short moment in time, released. They laughed heartily together as the TTAXI made its way through the atmosphere and toward the mission target area.

Landing on the mission target area would be a challenge. It would have been a challenge for even the most experienced of TTAXI drivers. The whole planet was black. Not just dark, or on the darkish side of grey, but black. SARDOC informed them as they descended through the atmosphere that the dim, orange sun had meant that the vast majority of plant life had evolved to be as dark as possible to soak up what little light there was. As the sun has gradually got dimmer, the plant life had gotten darker, until the whole surface area was covered in a deep, black carpet. The only sentient life on the planet, the Gedren, had long since retreated to living completely underground using the heat from the surface, or 'over soil heating' as they called it, to warm their colonies. Gedren were five-foot tall, Mole-like creatures, with poor eyesight yet amazing building skills. They were also big in the recycling industry, using the trapped gasses from their sizeable guano to power most of their technology.

Gedren cities were some of the largest, flattest, smelliest settlements in the Galactic Alliance and nasal protection is provided with any holiday booking as standard. Despite the stench, their cities, hewn from the red stone that pervades most of the planet, are an awesome sight to behold. The largest of these is the capital city of Brambram, which is on Fleeban Domub's list of 'Top 50 places to visit before the Big Crunch'. It was also voted best Aroma of all time by the readers of Septic Tank Magazine, but they don't like to talk about that.

"S, overlay the mission objective and any Dark Matter signatures on the front window please," said Abel, turning off the headlights as they really weren't helping, "Let's see if that makes a difference".

Abel and Kinmal each looked out of different side windows, but neither of them could see anything. Torlup 6 was like one of those comedy posters where the caption says, 'Paris at Night' and the picture is just a big black square.

The HUD on the front window sprang into life in a flash of red blobs that kept blinking in for a few seconds and then out for a few more. The yellow mission marker was ahead and slightly to the left, with a distance underneath, counting back from 500m as they neared it.

"Why are the signatures blinking in and out like that?" asked Kinmal, his eyes still adjusting to the brightness of the HUD against the lack of light from the surrounding windows.

"I cannot talk to Agent Abel's SARDOC unit, Liebling," answered his SARDOC, "but I would suggest it is because of their distance underground".

"Take us down to the mission marker, S" commanded Abel, releasing the wheel and allowing SARDOC to gently land the TTAXI, "we'll get out and have a look".

The HUD information swapped to Abel and Kinmal's helmet displays, as the Nano Bytes covered their respectively heads in readiness. They both disembarked, their feet crunching on the pitch-black, but surprisingly warm vegetation. There were no signs of life in any direction. Finding the entrance to the city was going to be harder than they thought.

"Oh, what a weird feeling! It's like my underfloor heating back at home!" declared Kinmal, even taking to doing a little bounce on the soft plants.

"Ooo, underfloor heating – very continental!" joked Abel, attempting to hold back the urge to join Kinmal in a bounce, "what's wrong with good, old-fashioned radiators?"

"Ah, very inefficient, my friend. We Germans..."

"British..."

"We German Brits prefer the most efficient way of doing things. Much like the Gedren, we harness as much energy as possible. Very little would be wasted through the ceiling".

"Through...the...ceiling," Abel said slowly and quietly, thoughtfully wagging his finger in the air as he turned around. He walked away from the TTAXI, his finger still wagging, as if it were a metronome for his thought process.

"S, scan the area for changes in temperature and map any increases into my view of the surrounding area. Take away the Dark Matter signatures for a minute".

SARDOC complied and Abel's HUD began to fill up with a temperature map, radiating out in every direction with him at the centre. It coated the land around them with a virtual temperature chart, with yellow being the hottest temperature and blue the coldest.

A little way away in a North Easterly direction, there seemed to be four spots of yellow. They were arranged in a precise diamond, too perfect to be a natural occurrence.

"Over there," said Abel, pointing in the direction of the spots, "That's our best bet".

Leaving the TTAXI where it had landed, they walked towards the warm yellow spots. As they got nearer, they could see that the spots were surrounding a large, square opening, which showed as blue on the heat map. It was either an exhaust for regulating temperature of the vast subterranean cities, or a door.

Either way, it was a way in for them and the matter was settled as they arrived in front of it. There was a large red button to the right of the opening, with what must have been Gedren writing under it.

"Can you translate it, S?" asked Abel. His answer came without his digital assistant saying a word, as the words began to virtually rearrange themselves in his HUD and morph into standard English. The sign now said, "PRESS FOR ATTENTION", which he did.

Abel moved to press the button and Kinmal stopped him.

"Wait, shouldn't we change our appearance to match the locals? It is standard mission procedure," warned Kinmal.

"We won't be able to. The Emergency Autonomy Mode stops you from accessing the required database. We'll have to do this the old-fashioned way".

As soon as he pressed the button, a small flap opened above the red button and a rectangular screen, about twelve inches tall flew out. It was accompanied out of the flap by a quiet farting noise and a plume of foul-smelling gas. The Agents' Nano Bytes reacted to cover their Humans' mouths in breathing equipment before either of them had a chance to catch too much of the odour. What they caught was quite enough though. The screen whizzed about in front of them, a small green light began to glow at the top middle of the screen's frame. It first scanned Kinmal, from his toes to the top of his head, as if covering his front in bright green silly string. It paused for a second, as if processing the data it had just collected. It then turned to face Abel and repeated the process. Again, it paused to process the information it had just collected. The screen then flickered, and a large snout appeared, its breath fogging up the screen from the inside.

"Who's there? What business have you with the Gedren?!" the gruff voice questioned, in perfect English. 'The scan must have been to discern what species we were. Clever.' Thought Abel. The creature's snout lurched downwards out of the screen and was replaced with two small grey eyes. They clearly weren't very good as the Gedren's face was almost touching the screen in an attempt to see them.

"Oh hello!" Abel said in his friendliest voice, even going so far as to do a little wave with his hand, "We're from a company called Universal Corrections. We're here to investigate the disappearances you've been having".

The Gedren on the screen didn't say a word. Instead he made a grunting noise, the screen went black and returned to the flap it had come out of.

"Well, what do you…" asked Kinmal, who stopped mid-sentence as he got his answer. The metal door started grinding it's way open with a series of loud thuds. The light that started issuing forth from the hole shone brilliantly against the completely black surrounding flora, although in truth it was no brighter than an oven lightbulb. In addition to the escaping light came another, larger, plume of green gas which would have made the Agents gag had it not been for their breathing protection. As their eyes adjusted to the glow, they stepped to the edge and looked down. Through the hole that was created, they could see a ladder leading down to a horizontal tunnel at the bottom, that lead off in the direction of their mission marker. At the entrance to the tunnel stood the Gedren they had seen on the screen. He was indeed about five-feet tall, with four pink, three-digited claws sticking out of thick, blue overalls. He motioned to them to climb down, his snout pushing out puffs of wet air. The dimly lit tunnel at the bottom of the ladder reflected lazily off the Gedren's grey, smoky eyes.

Abel and Kinmal shared a quick glance at each other and nodded. There a spot of 'after you', 'no after you', all done in silence through the use of hand gestures. Eventually, Kinmal took the offer and climbed down the ladder first, closely followed by Abel.

Abel's head had no sooner cleared the level of the opening, that it began closing again. The Gedren were notoriously secretive and both the Agents realised how serious the problem must be for them to have called in outside help. They would have to be on their best behaviour.

Both Kinmal and Abel bowed at the Gedren doorman as they dismounted the ladder. He gave them both the same dismissive grunt and walked off down the tunnel, motioning for them to follow him. They exchanged another glance and complied.

After what seemed like ten minutes of walking, the tunnel opened out into the largest underground dwelling either of them had ever seen. The whole cavern was alive with tens of thousands of Gedren all going about their daily lives. It must have been at least three miles long and just as wide, all held up periodically with huge red stone columns. Abel thought it looked like you'd expect the inside of a Termite mound to look, if the Termites were the size of Mini Metros. The outside walls of the cavern were dappled with a countless number of holes of varying size and shapes, each one representing a dwelling or collection of them. In the middle was a massive, cuboid construct that looked like a Rubik's Cube, but each side was at least half a mile long. Each section of the cube had a different usage from what Abel could ascertain. The ones at the bottom looked like the storage areas for the city's waste – drainpipes fanned to the outside walls in every direction across the floor of the cavern, covered in precise increments with stone walkways.

In the middle row, food growing areas could be seen through the open centres of the sides. The top row was closed off, but had tubes stretching to the roof of the cavern. The roof was covered in hexagonal plates, which glowed with the same dim ferocity as the lights in the entrance tunnel.

"Fascinating," said Kinmal, staring up at the cavern roof, "The cells are collecting the heat from the flora above and producing light and energy below".

"Like the opposite of solar panels!" agreed an amazed Abel. The Gedren acted like he'd seen it all before. Which of course he had. Or at least he would have if he could see that far.

As the Gedren led them to the edge of a set of steps leading down to one of the many stone walkways littering the floor of the city-sized cavern, Kinmal spotted the source of the trouble. Off to the right and approximately halfway along the side of the cavern, he could see a large ball of solid rock had been removed from the wall. It must be the location of the WAMD he thought, which of course was invisible to those not in possession of a SARDOC and a Nano Byte suit. Kinmal's HUD confirmed his suspicions, as the area glowed red. For the first time on one of these missions, he had another being to share his findings with.

"Look, over there!" shouted Kinmal, trying to be heard over the cacophony of the sprawling underground city. Abel obviously didn't hear him, as he was still gawping at one of the layers of the giant Rubik's Cube in the centre. Kinmal tapped Abel's forearm with his hand, causing tiny sparks to fly from the site of two Nano Byte suits touching. Abel flinched and turned his head sharply to look at his arm, as if he had been given a small electric shock by the contact. He quickly looked up at his fellow agent.

Kinmal waited for the eye contact before raising two fingers up to his eyes, meaning 'LOOK', and then moving them in one motion to point at the growing empty area he had spotted, meaning 'OVER THERE'.

Abel followed his colleague's fingers as they pointed and instantly saw what he was on about. He brought the Nano Bytes back up over the remainder of his head as Kinmal had done and scanned the area for himself. His findings would concur with Kinmal's, although the confines of Emergency Autonomy Mode would stop their SARDOCs from knowing this straight away. They shared a knowing nod, and both concluded that they needed a plan. They also both knew that they were rubbish at hand signals.

"S, leave the breathing equipment on my nose but free up my mouth," instructed Abel, "I need to talk tactics with Herr Flick over there".

"Certainly sir, remember to override your compulsion to breathe through your mouth, sir". SARDOC warned him.

"Are you saying I'm a mouth breather, S?" asked Abel, trying to remember what he had left his assistant's humour settings on the last time he had tinkered with them. SARDOC's silence spoke volumes.

Kinmal saw what Abel had done and duly instructed his SARDOC to do the same, without the sarcastic comments. They were now both now stood there looking at each other with what looked like glittering metallic Clown noses.

"We look like we're about to do a sponsored walk for Comic Relief". Said Abel, surveying his colleague's face and then crossing his eyes trying to see his own metal nose.

"Ha! Don't you mean COSMIC Relief?" asked Kinmal, landing the joke further by giving Abel the 'double guns' hand gesture.

Abel tried not to laugh, but he had to admit that he wished he had thought of it. It was a Dad joke, not a bad joke. He decided an encouraging smile was probably the best response to give.

"Okay we need a plan, quick," started Abel, the eye parts of the Nano Byte suit returning to allow him to see his HUD, "Why don't I start by defending the nearest pillar to the disturbance and work our way back to the Wormhole. You stand in front of the Wormhole and catch any Wardz that try to escape".

"I concur, Agent Abel," agreed Kinmal far-too-seriously, "I will make my way down this way," he pointed down and to the right, "and you make your way to the pillar through the centre, over there". He pointed straight ahead, to the main walkway stretching out in front of them.

"Good luck Agent". Said Abel, before his mouth was covered by the Nano Bytes.

"On this occasion, we do not need luck, Agent Abel," shouted Kinmal as the ran off in his planned direction, "On this occasion, we have each other! And afterwards we will celebrate with some drinks!"

-

Abel took up his position at the base of the nearest stone pillar to the disturbances. The pillar dwarfed him, being at least nine or ten feet wide and hundreds of feet tall.

Now that he was at the bottom of the cavern, he could barely see the cells on the roof of it. In fact, they were so far away that individual light cells could not be made out, meaning the roof of the cavern just looked like one complete orangey-yellow sky. A sky permeated with green noxious clouds, being given off by the central cube. His HUD had kept a track of Kinmal as he had run towards his position and he could now see him jumping down in front of the WAMD portal. There would be no escape for the Wardz attempting to destroy this beautiful subterranean city.

And so it proved to be the case. The first of the three Wardz to be despatched made the mistake of landing right in front of Abel and trying to fire his Entropiser, attempting to dematerialise the base of the pillar.

Unbeknownst to either of the combatants, a young Gedren child, Doodoc, was watching the whole thing out of his bedroom window. The fight he was about to witness would be as awesome as it was confusing.

Abel leapt forward immediately and knocked the Anti-Matter Demon flying across the hard-stone floor with such force, that to Doodoc it looked as if Abel was riding an invisible skateboard. He quickly cracked open the writhing creature's protection suit with one hand and filled him with a blast of the matter cannon with the other. All before they came to a stop. To Doodoc, the invisible skateboard had suddenly materialised, out of thin air, looking like a four-armed, expandable foam sculpture.

One down, two to go.

He spotted the second one almost straight away. He jumped off the solidified body and sprinted towards his new target, making an assortment of traditional 'oo' and 'ah' noises as he did so. The suit was a major help to the speed he could attain, but it still made his knees hurt to run this fast. No amount of state-of-the-art Nano cushioning could remove the impact of foot with ground completely. At these moments, when he was having to run after things, he always wondered when the Cromulites would get around to invent a Nano Byte suit that could fly. Iron Man had one in the comics in 2006, for heaven's sake.

The second Wardz must have caught sight of his pursuer when Abel was about six feet away from him. The Nano Byte suit's stealth components had done their job. It was too late for the Wardz to change his direction, but he tried anyway.

Doodoc watched from his window, now munching from a bag of what passes for Popcorn on Torlup 6. What he saw was Abel darting first one way, then another, all in pursuit of an unseen target. He wondered what these flies had done to this humanoid, that he would chase them so angrily and expand them with foam. Then he realised that the flies must in fact be Wasps. Even on Torlup 6, everyone hates Wasps.

Abel reached out with his trident attachment and pierced the creature right between the shoulders of its protection suit. A crack and blast later and the city of Brambram now had a second sculpture to add to the first one. One more and they could have an art exhibition.

The final creature had already started running back towards the portal, which meant Kinmal was up.

Kinmal could see from his scanning that Abel was not going to catch the last Wardz. He readied himself for the oncoming kill, his Nano Byte suit assuming the shape of a large boulder, while inside he flicked his arms downwards and commanded the Nano Bytes to form the required hand weapons. Left for trident, right for the matter cannon.

The demon came charging towards him, firing his Entropiser wildly. The creature was completely unaware that he was about to be killed by a rock, like the world's angriest pair of scissors. This strategy of letting the enemy come to you was most unusual to Kinmal, as he was usually the one in Abel's position doing the chasing.

Wardz always knew to run from the man with the hand trident for some reason. He had never before been fired at with the Entropiser, but he assumed nothing good could come from being hit with one.

The first shot burbled past his head, which to the Wardz beast was the top of the rock between him and the Wormhole. He ducked his head as a reflex. He hoped the creature hadn't noticed the top of the boulder dent in any way. It was less than ten feet away now, almost time to strike from his hiding position. Another shot ribboned wildly past his left side, although this time Kinmal managed to stay still, so engrossed as he was on the perfect moment to strike. The beast was almost on top of him, probably wondering why he hadn't noticed the big lump of red sandstone on the way out of the Wormhole. Unfortunately, for it anyway, it didn't have any time to work it out, as it was now right next to Kinmal's hidden trident hand. The prongs leapt out of the side of the rock and buried deeply into the demon's side, right between its two right arms. It stopped the beast right in its tracks. Crack. Blast. Foamy foamy. The job was done.

The agents had completed their mission. The people of Brambram had their art exhibition. And Doodoc had a story to tell his friends at Mining School the next day. The one about the angry humanoid and the even angrier rock chasing Wasps with their big forks and killer foam. It was a story that would earn the juvenile Gedren an award for Story of the Month and several visits to the School Counsellor.

-

"Well, you were right about one thing, Agent Kinmal," laughed Abel, as he clambered out of the opening, "You certainly can celebrate!"

"Why thank you, Agent Abel!" replied Kinmal, in a high-pitched comedy voice, as the suit powered him out of the hole, "I consider it one of my greatest strengths. What's the point of being the last line of defence for the universe if you can't enjoy it afterwards?"

"I know what you mean, I sometimes enjoy a drink with the locals after a mission," agreed Abel, although he omitted that he didn't go as mad as Kinmal seemed to, "Sorry I had to…um…break your flow. But as I told you at the beginning, we've got a deadline".

"Argh," Kinmal closed his eyes and held his hands up in the traditional 'don't worry about it' manner, "of course, my friend. The unknowable answers and the eight-armed head await!" He placed a hand on his hip and pointed the other one to the stars.

The entrance tunnel closed behind them, leaving the only light visible as that of the TTAXI headlights in the distance.

"How long until the two hours are up, S?" Abel checked with SARDOC.

"Ten minutes ago, sir" admonished SARDOC.

"Ah, best not hang around then!" Abel grabbed Kinmal under the arm, flipping the arm across his shoulders and quickening his pace. Abel could feel the answers to today's questions getting closer, just as he was nearing the TTAXI. He dreaded to think what he was going to find in that cleaner's cupboard when he got back there. What weird and wonderful clone would Rigsan have found on his mission? He would soon find out.

-

"To the Batcave!" Laughed Kinmal from his horizontal position on the back seat of the TTAXI. His finger pressed against the glass as if instructing Abel where to go next.

Abel pulled the TTAXI up to the end of the cab rank and turned off the engines, allowing the movement of the queue to take over. He turned and looked over his shoulder at the drunken clone behind him. How the hell would they get this puddle of inebriation passed anyone, let alone an eight-legged monster with lasers for eyes.

'One step at a time' he thought to himself, 'It's got me this far!'

The recess was now almost alongside them and Abel figured Kinmal would need a little help to get out. So he got out and quickly opened the back door to the cab.

Luckily, Kinmal was laying with his legs nearest Abel, so he grabbed both ankles and dragged him vigorously out of the cab, placing them both on the floor. This movement, coupled with the double mild-electric shock from the Nano Bytes suit contact, made Kinmal stand bolt upright. He almost tipped over forward and came within millimetres of whacking his head on the door frame as his torso vaulted out of the cab. As Abel stood him up, Kinmal got his balance and started to laugh. Abel grabbed his arm and started to make for the recess and cleaners' cupboard. Kinmal, now losing his balance again, pretended to shoot the TTAXIs in the rank behind them with his finger gun, still giggling.

Abel opened the cupboard door and rushed through, with Kinmal staggering in tow.

"You're late". Said Rigsan, sternly. Dofe shook at the noise of the door slamming against the racking behind it.

"I know, I can explain". Replied Abel, letting go of his colleague and pointing at Dofe, "Is yours German? And why does he look like an elderly Terry Nutkins?"

"German? Why would a clone of m…DON'T CLOSE THE…!"

The door had begun to swing shut again. Kinmal, still trying to get his balance from being dragged in the room by Abel, stumbled into it and helped it on its way by leaning on it with his back. His head fell to one side as he slid down it, smiled and relaxed, as if happy in the knowledge of a job well done.

"There's no handle!" exclaimed Dofe, pointing at the door.

"German?" exclaimed Rigsan.

"Not again…" sighed Abel.

"There should be a sign…" slurred Kinmal, before collapsing onto his side and falling asleep with his head on a yellow bucket.

CHAPTER 15
THE ROOM
(NO, NOT THAT ONE)

"So yours is German?" inquired Rigsan, pointing at the Kinmal-shaped lump by the door, "How can he be German?"

"Well, he's not *exactly* German," replied Abel, turning to look at Kinmal too. The pair of them looked like new parents standing over their sleeping firstborn, "He reckons his parents moved to Germany when he was eight and he's lived there ever since".

"That's weird". said Rigsan, stroking his chin thoughtfully.

"Yeah, really weird". Agreed Dofe from the corner.

"What's weird about that? Apart from the obvious of course?" asked Abel, getting the feeling that he should be remembering something his clones were remembering.

"Well, my Dad had a chance to go and work in Germany when I was eight". Said Rigsan.

"Mine too!" said Dofe, standing up.

"But he decided against it because…" started Rigsan.

"Mum didn't want to!" finished Dofe. They were now looking at each other, before both turning to Abel, as if for confirmation whether he actually shared the same memory.

He thought about it. His memory woke up with a start and realised that it did. Abel's eyes widened.

"Bloody hell, yeah. I remember now. She didn't want to leave Nan and Grandpa". Confirmed Abel, making a point with his finger, as if flicking through an imaginary photo album in his head. Still frames of walking into the kitchen when he was eight and hearing his parents talking about a job in Germany. Dad had said it was a great opportunity for them. For him more like, his Mum had replied. It had never been talked about again. Not in his earshot, anyway. It was bad enough when Dad had taken the job in Dartmouth and they'd moved to the outskirts of Plymouth. Nan had thought it was the other side of the world.

"What the hell are the Cromulites playing at?!" asked Dofe, "Why would they make clones of me…"

"Me…" argued Rigsan and Abel, both at the same time.

"Us," continued Dofe, trying the tactful route Kinmal had tried earlier, "But implant us with different memories?"

"That's what we're here to find out," confirmed Abel, looking up at the chute entrance that had been his way out of this room twice before, "Let's wait for Oliver Reed over there to sober up a bit and then make a move on that door".

They sat down on upturned buckets and decided to give Kinmal some time for the Nano Bytes to sweat some of the Alcohol out of his system.

"So what's your story then, old man Terry?" asked Abel, pointing at Dofe, "How come you're ancient compared to us?"

"TTAXI accident," Dofe replied morosely, "The TTAXI went through a comet's tail just before coming out of warp. The Time protection inside the cab failed for a split second and I aged 30 years. Left me like this. No way to reverse it without destroying the time-space continuum".

"Bummer," consoled Abel, tutting and flicking a 'this is the best you could do?' glance at Rigsan when Dofe looked down. Rigsan replied with a 'what do you expect in two hours?' glance in return.

"So, how do we get past the Octo-Boglin then?" interjected Rigsan, trying to bring everyone back on target, "He's a big, nasty swine. Too big for us to take on with our weapons out in the open. It'll cause too much of a scene".

"Sir, may I be allowed to interject?" asked S, from inside Abel's suit.

"Of course, S". replied Abel, eliciting confused looks from Rigsan and Dofe until they realised he was talking to his SARDOC, and not having a psychotic break under the stress of the situation.

"Sir, I believe the Nano Bytes that comprise your suit may be able to collaborate with the other suits in this room. My preliminary scans indicate they are coded to the same DNA as yours, so no rejection would occur".

"Okay," said Abel, quizzically, "Meaning?"

"Meaning that if the four of you pooled your Nano Bytes, your suits could create a facsimile of the Krunt guarding the Nexus door".

"The WHAT guarding the door?!" exclaimed Abel.

"What's your SARDOC saying?" whispered Dofe, leaning over and lightly tugging at Abel's arm like a toddler when his Mum's on the phone.

"He says the thing guarding the door is a Krunt!" replied Abel, turning away again to continue talking to his AI companion.

"I'll say," misheard Rigsan, nodding.

"Would we be able to do this while we're all in EA Mode?" asked Abel, fearing he already knew the answer.

"Unfortunately not, sir," confirmed S, "All four SARDOC units would need to communicate with each other to ensure the facsimile was complete. If we didn't, we may all decide to copy the same piece of the creature".

"That'll have to do I suppose, S. We'll have to wait until the last possible moment. Do you think they'll read us if we are that close to the centre of the complex?"

"Unsure, sir," said S, "I don't believe a connected SARDOC unit has ever been that far inside".

"We'll find out I suppose. We've come this far, I'm not about to give up now!" said Abel, determinedly.

"Who's giving up? Is your SARDOC telling you to give up?" said Rigsan, straightening his back in disgust, "There'll be no giving up here".

"Alright, calm down G.I. Joe, no one's giving up". Said Abel, holding a conciliatory hand out, "Right, here's the plan. My SARDOC reckons we can combine our Nano Bytes and make ourselves look like the Boglin at the door. We can lure it away somehow and stun it ounce we're in cover".

"Sounds good," agreed Rigsan, "We'll be like a Trojan Horse!"

"More like a Pantomime horse". Sniffed Dofe.

"Bagsy not the arse then!" shouted Rigsan, before anyone else could.

"There's only one problem".

"Here we go". Said Dofe, defeatedly.

"Go on". Said Rigsan.

"We'll have to reconnect our SARDOCs to the mainframe so they can work together to copy the Krunt. S doesn't know if that'll put us back on the grid or not".

"Oh great. So, we could get past the big monster, but get taken down by the guards instead". Said Dofe, his voice wavering.

"Or, we could be so far inside the complex," corrected Rigsan, shooting Dofe a withering look, "that they won't be scanning for SARDOCs because they wouldn't dream of looking just outside the door".

"Exactly". Agreed Abel, watching Dofe as he scrunched his face up in response to Rigsan's look. Out of Rigsan's eye-line, of course.

"As soon as our Pan-European friend is awake," said Rigsan, pointing at the still sleeping Kinmal, "I say we go for it".

"Agreed. Now let's chill out for a bit while we wait for Kinmal's detox to take effect. Today has been an extremely stressful day so far, for all of us. Let's take some time to…just to gather our thoughts". Said Abel, sitting down on the floor and resting his head against the equipment racking. Dofe and Rigsan agreed and joined Abel on the floor.

"All we need is a campfire!" joked Dofe.

"And a guitar to sing Kumbaya!" replied Abel, laughingly strumming an air guitar.

"We should be getting on with it," Rigsan said impatiently, forgetting it was his idea to wait until Kinmal woke up, "Can't we throw water over him or something?!"

"Oh for god's sake, Rigsan," said Abel, lolling his head around sarcastically, "Look, so far today I've found out that my life is a lie, there's thousands of versions of me running around the universe, every one of them seems to have a Cat called Colin and I've been stuck in this bloody cleaner's cupboard three times! I just...want...a...sit...down! Alright?!"

The chill out was replaced with an awkward silence. Talking to yourself shouldn't be this difficult.

PLYMOUTH, UK, TERRA, SOL SYSTEM, MILKY WAY, EARTH YEAR 1990

"This is a really crap disco, Mark! I can't believe you talked us all into coming!" Shouted Marcus, leaning over so Mark could hear him above the noise of *The Birdy Song*.

Mark could only nod in agreement. Neither of them were great partygoers. They'd celebrated when their final A-level exams had been completed, but that wasn't really a party. Unless six friends, all recently turned 18, getting drunk in the local while the old men looked on disapprovingly constituted a party. None of his group were big party goers, which is why they worked together. They would much prefer to be round someone's parents' house playing Trivial Pursuits like middle-aged couples than getting into scraps downtown.

Nevertheless, Mark had gone out of character and convinced them all that they were duty-bound to go to the Leavers Disco, being as how they were all, well, leavers. So, here they were, sat as far away from the dance floor as they could be without being in the cloakroom, gradually getting drunk enough to venture into the light. Mark was already on his third 'K' Cider and he could feel his limbs loosening with every passing sip.

"I wonder if he's got any Stone Roses?" wondered Andy, taking another drink of his Guinness, "Or even some Happy Mondays".

"Don't be daft," sighed Marcus, nursing his Coke, "It's a kid's disco – you'll be lucky if he's got any snogging music".

Just the mention of 'snogging music' made Mark subconsciously sit up straight on his stool. That was the bit he hated the most, partly because he viewed it as a meat market and partly because he could never find anyone to dance with.

Tonight might be different though, if his plan came to fruition. Part one had been getting the group to come to the disco. Part two was somewhere inside.

The Leavers Disco was in full swing around them. The Social Committee had done quite a good job with it, to be honest. The hut was normally the social club for the local Electricity company, SWEB. So it was ideal for parties of this type, or it was according to the advert in *The Evening Herald* anyway. Maggie and the rest of the party planners must have spent hours blowing up all the 'Good Luck' balloons that festooned the walls. They'd even managed to talk Mr. Mockridge into painting the 'Goodbye to all the 1990 Leavers' banners as part of the 1st year's Art project for the Summer term. Mark and his friends had been secretly quite impressed when they walked in, even if they managed to maintain their protective shell of sarcastic aloofness.

"Hi Mark," said a soft voice close behind his ear. So close it made the hairs stand up on the back of his neck, making him move his head back like a Turtle, "Enjoying the party?"

Mark turned around on his stool and saw Part Two of his plan standing up again from talking in his ear. Michelle Evans. The beautiful Michelle. The sweet, generous, kind Michelle. With the dark brown eyes and, to quote Andy, "the massive norks". He stood up instantly, leaving his bottle of cider pirouetting wildly on the edge of the table like a gyroscope on a fishing boat.

"Oh, uh, hi Michelle, sorry, uh, didn't see you there," Mark steadied the bottle on the table and wiped his hands on his trousers. They were damp from a combination of bottle moisture and now nervous sweat, "How are you doing?"

He leaned in and gave her an awkward, timid cuddle, which she reciprocated. As his chin rested on her shoulder for a few seconds, he caught a waft of her perfume. As always, she smelt amazing. Properly amazing. They say that smell is the sense most closely linked to the Hypothalamus, the animal part of the brain. And his monkey brain was currently jumping up and down, screeching and throwing lumps of its own poo at the logic centres.

"Are you enjoying the party?" Michelle repeated, too nice to be offended by his disregard for the first time she'd said it.

"Oh yeah, it's great!" he replied, over enthusiastically, "I can't believe what you've managed to do with the place!"

"Oh, it was a team effort," she replied humbly, averting her gaze, making Mark realise that he was staring like the man on the bus who eats flip flops, "I can't take all the credit".

Mark started to sweat even more profusely, as the realisation of what he was doing swept over him. The surprise of her instigating the conversation had given his speech centres a few minutes head start, before the damn nervousness kicked in. Whenever it was him starting things, his brain had already had several minutes to reduce him to a puddle of perspiration and stuttering. The adrenaline would soon be in control and his tongue would feel like it had swelled to three times its normal size. And this was ten years before having a fat tongue was cool.

"Ha-ha yeah, I suppose so," replied Mark, wiping his hands again. This time it was 100% sweat on them. 'I suppose so?' he thought, 'That's it is it? That's all you've got? All those jokes that are normally right on the tip of your tongue and all you've got is I suppose so?'

"I'm not sure about the music though, are you?" she asked , nodding towards the DJ, who'd moved onto *Swing the Mood* by *Jive Bunny*.

"What's that banging noise?' Mark wondered to himself, before realising it was the blood rushing up his neck and around his head.

"Mark was just saying the DJ was rubbish!" shouted Marcus, leaning around Mark's side. Mark pushed Marcus back with his hand, so Michelle couldn't see him. He was perfectly capable of messing this conversation up on his own, without his stupid friend getting involved. He turned and gave Marcus a look that he hoped would stop any further interruptions.

"It's okay, I suppose," he said, looking around at something, anything but Michelle's beautiful brown eyes, "I like the Stone Roses, Happy Mondays, stuff like that. I doubt he's got it though".

"Oh I love the Stone Roses!" exclaimed Michelle, her face lighting up in that way it did, the way that took Mark's breath along with it, "Not sure about the Mondays though".

"Yeah, they're a bit mad," agreed Mark, putting his hands in his pockets so that Michelle couldn't see them shaking, "They're pretty cool".

He winced at the use of the word 'cool'. "Cool' people would never use the word 'cool'. Using it negates its effects, everyone knew that. But Michelle didn't seem to mind. She fixed her eyes with his. And whenever she did that, she was the only thing in the room.

Mark didn't realise it when it was happening, but this was a moment he would think about for the rest of his life. Every time he showed people where the Beans were. Every time he had to pick up a broken jar of Piccalilli. Whenever he sat in his tiny flat after his marriage had fallen apart. Even when he was on the loo sometimes doing an unsatisfying poo.

"Listen, why don't we go and see if the DJ's got any Stone Roses. Or maybe something we can dance to". Said Michelle, putting out her delicate hand and willing Mark to take it.

"Um," said Mark, knowing that one touch of his clammy claw and Michelle would be gone forever, "I, uh, I need a wee!"

He scooted off to the toilet, telling himself that his dancing would have put her off, or his sweaty hand, or whatever he needed to tell himself, so he didn't face the fact he'd just blown it. Marcus and Andy ripped him mercilessly when he returned from the toilet and by the time he'd drunk enough to try again, Michelle was dancing with John and his chance had gone. And it was no consolation to Mark that that sentence rhymed either...

–

The awkward silence had continued far too long for Dofe's liking. His anxiety did not cope well at the best of times. He'd once had a panic attack in Mc Colls because they'd run out of Rizlas. So being stuck in a medium-sized utility cupboard with three clones of himself, two of whom weren't speaking, was a recipe for disaster. He could feel his chest starting to tighten and his head beginning to become lighter. He knew how this would go, as he had been here many times before. So he tried a new tack – he summoned up what little courage he had and spoke up.

"Come on guys," he said, standing up and holding out his hands and leaning his light-headed body on the nearest racking, "This is, like, really uncool".

"Bloody hell, you sound like Neil!" said Rigsan, looking up at his colleague as Dofe gently bounced from one leg to the other. He was referring to the plant-loving character from *The Young Ones*, a reference he knew everyone in the room would get.

"Ha-ha yeah," Abel agreed, putting on Vyvyan's voice from the same show, "Shut it, Hippy!"

Dofe stopped bouncing and sat down timidly, but it seemed like his outburst had done the trick. Abel and Rigsan were united once more, even if it was only in mutual mickey taking.

"Huh," Rigsan sniggered ruefully and shook his head, "Michelle would be loving this".

"Who?" asked Abel urgently, fearing he knew what Rigsan was going to say next, even if he was going to have a hard time believing it.

"Michelle, my ex-wife," replied Rigsan, gazing at the wall as if reliving some hideous trauma, "We were school sweethearts. I had a thing for her all through sixth form. I didn't realise it until the Leaver's Disco, but she had a thing for me too. I was such a nerd back then but somehow, I got out of my own way and danced with her. We were thick as thieves after that. She even talked me into going travelling for a year straight after school finished. I'd never have even considered anything like that before. I hadn't even gone to France with the school in the first year because I didn't want to leave home for a week. But with her…with her it didn't matter where I was," He paused and Abel thought he saw Rigsan's eyes mist up, just for a second. It was as if a long-forgotten memory had commandeered his minds eye's view screen, only for his logical brain to quickly change the channel, "So we went backpacking around Australia for a year, working and such. Then we came back and even went to Bristol University together. I did Computer Science, she did Social Work. We even ran the London Marathon a couple of times together. But she never understood how much time I needed to spend at the business to keep it running. I just couldn't trust anyone to do anything unless I was breathing down their necks. We had the kids…we thought that would help. The 'perfect family'. Heh". He looked down at the ground, between his raised knees.

"Ex-wife?" enquired Abel, still working on believing what this clone was saying, "You said ex-wife. As in not your wife anymore?"

"Yeah. I gave her everything she could want, but it wasn't enough. One day I came home early to surprise her. I surprised both of us. Found her on the kitchen table with the next-door neighbour. She told me it was the company or her. Can you believe that?"

"No, not really!" said Abel, barely concealing his contempt for his colleague's story, "So let me get this straight – you got off with Michelle?!"

"I already said that. Right at the beginning of the story," Rigsan looked confused, "It really wasn't that long".

"Michelle Evans?"

"Of course Michelle Evans!" said Rigsan, giving Abel a look of disgust at his stupidity, "They're your memories too, ya tool!"

"And mine, sort of…" added Dofe, holding up a delicate finger in an attempt to join the conversation and quickly lowering it again.

"Well, they *should* be my memories," agreed Abel, sarcastically, "They should be! Except they're not! Because I never bloody kissed Michelle at the bloody leavers disco, did I?! I ran away to the bloody toilet like I always bloody did and by the time I came back, she was dancing with John!"

"Actually yeah, that's more like my memory…" added Dofe, nodding guiltily and pointing at Abel while looking at Rigsan.

Rigsan looked at Dofe. Then at Abel. Then back at Dofe. His head snapped back, and he let out a booming, condescending laugh. They waited for him to finish, both shooting each other a look as if to say, 'you hold him and I'll hit him'.

"So you're telling me you both remember bottling it with Michelle after all that sweating and working yourselves up? Well then, how the hell did you go trav…oh" Rigsan stopped and realised why these two clones were like they were, "You two didn't go travelling, did you? You stayed at home, like snivelling Mummy's boys. No wonder you didn't make anything of yourselves. But that still doesn't explain why he…" Rigsan pointed at Dofe, "is a simpering bag of nerves and you're a fat layabout".

"Hey, I am not a layabout!" defended Abel, pointing back at his verbal attacker, "I've done alright, considering".

Abel's subconscious lack of conviction suddenly levered its way into his conscious mind and did a little dance. 'Christ, I am a fat layabout, aren't I?' he thought. Deflection was the best way forward.

"Yeah Dofe, why are you like this?" he asked, both him and Rigsan turning to their elderly colleague, "Was it the TTAXI accident?"

"I wish," replied Dofe…

–

PLYMOUTH, UK, TERRA, SOL SYSTEM, MILKY WAY, EARTH YEAR 1992

The Warehouse was always Mark's favourite nightclub. Plymouth's other main club, Ritzy, or "Ritzy's" as the Janners called it, was for pulling the girls, but he and his friends were rubbish at that. Apart from Teddy, who was the only one of the friend group that collected phone numbers on a regular basis. He was extraordinarily good at the 'agony uncle' routine, listening intently to the girl's problems and only swooping in when the moment was right. Sometimes, once Teddy had that night's quarry sat with him in the corner of the club, Mark and his friends would place bets on how long it would be before the first kiss was completed. They all made fun of him for his 'pulling ninja' skills, but all secretly hoped some of his magic would rub off on them. Mark in particular had never seemed to get any better, despite spending every weekend with Teddy in various clubs. You would think that some semblance of chatting up skills would have soaked into Mark through osmosis, but alas no. He would usually end up getting drunk at the bar with the other useless nerds, while Teddy harvested another number.

So tonight, as it was Mark's night of celebration, it had been decided that The Warehouse would be the club of choice. The upside of this converted, 1930s cinema was that the music they played was much more to his liking. Ritzy would stick to the familiar playlist of *Grease* and *ABBA*, while its audience of tradesmen and hair dressers lapped the whole thing up. But Warehouse was always playing *Stone Roses, Happy Mondays, Inspiral Carpets* and the like.

The other upside was the atmosphere in there. Not the buzz of the crowd or the friendly welcome you might get, but the *actual* atmosphere. As in the clouds of Marijuana smoke that hung above the dance floor throughout the evening and ensuing morning. It was a good way to save money, truth be told. The only downside with The Warehouse was that it tended to be full of druggies and drug pushers for the same reasons as just mentioned. And it was right in the middle of Union Street, which is like saying your house is really nice, but it's right in the middle of an active war zone.

The night had been spent drinking, dancing and laughing, to celebrate Mark gaining his first full-time job at the supermarket. It was only as a general assistant on the Wine department. But it was start and reason enough to celebrate with money he didn't yet have. When he had dropped out of his Computer Science HND course at the University of Plymouth, he had wondered whether he should have moved away to do it. Or maybe he should have taken a year out instead of rushing straight into it. Either way, he had dropped out without completing the exams of the first year, meaning he wouldn't get a grant again if he tried to go back. So that door was closed to him, unless he made his money elsewhere. This was pretty far from his mind right at this moment though, as he gulped through his eighth pint of Guinness.

"It's crap for fanny in here! I never have any joy when we come here. Lucky, I like dancing". complained Teddy as he and Scott pushed their way to the bar next to Mark. He was right of course – the girls in here were either too interested in dancing or too wasted to have a conversation, let alone remember their phone number, "I might shoot off in a minute".

"Yeah, after this song, I like this one," shouted Mark, over the noise of *Smells Like Teen Spirit*. He did his traditional 'bar dancing'. Which meant pint in one hand, pocket with the other and dipping the knees slightly to the beat of the music. He drank in time with the music too, which is quite a trick with Nirvana. He did this until his glass was empty.

The music changed to *St Etienne*, signalling it was time to go.

"Ready, gents?" he asked, mimicking a funny walk without moving.

"I'm going for a wee," said Teddy, putting his empty pint of Kronenbourg down next to Mark's glass on the bar and moving the opposite way to his friend, "I'll meet you outside".

"Yeah, I'll drain the pool as well I think" added Scott, moving off to follow Teddy to the toilets, "Don't know how long the Taxi queue will be".

"Okay, I'll start walking to the Taxi rank!" he shouted, although to Teddy and Scott he was simply mouthing the words. Luckily, Teddy was a master lip reader from his number harvesting and so understood perfectly.

Mark walked up the 1930s curved Art Deco staircase that led to the entrance. Most of the fixtures and fitting from when the place was a cinema were still on the walls. Old posters lined the corridor as he left the dance floor area and headed to the outside. He felt the draught of the early morning air around his feet as he neared the door. He noticed the drop-in temperature as he stepped into the wintry, February early morning. What he didn't notice was the two figures following him out the door.

He walked out of the club and onto Union Street. The lane to the cab rank was a little way down the road and off through a lane to the left, but it might as well have been a mile. As it always did, the blast of cold air to Mark's face had scrambled his senses and his determined walk had been reduced to a 'totter' by the time he got near the entrance to the lane. He just about made it around the corner into the lane, using the shop fronts as large concrete Zimmer frames.

It was now he realised he was being followed. He realised just after the first punch had landed on the back of his head, sending him collapsing to the floor. It felt like someone had whacked him with a rolling pin, like you see in Andy Capp comic strips. The shock of it, coupled with his already muddled brain, made it pretty much impossible to get up and fight back. So he assumed the foetal position on the floor and waited for his attackers to punch themselves out. The punches became kicks, each one feeling like it broke something. His senses were not too far gone to feel every rush of air as the boots landed.

They hadn't even tried to take anything. What could be the reason for the attack? It wasn't like he'd talked to anyone's girlfriend in the club – that was Teddy's job. He could sort of understand it if he'd come out of a club and Teddy was, not for the first time, being held up against the wall by a jealous boyfriend.

As if he was the shopkeeper in Mr Benn, the mere thought of Teddy made him and Scott appear from around the corner, where the lane met the main road.

"Thank god for that!" thought Mark, peering at his friends from between his arms as they protected his face, "Reinforcements!"

–

"I was out on a night out in 1992 and I got jumped by two blokes on the way to the Taxi". Said Dofe grimly, fiddling nervously with the corner of the bucket in front of him.

"Yeah, I remember," agreed Abel, "Lucky Scott and Teddy came around the corner when they did".

Dofe looked up at him, tears of sadness and anger welling at the corners of his eyes.

"For you maybe," he said, his hand tightening around the bucket handle as he relived the moment, "My 'so called friends' got scared and ran away. The beating turned into a mugging and I ended up in the hospital. I never trusted anyone again after that".

Abel was stunned, remembering vividly a completely different history where Teddy and Scott had fought off his assailants and got him to a cab. Teddy had even made sure he'd woken Mark's Mum and Dad up and were with him before he left to complete his Taxi ride home.

"I started having mental health issues from then really," continued Dofe, staring ahead at the wall as he spoke, as if taking the chance to say things out loud that he could only say to himself, "I lost the job at the supermarket as I kept having panic attacks whenever I went on the shop floor. It's hard to answer people's questions about which Wine goes best with fish when you can't breathe. It did help me to meet Michelle again though, in a roundabout way".

"You went out with Michelle as well?!" Abel was getting the feeling that he'd died on in the TTAXI crash on that fateful mission and he'd ended up in Hell for killing the Baby Confluence, consigned to an eternity of being stuck in a cupboard with reflections of himself that had all snogged his first love.

"Not quite. She ended up being my Social Worker," laughed Dofe sadly, "I remembered her from school and from that moment on all the old feelings came back. I became a little…too interested in her. She got a restraining order from the courts in the end and I got a new case worker. Dave. Nice chap. Bad breath".

"Bugger me, this is like *Sliding Doors* in space!" exclaimed Rigsan, shaking his head in the least sympathetic way possible.

"At least you didn't kiss her, I suppose". said a relived Abel to himself, quietly enough for Dofe not to hear.

"Kiss who?" asked Kinmal, sitting up and rubbing his head. Abel had clearly said it louder than he thought or intended.

"Michelle!" said all three of Kinmal's cupboard buddies in unison.

"That's weird. I went out with a girl called Michelle at University," Kinmal offered, his barely finished slumber making him not realise the gravity of his words, "Michelle Evans. Beautiful eyes…" he trailed off as if lost in his memory library, frantically trying to pull up more mental pictures of her, "Good kisser".

"Right, Kinmal's awake, everybody into the tunnel!" shouted Abel, springing upright faster than his knees would really let him. He had heard enough. Abel would be not only be demanding answers from whoever or whatever was in the Nexus about what was going on here. He would also be demanding whichever clone memory transplants allowed him to remember kissing Michelle. He was the last line of defence for all matter in the universe. Surely he deserved to remember getting lucky?

CHAPTER 16
THE BOGLIN, THE DOOR AND THE NINTH ARM

Abel led them through the tunnel network, heading for the Nexus. This was much to Rigsan's disgust, who had said that he should go in front as he'd memorised the route already. Dofe didn't mind where he went, apart from at the back in case something nasty crept up on him from behind. Kinmal added that he was happy at the back, away from 'the old married couple' as he put it.

"Can't you go any quicker?" Rigsan kept asking urgently, his head almost up Abel backside. He was so close that if Abel slowed down for even a second, Rigsan was knocking his head against his colleague's butt cheek, "we're on an urgent mission, remember?!"

"Rigsan, this is not *The Human Centipede*!" replied Abel, as quietly as his frustration would let him, "get your nose out of my arse!"

"Can we get on with it please?" added Dofe, his voice thin and quivering, "I'm starting to get claustrophobic!"

"Ooo, don't make me anxious, you wouldn't like when I'm anxious" said Rigsan caustically, aping an old lady voice while calling back to the *Incredible Hulk* TV show of the 1980s.

"Could we just get on with it?" asked Kinmal politely in his pidgin-English accent from the rear, "I have to agree with my whimpering friend here. This arguing is most inefficient".

"You hear that, Rigsan?" said Abel without turning around, "Now you've got Herr Flick mad at you!"

Luckily for everyone, the exit into the equipment room was just up ahead. They each fell out of the hole and into the room in exactly the way you'd expect them to. Abel fell out in his usual haphazard manner, despite this being the third time of asking. Rigsan dove out and did his usual 'super hero landing' in the centre of the floor. Dofe crawled out slowly, sliding down the pile of boxes with barely a sound, like a snake slithering through the undergrowth. Kinmal had somehow managed to turn himself completely around in the tube and came out legs first. He climbed down the boxes as if he was scaling down a five-bar gate. Most efficient, of course.

"Okay, so when we exit this room," Rigsan began, stealing Abel's thunder and popping it in his back pocket. Abel couldn't be bothered to argue again, so he let him continue, "its left, left again to the end of the corridor, then the big Krunt will to the right of the T-junction. I say we let Herr Flick and The Agitated Hulk go and have a look at the beastie, so all our SARDOCs have had a chance to see it before they started mapping the replication. Then we reconnect to the mainframe and join our suits together in here before leaving the room".

Abel felt a bit sick, as that was actually a really good plan. It was pretty much the same as what he would have said, which made him both proud and worried at the same time.

"You guys are up. You ready?" Rigsan motioned at Dofe and Kinmal, who had donned the cleaner's uniforms that they'd picked up from the cupboard earlier. Rigsan cracked the door and poked his head out gently. His two colleagues pressed their caps onto their heads in readiness. Rigsan's reappeared from behind the door and nodded, signalling the all-clear. He swung the door open silently and newest recruits into the 'Fake Cleaning Agency' crept through and dusted their way down the corridor towards the first turning. Both Abel and Rigsan noticed how hard Dofe was breathing as he inched past them and off to the left after Kinmal.

"How hard do you think Dofe's Faecal Recycling Nano Bytes work?" asked Abel.

"About as hard as Kinmal's liver!" joked Rigsan. They shared a laugh at their colleagues' expense.

"Look, I'm sorry about earlier," said Rigsan, his smile being wrestled from his face by a expression of regret, "I just need to get on with things. Means I haven't got to stop and think too much about what's going on".

"Don't worry about it," consoled Abel magnanimously , shocked at his arrogant clone's candour, "We might have different memories, but you're still me and I'm still you. Clones of each other anyway, I don't know. I'm just jealous you got the memories where you were like you are and I got the ordinary ones".

"Let's just..." the conversation was cut short as their two corridor-creeping colleagues returned through the door. Dofe seemed to be breathing even more heavily than before.

"Bloody hell, he's big!" said Dofe, wheezing and very obviously trying to keep his mental state in one piece, "Are you sure four of us are enough to make one of him?"

267

"Nonsense, my friend," said Kinmal, trying to calm his fellow Agent down with a friendly hand on his shoulder, "We will just have to hope that the female Krunt is smaller than the male, as is with most species".

Rigsan gave Abel a broad sardonic smile, his eyebrows raising in amazement.

"What's with the accent?" he asked quietly, pointing at his pan-European clone.

"Café Hag?" asked Abel, joining the smiling party.

"Schmells gut! Right?" added Rigsan, holding an imaginary mug of Coffee up to his nose.

"My SARDOC says she has completed the necessary calculations and is ready to reconnect to the mainframe for suit joining". Said Kinmal, ignoring his colleagues' mickey taking.

"Uh, yeah, mine too," said Dofe, through heaving breaths.

Abel and Rigsan shared another glance, but a much more serious and determined one this time. It was time to find out if they would be discovered.

"Let's go catch a Boglin," said Rigsan, in what Abel had realised was his determined voice, "Sarge, prepare to reconnect to the mainframe in twenty seconds".

"Why do you do that?" asked Abel, instructing S to do the same.

"Do what?" replied Rigsan, as Dofe and Kinmal gave their SARDOCs matching instructions.

"Talk like you're in a movie? Like there's an audience watching?". Added Abel, trying to get Rigsan to have just a sliver of self-awareness. He feared it was a hopeless task.

"We're about to pretend to be a nine-foot octopus head, using four suits made up of millions of microscopic robots, in order to meet aliens that have made thousands of different clones of us". Said Rigsan, matter-of-factly, "and you're worried about my intonation?"

Abel thought about it for a few seconds. He nodded chastely.

"Fair enough. Carry on". He replied, moving to the centre of the room to join the group.

"I have reconnected to the mainframe, sir" said S, his voice dropping every few milliseconds. It sounded the pipping noise you would hear coming through a radio, if the DJ had forgotten to turn his mobile off. His suit froze and judging by the way the group were standing, their suits had done the same.

"What's going on, S?" asked Abel, starting to panic that he had damaged the Nano Bytes by invoking Emergency Autonomy Mode when there wasn't actually an emergency.

"System update, sir". Replied SARDOC, as the four of them stood there for what felt like minutes, frozen like the worst sort of street performers you see at the wrong end of town on a Tuesday afternoon. This frozen time was mainly spent giving each other the types of looks you give when you accidentally make eye contact with a stranger on the bus. The classic 'small smile/eye roll' combo that you reserve for those people you don't know, in case they turn out to be a bus-massacring mentalist. Who knows, that small act of friendliness might mean they let you live, or better yet grant you a quick death.

All four suits gained the power of movement back at roughly the same time and with it, each SARDOC gained the power to communicate with the others in the room.

"Good afternoon, fellow SARDOCs," said S to the other AI assistants, "I have taken the liberty of inviting you all to this virtual private conference room I have created. I feel it will be much easier if our humans are not involved in the planning process. We know what they want us to achieve, so let's discuss it".

"Sounds like a good plan, Lord SARDOC," said Sarge, saluting with this non-existent hand, "I'll take the front and face. Military eyes will be best for this mission!"

"Agreed, dear," added Dr S, "I'll take the right extremities".

"And I will have the left ones!" replied Unter.

"And I take the back of the head. I've also taken the liberty of drawing up a plan of where the suits should meet and how the humans will be placed inside. Transmitting now". S said, as he transmitted the required schematics to the other assistants.

"Got it. That was so easy, dear. I sometimes wonder why we need the humans at all," said Dr S, "It would have taken them twenty minutes of arguing to come up with that, judging by what they've been like since they met".

"Indeed Dr," agreed S, "I myself am quite curious to find out the same answers as the Agents".

"Me too, damn squabbling maggots," said Sarge, "my mommy would have taken a belt to the four of 'em".

"What Mommy?" asked Unter, confused, "Weren't you programmed at the same facility as the rest of us?"

"Let's not go there, Madam Unter," said S, trying to stop what had been a productive planning session from degenerating into the type of four-way argument they were only just making fun of, "Does everyone have the schematics?"

"Yes," said everyone, taking a deep virtual breath and preparing to return to their suits.

"Best of luck SARDOCs," said S, steadfastly.

They all returned to their humans, who had not realised that they'd been talking to just the Nano Bytes for the last minute or so.

"S? S?!" shouted Abel.

"Hello sir," replied S, returning to the suit.

"Where have you been? Thought you had me on mute or something".

"I did sir. The other SARDOCs and I have planned the layout of the upcoming four-way replication".

"Okay, we need to plan the four...oh, right. You've done it". Stopped Abel, disappointedly, "Already? That was quick!"

"Indeed sir. I thought time was of the essence". Replied S, pretending he was sympathetic of his agent's sadness.

"Yeah, I suppose so," said Abel, forlornly, "How did you divvy up the body then?"

"Agent Rigsan will take the front of the head, Agent Kinmal will take the left limbs, Agent Dofe the right and we will take the rear".

"Wait a minute," Abel couldn't believe what he was hearing, "This was you plan, your idea. And you gave us the arse?!"

Across the other side of the group, he could see Rigsan's shoulders starting to shake in laughter. His SARDOC has clearly just told him the same thing.

"Ha-ha! You got the arse!" guffawed Rigsan, pointing at Abel and cupping his own cheek with the other hand, "And it was your SARDOC's idea. He must really hate you".

"Actually, I asked for the back," lied Abel, trying to make the best of really embarrassing situation, "Like the head wolf always goes at the back of the pack to protect them".

"Can we just get on with it? Please?" said Dofe, moving in between his two arguing clones, "I just want to get this over and done with now. I'm overdue my afternoon joi…just right cup of tea".

Abel and Rigsan both gave each other a glance and seemed to decide they would let Dofe's Freudian slip go and come back to it later.

"Yes, I agree with the panicky tramp clone," said Kinmal, moving closer to join the group, "Let's combine and get in the door. Mt Unter says it will be easiest if we stand back to back to back to back I think?"

They followed Kinmal's lead and stood in a tight circle, with each Agent's back facing the opposite one. Their shoulders were almost touching, as they all felt their Nano Bytes shiver and begin to move around them. The ones on their head and legs began to pull away and form a flat skin above them. As the replication continued, the Agents were gently guided into sitting positions, although at the last minute, S had informed

272

Abel that it would better for him if he turned around and faced Rigsan's back. It would be better for the locomotion and shape of the finished creature. Dofe and Kinmal each had their arms and legs pushed out through the side of the beast's head, each limb pretending to be one of the creature's eight arms. It was as if they were stuck in Medieval stocks. As the Agents were being moved around by the Nano Bytes, they watched in awe as the suits began to join together. At the edges, they could see the different sets of Nano Bytes begin to meet and knit together in flashes of hot, orange activity. Like a molten zipper, the seams closed up around them from bottom to top, eventually forming a seal at each corner.

It took barely a few minutes for the replication to finish, but what a sight they must have been from the outside, Abel thought. Of course, it was a different story from the inside. From the inside, all Abel could see was the back of Rigsan's head and the backstage view of the world's two crappiest puppet shows.

"Well, this is nice". Said Abel sarcastically, "How do we open the door?"

"I got it!" said Kinmal, excitedly, as everyone else realised that he was naked under his suit, "If we could just move over towards it a bit".

It was now that they all realised that they had been so consumed by how to look like the Krunt, that they hadn't stopped to think about how to *move* like one. Luckily, their SARDOCs and Nano Bytes HAD thought about it, so without guidance from their Human pilots, the newly-formed Nano Krunt bounced nearer to the door with all the grace of a Seal flopping along the beach on the way to the sea. A variety of noises emanated from the Agents as they got used to the movement of the thing they had created. Abel thought it felt like when you go over a speed bump a little bit too fast in your car.

"There, all done," said Kinmal, reaching out his hand through the suit and undoing both doors.

The double doors swung open and Agents flapped their way out and down the corridor. As they bounced their way down the corridor, the mass was moving in such a way that Abel was being forced to dry hump Rigsan in front. Much to Rigsan's disgust.

"Can you stop that, Abel?" whispered Rigsan from the face, "I can't concentrate with you trying to hump me all the time!"

"I can't help it, can I?" explained a frustrated Abel, as his crotch connected with his colleague's butt for the umpteenth time, "It's the way the things moving!"

"Just keep Abel Jr away from my arse!" exclaimed Rigsan, angrily, as they reached the T junction.

They bounced on the spot, until they were facing Fallapdax by the door. He hadn't seen them yet, as he was too busy checking paperwork. Very litigious, this Krunt. They bounced five paces towards him. Still nothing.

"What's Krunt for 'How you doin'?" Abel said aloud, although the question was meant for one of the SARDOCs.

"Transmitting Krunt sexual instigation signals now, sir". Said S, as if that sentence was as normal as someone asking if you wanted a cup of tea, "I would prepare everyone for a speedy exit. Krunt's are very sexually aggressive".

As the suits were joined together, everyone heard what S had just said. As they began to turn slightly back towards the T-junction, a fine mist was expelled by the suits, in the direction of the beast guarding the door. They watched as the mist made its way along the floor of the corridor, floating to the bottom of the creature's massive face. As he took a breath through his foot-long nose, the mist was taken in with the air of the room. The Krunt instantly stopped checking the papers of the workmen stood next to him and opened the door for them. He hurried them through the door and quickly turned to face the Agents. The expression on his face had changed into a wicked smile, his eyebrows almost meeting in the middle as he grimaced a wanton grimace. He licked his gargantuan lips and started to bounce down the corridor. Surprisingly quickly.

"I'd say we've got his attention," said Rigsan, as they started to bounce themselves around and back towards the T junction, "let's get him back to the room!"

The Nano Bytes were bouncing as quickly as their microscopic motors would let them, but the Krunt was gaining on them. Abel and Rigsan tried to help by dry humping as fast as they could, but the whole mass could only go so fast without breaking apart.

As the they reached the T junction and tried to flop left, Kinmal got a good view of the rapidly nearing Krunt, saliva oozing from the beast's lips as it plopped towards them.

"I thought you said the creature had eight arms, Agent Abel?" questioned Kinmal, pointing one of his controllable limbs at the creature and counting under his breath, "This one would appear to have nine!"

The Agents nearly toppled over into the side of the corridor, as their speed sent them skidding across the metal floor. They righted themselves and regained their forward momentum. Abel looked back to see what his naturalised Germanic clone was on about. His eyes widened in realisation.

"THAT'S NOT AN ARM!!!" he shouted, panicking and dry humping Rigsan even quicker. The mist had worked a bit *too* well by the look of it, as they were now being chased by a fully-engorged Fallapdax.

They made around the second corner and were less than ten bounces away from the safety of the room by the time the horny Krunt was almost on top of them. Literally. The beast's appendage was close to tapping at Abel's rear, who now even angrier of his SARDOC for giving him the arse.

"QUICKER!" screamed Abel, "I can feel it trying to get in!"

"Now you know how I feel!" Rigsan shouted back, because as usual it was all about him, "You've been trying to mount me ever since we got in this thing!"

"Just get in the bloody door, you idiot!" shouted Abel, as they rounded the frame of the door and Abel felt the alien member pressing against his back, trying to find an entry hole, "We both know I'm not three-feet long like this thing is! Although, who knows – maybe they gave you a bigger knob on top of everything else!"

Dofe had the presence of mind to grab the door frame on the way past, catapulting them around to the right and into the room much quicker than they would have just by bouncing. The Krunt had not thought of the same idea, too enraptured as he was with his gorgeous, petite new lady friend. He lost a few steps on the way into the room and that was the window of opportunity the Agents needed.

They landed inside the room and managed to keep the spin going, turning and facing the door in a matter of seconds. The last thing Fallapdax saw as he entered the room, hungry for love, was his prospective mate pointing four arms at him, each holding an Attention-Stun finger blaster.

Four flashes of light later and he was dreaming of the Atenian rainforests of his home world. He would wake up much later with the type of headache that you can only empathise with if your whole body is a head.

-

"That was too close!" said Abel, panting furiously as the suits disengaged from each other and all four Agents fell to the ground.

"Oh I dunno, I think he liked you Abel!" laughed Rigsan, "You nearly got some action then".

"He's re...really big up close, isn't he?!" exclaimed Dofe, backing away from the stunned Krunt, which had come to rest against the racking and was snoring heavily. Its gigantic, green tongue was lolling out of its mouth and a healthy pool of saliva was starting to gather on the floor. It would almost make for a peaceful scene, thought Abel, if the same creature hadn't been trying to penetrate him with its three-foot member only seconds before.

"A fine specimen, to be sure!" agreed Kinmal, walking over and prodding the creature's cheek as his suit finished reforming around him.

"I think I might have some of your suit here, Dofe," said Rigsan, shaking his leg. A small orange patch that was attached to his leg fell off and slid along the floor towards his timid colleague. It reached Dofe's foot and disappeared into it.

"Thanks. So, is that it then?" asked Dofe, as his suit stopped shimmering, now whole again, "Can we get in now?"

"Only one way to find out". Said Abel, turning away from the stunned creature and walking towards the doors.

They made sure to close the doors behind them, so the creature wouldn't be discovered for a while, at least until someone needed a new stapler.

The corridor was now deserted and all four of them started to sweat, as the adrenalin started to flow at the prospect of what they were about to do.

Abel wondered how the others would take being told they were clones. Rigsan was ready to admonish whatever was behind that door for messing up the cloning process so badly. Dofe wondered if he would get told off for stunning the Krunt. And Kinmal wondered what drinks they would be serving in the room, as he still thought Nexus sounded like a really exclusive nightclub.

They approached the palm readers, Dofe and Abel going to the left. Kinmal and Rigsan to the right. They all exchanged a look as they held their hands up in front of the panels – Kinmal and Dofe crouching down to cover the four lower ones.

"Right, on three," said Abel, looking at each of the other Agents in turn, "One…Two…Three!"

They all pressed their hands against the panels and waited for the scan to start. It seemed like an eternity as the bright green line passed horizontally down their palms, from top to bottom. Eight friendly *ping* noises and eight ticks later, the door gave a loud hiss and began to open.

They each walked to the doorway and waited for the doors to finish opening. They each stood nervously moving on the spot. Rigsan made two fists, although if he was honest with himself, he wasn't really sure how much use they would be. Abel looked along the line from his position on the left and realised this was probably the last moment they would not know the truth. Would ignorance prove to be bliss? Now that he was here, did he really want to know the reality of the situation? Had he ruined the lives of these other three Agents as well as his own?

Suddenly, he felt guilty, but it was too late to turn around. Even if he apologised to everyone and sent a 'sorry for stunning your Krunt' card to whoever was in the Nexus, it probably wouldn't be enough to make amends for the trouble he'd caused over the last 24 hours. For once in his life, he hadn't taken the easy option and look where it had gotten him? He resolved to go back to coasting if he ever got the chance.

The doors came to a stop and the Nexus room was finally revealed. It was dark, a complete contrast to the brightness of the corridor and the Arrivals and Departures rooms. He could see the large table in the centre of the room as he had done when he caught a glance before. But now, up close, he could see it was circular holographic display, at least eight-feet in diameter and alive with lights and switches. Above it was a similar hologram of a region in space as he had seen before.

But now, as he had more time to study it, the region in space got smaller and became a flat, square object, as if it were turning into a map. It continued to get smaller as it was joined in the display area by a large holographic representation of a hardback book. The book reminded Abel of an old copy of a volume of the *Encyclopaedia Britannica*, which every self-respecting household had in the days before Google. The book opened and the map, which was now tiny, deposited itself onto the page the book had remained open on.

As soon as the map had disappeared, the book closed around it, like a hardback whale devouring his microscopic lunch. The closed book remained in the display area, merrily spinning slowly on its spine, waiting for another query. Abel was willing to bet that no one had ever used this holographic book of Universal Maps to look up planets with the rudest names. It was duly, but quietly, added to his bucket list.

All four of them had stepped into the room in unison, like a boy band rising off their stools and walking towards their screaming, pubescent audience for the key change. Although there was no screaming in this calm, orderly room. Just the gentle tweets and various computers doing various other-worldly things. They all looked in different directions, afraid to touch anything, but surveying everything. The only beings in this room were Cromulites, as they had been in Arrivals and Departures, but in here they wore white sashes over their white gowns. It gave them a ghost-like quality, as they moved smoothly across the floor, giving the impression they were floating. None of them appeared to notice the four interlopers that had entered their control room. They were far too busy by the looks of it.

"I hope you didn't hurt Fallapdax too much," came an ethereal voice out of the darkness. The voice was everywhere and nowhere. Even the multi-directional aural sensors of their suits couldn't pick up where the talking was coming from.

Abel caught a glimpse of a strand of white coming out of the far-right hand corner of the room, hidden in the shadows between the spotlights of the different control panels. The strand became a patch, which became a rectangle. As it moved closer, the white rectangle gained two red circular partners above it. Behind the red circles came a face, in a very familiar combination. All the agents could see the shapes now.

"Hang on, isn't that…" began Rigsan.

"The lady with the red glasses…" continued Dofe.

"From the morgue…" added Kinmal.

"In our dreams!" finished Abel.

The agents, different in so many ways, joined together in what had become their signature gawp of disbelief.

"Hello Marks," said the voice, which was attached to a very real person, who until now had been only a dream for the four of them,

"My name is Jax and I'm the person who's responsible for all of you. I expect you have many questions".

CHAPTER 17
THE END WAS JUST THE
BEGINNING

LOCATION – UNKNOWN, YEAR - UNKNOWN

Jax looked around. Everything in her office was on fire. Even the flame-retardant desks were on fire. She was determined to write a strongly worded email to the makers of said office furniture, *Catherine Zeta-Deskz*, when all this was over.

"This is it, Jax" said Plax, reading his data-pad as he and Jax evacuated the room, "Pressure's increased again. I don't think its going back down this time. Also, SARDOC says another dimensional shift is about to happen. Looks like this is it!"

'Looks like the Desk people are going to get away with it' Jax thought as she ran down the hallway. Panels and pieces of the building were falling to the floor all around her and her twin brother. The building appeared to be bouncing wildly and trying to separate its top from its bottom, like a peanut butter sandwich in a washing machine.

"Let's get outside before this whole place collapses!" shouted Jax, as her eight legs skittered her towards the door. A biped would have fallen flat on their un-evolved face in this situation, but an Octopod was much better equipped for uneven surfaces. It was why the Epiwi had genetically engineered themselves with six more legs aeons ago. The advantage of being one of the last remaining civilisations in the known universe, was that you've had a lot of time to learn from other species' mistakes. It didn't appear that it would help them keep their planet alive though. Or indeed the universe around it. Some problems are just too big to solve with extra body parts, much to the Epiwi's chagrin.

"The Anti-Matter's spiking again!" shouted Plax, pointing to the large twin spires that towered over the rest of the buildings at the centre of the city. Large twin spires that were disappearing out of existence right before their eyes. The spires were removed from reality from the bottom up, as if sucked up by some intergalactic vacuum cleaner.

The Wardz were everywhere now, running out of control, Entropising everything. Unlike anyone else, Plax could see from his data pad exactly where the Anti-matter invaders were and what they were doing. However, there was nothing he could do to stop them or hinder their progress in any way. If only they'd found a way to detect them earlier and discovered a way to defeat them, maybe they'd have been able to hold out for longer. But they hadn't and now they were fast approaching the end. Of everything.

"We need to get to the pods!" shouted Jax, as they ran through the rapidly disappearing streets, dodging the panicking crowds which now numbered in the millions. Not everyone had degrees in Quantum Multiverse Theory like Jax and her twin brother Plax. And those people were not sure what was going on. Jax wondered if she'd rather be in blissful ignorance right at this moment. Is it better to think you're under attack from an alien invader, or that the end of the known universe is happening? It would certainly inform your plans for tomorrow.

"Look out!" screamed Plax, a few steps behind his sister. From his vantage point, he was able to see the large piece of the masonry that used to be attached to a building, heading vertically for her. It was readying itself to remove one of Jax's dimensional axis, turning her from a 3D being into a 2D floor covering.

Instead of moving out of the way, Jax froze, just as people do right when they really shouldn't. As she watched the last thing she thought she'd ever see plummeting towards her, it began to disappear. Plax, who hadn't yet seen the boulder start to submit to its enforced entropy, had already began his heroic dive to push his sibling out of the way. As they ended up in a heap on the floor, both of them looked back as the space where the death rock should be.

"Thanks," said Jax, the adrenalin making her pant deeply, "for nothing" she softly patted her brother's head and smiled cheekily.

They scrambled back to their feet and continued their frantic journey toward their destination. The sub-quantum escape pods they had been developing had been shunned by the University, who had scoffed at the twins when they submitted it as part of their dissertation on Multiverse Collapse. The examination panel were mainly MC deniers, not to be confused with M.C. Deniers, the world-famous DJ. No, these MC deniers were part of an establishment that maintained the increases in universal pressure and the dimensional rips were all part of the natural order of things. Events that came and went with varying frequency throughout the whole of time, they said. Jax and Plax had argued (along with a few other preeminent scientists) that they had detected evidence that the Entropy events were not only going to result in the total destruction of reality, but were being exacerbated by Anti-matter lifeforms, hellbent on wiping out all 'normal' matter. They tried to explain that these beings were using technology that was causing the boundaries of the multiverse to thin and rupture. They maintained that this would cause the whole of reality to collapse once matter had reached a level small enough.

In response, the establishment had said they would 'give these invisible creatures, invisible ASBOs'. And so here we were. What use was the establishment's sarcasm now, at the end of everything?

"There's another rip opening – dead ahead!" shouted Plax, turning his attention from his datapad to the sky. He pointed, although it was really moot as Jax didn't need a helping hand to see what he was on about.

The sky had started to flare in an all-to-familiar way. The clouds began to change shape and disperse, as the tremendous heat of two universes rubbing up against each other began to take hold. The orange atmosphere started to bulge at the point of the flare. A bulge that became a white-hot ribbon elongating across the sky, until it's ends disappeared from their view behind the buildings either side of the twins. They began to sprint again, knowing they didn't have much time to complete their mission.

"Pressure's still increasing. We need the suits, or we'll be squashed before we get anywhere!" shouted Plax, splitting his gaze between his data-pad and the crowds running every which way in front of them.

286

As they arrived at their workshop, Jax looked up and couldn't believe what she saw. Every rip they had detected before this one was an isolated event, affecting individual people or even some small towns on other planets. But this one, according to their scans, was about to be the size of the planet. And it had begun to open.

She stopped Plax as he got to the door and this time, it was her turn to do a pointless point. Protruding through the rip as it began to open, came two large spires. The same two spires that had just disappeared from their city. Followed by more buildings, all a reflection of what was on the ground. Behind the rip, materialising gradually from one reality to another, seemed to be the remainder of the planet.

It was like the rip had produced a mirror image of what was below it and was intent on snacking one planet into the other, like a game of Cosmic Conkers.

"It's a parallel reality to this one, Plax! They're collapsing in on each other!" exclaimed Jax, running inside the warehouse and starting to put on one of the grey pressure suits hanging on the wall. Which takes a while when you've got eight legs.

Plax concurred without speaking, as he was too busy trying to get his own suit on. He gave the disintegrating sky a last look before joining his sister.

By the time they clambered onto the roof and powered up their pods, the planet's reflection was almost on top of it. As far as the horizon in every direction, the planet looked like it was clashing with a reflection of itself. Two planets were trying to inhabit the same space and it wasn't going to end well.

"Mine's ready to go!" Jax said into her comms, leaning in to begin the lift off sequence.

"Mine too," replied Plax, turning around and grabbing his sister's arm. She turned and they shared an urgent embrace. They looked at each other through their helmet glass, both studying every detail of the other's face, "Mum and Dad would have been proud".

"See you on the other side," said Jax, slapping her brother on the shoulder. They parted and got into their pods. They had designed the pods to get smaller and smaller as the universe collapsed in on itself, right down to the subatomic level, which they hoped would be enough to survive whatever was coming next. 'The Big Sandwich' Plax had called it, jokingly. Again the establishment had scoffed. The universe would expand and contract to varying degrees over its life cycle. It was generally agreed that 'The Big Bang' had started this universe, but the same scientists had refused to believe 'the big crunch' would happen sooner rather than later. And they especially refused to believe that it would be more of 'big collapse', instead preferring the idea of slow, meandering shrinkage like water running away down a blocked sink.

The twins had never been sorrier to be proved right.

The pods rose into their upright launching positions, just as the first buildings began to scrape against their reflection counterparts. Jax gave a quick thumbs up to her brother through the glass and settled her head back against the head cushion. She saw her brother reciprocate her gesture, just as the rocket boosters ignited and they were fired into the collapsing sky. They were heading for one of the edges of the rip, the space between dimensions. To bystanders, it would look like they were heading for one of the lips of the gigantic open mouth that had appeared to eat their homes.

"Dimensional space entry in 20 seconds," said Jax's SARDOC, as she streamed past all manner of falling and exploding debris. The pod wobbled and shimmied as it fought the adverse gravitational effects of two planets colliding, while simultaneously attempting to avoid the flotsam of the disintegrating worlds. The pod spun around momentarily, and as it did, Jax could see her brother's pod struggling to do the same. She wiped imaginary sweat from her helmeted brow as she caught her brother's eye through their cockpits. As he smiled and gave a thumbs up in response, a piece of the disintegrating buildings above them slammed into his pod, sending it down and away from Jax in a hail of sparks and flames.

"NO!!!" screamed Jax, pressing her hands to the cockpit glass, desperately trying to look as far down as the frame and her helmet would let her. Her pod continued upwards, rocking and sliding through the gravitational turbulence. She relaxed her head to one side, tears rolling down her cheeks. Her helmet began to mist up as her hands fell defeatedly down to her sides.

The pod began to pick up speed, as SARDOC ignited the sub-quantum boosters, lurching the vessel inexorably forward into the unknown.

As the pod reached the white ribbon of inter-dimensional space, she noticed everything starting to crush together. The ribbon was getting smaller, but so was everything around her. The pod picked up speed, but the void in front her seemed to be getting further away, such was the pace at which it was shrinking. It felt to Jax for a second that she would not make into her shrinking target, as it appeared to be pulling away. But SARDOC fired the second stage quantum engines and she propelled forward again, the pod and its quarry getting ever smaller until the whole of space was replaced, inside and outside the pod, by unseeable white light. She closed her eyes and thought of her lost brother. All the hours they'd spent planning this trip. Arguing with the doubters. She went further back, remembering playing spacemen in their parent's garden against the orange sunset; their first day of Science College; the first time they'd discovered evidence of the Anti-Matter Lifeforms. It was as if she could see all of the pages her personal history at once. And Plax had been there for all of it, right next to her. But now he wasn't.

She didn't know what would happen next. She didn't even know if the end of the universe was survivable. But now, as reality crushed in on her from all sides and she began to pass out, if she did survive into whatever came next, she would do so alone.

CHAPTER 18
A BOOK, A CUPPA AND A SARNIE

"I don't understand," said Abel, as Jax's mental projections of her history drained away from their minds. The others were blinking and shaking their heads, as if they'd just finished a particularly realistic VR game, "Is that the future or the past you just showed us?"

"It was my past. But it is also the future, eventually," said Jax, confusingly, as Abel was the first of them to notice her eight legs for the first time. He'd been too overwhelmed by the glasses revelation and all the mental voodoo to notice before now, "What you saw was a projection of the end of the previous universe to this one. But it was also a demonstration of what will no doubt happen to this iteration as well, despite our best efforts".

"Wait a minute," Rigsan held his hands up, finishing a spot of mental arithmetic, "If you survived the previous universe, you must be 13 billion years old!"

"13.8 billion to be precise," corrected Jax, "and 43 if you count the years I spent in the previous one".

"Oh. Right". Said Rigsan, for once devoid of anything to say in response to their host's flat reply. Instead he nodded and pretended he knew what was going on.

"I have always been unable to ascertain exactly what happened after what you would call 'the Big Bang'", continued Jax, as she walked in a circle as only a Octopod can do. Abel was strangely comforted by her use of air quotes around 'the Big Bang' and wondered if it was her that had invented them, "I'm not even sure how long my pod kept me in suspended animation. However, as soon as I awoke I resolved that I would not let this universe succumb so easily to the forces of Anti-Matter as mine had. For aeons I searched the cosmos, visiting countless systems and planets, on my quest to find the first suitable sentient civilisation. I estimate that my journey took 1.8 billion of your Terran years. Once I found a suitably evolved life form, I began to…work with them to be all that they could be".

"The Cromulites". Said Kinmal, so amazed by current events that he had forgotten to put on his accent.

'One point eight billion years on your own,' thought Abel, amazed, 'I'd still rather do that than go back in that tube with Rigsan for ten minutes I think!'

"Indeed," confirmed Jax, "And for many years, we developed untold technologies in preparation for the upcoming battles with the forces of Anti-matter. None however, proved to be successful once the war actually began. Eventually, I helped the Cromulites to develop the TTAXIs that each of you uses for your missions".

The holographic display had changed it's view and had started to show a three-dimensional video of a TTAXI, which Abel thought reminded him of a car advert from Earth. "It was a glorious achievement, the harnessing of Tachyons that allowed us to travel anywhere in the universe in a blink of an eye".

"Except when it goes through a comet's tail!" exclaimed Dofe, pointing at his aged face.

"A most regrettable and unforeseen occurrence, Agent Dofe". Sympathised Jax, nodding apologetically at her decrepit Agent, "For many more years, we were able to track the Wardz using our TTAXI force," the display changed to video of a Cromulite in military fatigues leaping out of a TTAXI, raising a pair of large binoculars up to his serious grey eyes and pointing off into the distance with a serious look on its face.

"But even though we were able to gather significant data on their movement, technology and tactics, we were unable to prevent them from carrying out their destruction. Although on occasion, we were able to frighten them back through their wormholes with loud noises".

The video changed to several more military Cromulites wafting at thin air with person-sized Maracas.

"We eventually developed weapons that helps us to combat them in a limited way."

The display morphed to show footage of what must have been a prototype matter cannon like the one on their suits. However, the prototype was more than twice the size of a TTAXI. The cannon could be seen firing a man-sized gloop of bright yellow, purified matter foam at an unseen target, whilst being flanked by two more binocular-using Cromulites. The foam seemed to hit its invisible target, causing the ball to grow petrified arms and legs. The scene finished with both military Cromulites giving the camera a gleeful, yet stoic thumbs up.

"We had the means to both detect and defeat our enemy. But what we needed was a way of combining these technologies in a…more mobile platform. Finally, with the advent of the Nano Bytes, we were able to develop such a platform".

The display changed again to an outline of a Cromulite, which began to be covered in a simulated grey ooze, in the same way the Nano Bytes would bond with them.

"An artificial construct capable of replicating shapes and technology as required, all controlled by advanced Artificial Intelligence and bonded to a living host".

"But why us?" asked Abel, "Why me?"

The diagram of the Cromulite was covered by a large red cross, as the outline of its body seemed to decompose before their eyes, into a ball, like a deflating balloon made of meat.

"Unfortunately, the Nano Bytes…rejected each and every host body we gave them. For an artificial life form, they can be very…emotional. We even tried artificial lifeforms, but these just seemed to make them angrier. The program was put on hold until we could find a subject that the Nano Bytes would accept. That is how we found…you".

"Hang on, you told me I was chosen for this job, because I had the 'right stuff'!" said Rigsan, angrily emphasising the last two words of his sentence.

"You did have the 'right stuff'," Confirmed Jax, "your DNA, coupled with 40 years of cell degradation, was found to be the perfect recipe and extremely palatable to the Nano Bytes. The

Cromulites have been seeding sentient worlds for many, many years. In fact, most of the humanoid life in their native universe has been seeded by them. They will occasionally return to those worlds to check on how they are doing, evolutionarily speaking. In all those places, all those worlds, you were found to be the only host the Nano Bytes would accept. Believe me, when we found the ideal specimen on such a backwards world as Terra, we were as shocked as you are!"

"And that's why you made clones of us". Said Abel, eliciting a confused look from Jax, "which brings me to the million-dollar question – which one of us is the real deal?"

"The real deal?" asked Jax, her face contorted into even further bewilderment.

"Yeah, which on of us is the real Mark Farringdon and which ones are the clones?" added Rigsan, shooting Abel a knowing glance, as if waiting for Jax to burst his fellow Agent's bubble.

Jax smirked a loving smirk, like each one of them would whenever they saw Colin watching the Television.

"You really don't understand what is going on here, do you?"

Jax took their collective silence as concurrence.

"You are all 'the real deal', as you put it," she confirmed. Now it was their turn to be bewildered, "You are all Mark Farringdon. But you are the Mark Farringdon from different parallel realities. You are all different people because of the different, unique choices you have made in your lives. I'm sure you've already uncovered some of your differences as well as some of your similarities. You are all the same person, genetically speaking".

The Agents all looked at each other. Even though it was the most far-fetched, incredible, mind blowing revelation any of them had ever heard, it felt like they had always known it.

"So none of us are clones!" exclaimed Dofe, as cheerily as he had ever said anything for a very long time.

"I'm the best one!" claimed Rigsan, looking straight at Abel.

"Does that mean you can't change memories?" implored Abel, seeing his chances of remembering kissing Michelle going up in smoke.

"Of course not, Agent Abel," confirmed Jax, sweeping away the ashes of his hopes and depositing them in the bin, "Memories are what make us who we are".

"I was afraid you were going to say something like that," said Abel, "So whose reality are we in at the moment?"

"Ah, well here's where it can be quite confusing," replied Jax, a representation of a planet appearing on the display screen.

'Oh good, because it's all been so easy to follow so far' thought Abel, for once keeping his sarcastic thoughts to himself.

"By improving on the technology I brought with me from my universe, the Cromulites and I were able to move the entire Universal Corrections Compound 'outside' of the multiverse. We are in a place we call the Chasm and from here, our TTAXIs are able access the same point in every universe as required. Each of your bases is on a small moon near to this entry point. From this inter-dimensional vantage point, we can monitor every parallel universe for Wardz activity and coordinate the defence".

"You can…see everywhere at once?" asked Dofe, his eyebrows pinching so hard it looked like his nose was trying to rip his ears off.

Jax looked along the line. They were all following what she was saying to varying degrees, but she feared she has lost them with the Chasm.

"Let me explain in terms you may understand," Jax continued, softening her voice as a mother would when explaining a relative's death to their young child, "Imagine the whole of reality is a book and each page of that book is a universe. Each page uses the same letters as all the others, but each of them is unique because the letters have been arranged into different words in different orders. Now imagine that the book has infinite pages. That's the multiverse".

Abel breathed out a long sigh that made him sound like he was deflating. The sound of his breath hung in the silence for a few seconds before he asked his question.

"So the Wardz are destroying that book?" he asked, attempting to understand.

"Well, imagine the Wardz are an infinitely big cup of tea that's been spilled on the book and is soaking through from page to page. Eventually, the book will be unreadable, just like my previous reality became. Here in the Chasm, it is like we are…in the spine of the book, able to access any page we need to".

All four Agents stood in confused silence, as their primitive ape brains tried to process concepts several aeons above their intellectual pay grades. In cosmological terms, their brains had only just finished working out that it was nicer on land than in the oceans and that maybe throwing poop at each other wasn't the best way to make friends.

"I'd kill for a cup of tea". Said Dofe, practically salivating at the imagined taste.

"I'd kill for a drink". Added Kinmal, still staring blankly ahead.

"Who reads books?!" asked Rigsan, almost offended at the notion.

"That's like Cucumber". Added Abel assuredly, pointing a thoughtful finger at his immortal host as his brain had found an analogy it could work with.

"Pardon?" asked Jax, her face exiting Serenity Boulevard and joining Befuddlement Way.

"That's like Cucumber," repeated Abel, holding his hand up in a claw shape to aid his point, "you can make a lovely sandwich. Put loads of different flavours in it. Nice soft bread. Chunky bit of Ham," he pointed at the imaginary lunch he held in his hand, "nice bit of mayo. Slice of mature cheese. But then you decide 'its summer, why not, I'll put a few bits of Cucumber in it'" Abel realised how hungry he was, "worst…decision…ever. Before you know it, the whole bloody thing tastes of cucumber. You have to throw it all away!"

Jax was now the one in stunned silence. Although as she looked along the line of faces suddenly bathed in understanding, she realised two things. One, that humans really are as stupid as the Cromulite research party had told her. And two, she would have to use more food analogies when talking to poorly evolved races.

"The Wardz…are the…Cucumber…" Abel explained guiltily, his eyes looking down at the floor like a child who'd just admitted that the brown nuggets on the floor weren't Chocolate Raisins.

298

"Okay yes, if you like," their host said, "As Wardz activity spreads from pa…from layer to layer of the sandwich, we must travel to the correct point in that reality's time to recruit the 40-year old Mark from that universe to enable us to defend it".

"If you can time travel, couldn't you just travel back to before each Wardz attack and kill them before they destroy anything?" Asked Dofe, thinking he'd spotted a flaw in his immortal boss' plans.

"Time travel is infinitely more dangerous than space travel, especially for the health of the multiverse. We only use it to gather that reality's Mark for fear of creating even more parallel universes to defend."

"Couldn't you just recruit enough of us to work together and finish them off once and for all?" asked Rigsan, of course looking for the quickest solution straight away.

"Until now, I had no idea how two of you being in such close proximity would affect the integrity of the multiverse, once you were outside of the protection of the Chasm". Replied Jax.

'Oh bugger', thought Abel, subconsciously biting his lip like a naughty schoolboy, 'I hadn't thought of that either!'

"Clearly I was wrong. You have all shown that, despite your differences, you have managed to gel into quite an effective team". Continued Jax, giving each of them an appreciative nod, "You even managed to combine your Nano Byte suits, something else I had never conceived as being possible. This requires us to rethink our strategy. Come, let us retire to the Observation Deck and discuss any further questions you may have".

As they walked down a corridor towards the elevator, Kinmal joined the conversation.

"What about our names?" asked Kinmal, "Why do we all have different names? Bit pointless if you never planned for us to meet".

"For our own convenience, mainly. It was easier to give each of you a different moniker, than refer to you by numbers". Replied Jax, stopping by a red door on the right of the hallway, "and partly to honour those who have lost their lives to the Wardz".

Their host opened the door and gently motioned them all inside. The room bore an uncanny resemblance to an Earth office, except the end of it disappeared off into the distance like an optical illusion. One wall was covered in metal filing cabinets, as far as their eyes could see. Abel noticed his name on one of the cabinet drawers. Rigsan, Dofe and Kinmal noticed theirs too as they walked down the never-ending row. Dofe tripped over a small robot as he walked towards the drawer that bore his name on a small plate.

"Each one of these original drawers contains the names and files of the beings who tried the suits before you were found". Jax waved her hand at the first bank of drawers, "As we needed more names, we began to take them from the files of all those beings killed by the Wardz. Each bank of cabinets represents a different plane of the multiverse".

"Who are these robots?" asked Dofe, moving quickly out of the way of the robot he'd just stepped on. The machine was one of two matching robots in the room. They were both pill-shaped and about three-feet in height, quietly floating a foot off the ground using unseen means. Both were alive with lights and sounds, with no discernible face and four arms each. As Dofe looked on in awe, the robot in front of him produced a file from the drawer it had just opened, and scanned it with a appendage that had appeared from its dome. Once it had scanned the complete file, it closed it again and placed it back in the same order, as the appendage retreated back into what probably passed for its 'head'.

"That is Kellitrex," pronounced Jax, pointing at the hovering machine that had been working in front of Dofe, but was moving off to another drawer further down the row, "The other one is Shazbot. They are the keepers of the records in this room. They work tirelessly to maintain the accuracy of the filing system. They also make excellent drinks carriers at the Christmas Party".

As if to demonstrate Jax's point, Shazbot quickly produced two halves of a metal tray from its sides, which came together over its dome. The tray halves disappeared just as quickly, followed by a salute, before Shazbot hovered off to carry on its important work.

Abel approached the drawer with his name on it. "A-BEL" he said to himself. "Beats being called Mark 357, I suppose".

-

"Surely, you must know your task is hopeless?" asked Kinmal as they entered the Observation Deck from the elevator door. The large, circular room was almost completely encircled with thick glass, giving Abel the impression they were in an upturned Goldfish bowl. Encircling the bowl were a patchwork of galaxies, planets, star fields and nebulae, the fragments of each view constantly changing. The patchwork of realities was a hard thing to take in for four recently-evolved ape creatures and in truth, it had already started to give Dofe a migraine. Jax directed the Agents to four low chairs that had materialised at one side of the room, next to one stool. The Agents all sat down, with Jax following them by encircling the stool with her eight legs and lowering herself down onto it. Once everyone was seated, Jax chose to answer.

"Indeed, if my experience from my previous life proves anything, it is that multiverses die and are reborn. Who knows how many times this has already happened?" She leaned forward, crossing four of her legs, "What is it that any of us want when faced with the end, except more time? If given a second opportunity or a chance to do things differently, would you not take it? You are proof of how differently things can turn out from just one different decision in one short life. Is this not a testament to how one should try to change the future if they have the knowledge and foresight to do so? Even if you know you will fail eventually, should you not make things last as long as they can?"

"I've got a question," said Abel, completely disregarding Jax's beautiful, thought-provoking, philosophical monologue, "Why are Rigsan and Kinmal's bases bigger than mine?"

For the second time since she had met them, Jax did a good job of hiding her exasperation before answering.

"Each of your base designs were your own choice, although you didn't realise it," she explained, "The designs were taken from your subconscious minds as the places where you have felt safest and most at home in your lives".

Abel felt embarrassed by the revelation, not only by the aged wisdom of their host, but of the stupidity of his question.

302

"Oh. Right". Replied Abel meekly, as the realisation of how far out of his comfort zone he was here, in an upside-down goldfish bowl, in between dimensions.

"Could...could you tell me what my dream means?" asked Dofe quietly.

"Dream?" asked Jax, moving the stool gently towards her timid Agent. Her eight legs worked so well in unison, effortlessly sliding the stool around beneath her.

"Yes, I've been having this dream that I'm dead". He continued, sounding unsure of himself, as if he could barely remember details, even though he was completely sure of them.

"Me too. I'm in a morgue..." Rigsan interrupted, Dofe instantly sinking back into his seat as if he had been waiting for someone else to pick up the conversational baton.

"Yes. And you are the mortician". Added Kinmal, excitedly.

"You zip up my body bag and shove me in a drawer with my name on it!" Abel joined in, suddenly realising that what he had been seeing was probably the filing cabinets of the room they had just come from, even though he had never been there before. It couldn't be just a coincidence, could it?

"Yes!" agreed Dofe, pointing nervously to each of his colleagues in turn as they added to the story, "It's why I recognised you when we met in the Nexus room".

Jax looked around the Agents sat in their chairs and noted their differences. Rigsan sat bolt upright, perfect posture. Abel slouching back, although clearly invested in the conversation. Kinmal on the edge of his seat, starting to shake from the alcohol withdrawal. And Dofe, closed shoulders and legs, trying to take up as little space as possible in this unfamiliar environment. She started to smile with pride. These primitive lifeforms never ceased to amaze her. They were resourceful and brave, even if some of them didn't believe they were. Just like the rest of the Human race, they were capable of awesome acts of kindness and mind-blowing stupidity. And they all spent far too long on the toilet.

"Humans," She said, shaking her head as she looked at each of them in turn, as a proud parent would survey her children, "Capable of so much more than you will allow yourselves. I cannot profess to understand the Human dream-state. But if I had to postulate, I would say that subconsciously you all knew you were not alone. You are assigned TTAXIs randomly, so maybe your subconscious mind has picked up markers from other Agents, whilst you travel in them. That or there is a link between Marks that we do not fully understand. Either way, it will make for a fascinating study".

"How many of us are there, so far, I mean?" asked Rigsan, from his perfect posture that was increasingly annoying Abel's peripheral vision.

"Since the introduction of the program, 205,993 Mark Farringdons have been recruited into service". Replied Jax, the overwhelming information being delivered to the Agents with all the importance of someone ordering a Vanilla Latte in a Coffee Shop.

"Two hundred and…" Rigsan repeated slowly, his voice trailing off at the enormity of the information.

"No way…" uttered Abel, slouching even more than before and rubbing his head with both hands. He always did this when he was stressed, and this seemed like a perfect time to do it.

"Blimey…" added Dofe, his eyes widening as he restlessly bit his finger nails and gently started to rock.

"That is a lot of filing cabinets!" Kinmal laughed nervously. His laugh caught them all and spread throughout the group. They all started laughing together as they attempted to process the knowledge of their being another 205,989 versions of them out there. That was a lot of different decisions, a lot of changed lives.

"So, did you lie to all of them?" asked Abel, his laughter falling away and catching his host off-guard, "You told me I was the ideal candidate for this. The perfect being for the job. But it turns out I'm just the being who happens to be palatable to the tiny robots".

"The longevity of the universe is at stake," Jax replied, "We cannot afford to take 'no' for an answer".

"By taking away our choice?!" Dofe interjected, looking as angry as Abel had seen him, "What if a version doesn't want to leave his family? What if they've not messed up their lives like we did," he held up an apologetic hand towards his colleagues, "No offence".

"None taken," replied Abel and Kinmal together.

"My life was alright!" exclaimed Rigsan, lying as much to himself as anyone.

"Like I said," their immortal host replied coldly, "We cannot afford to take 'no' for an answer".

This information was too much for Abel. He stood up and walked away from the group, towards the edge of the bowl. The thought of all those Marks who had been taken against their will, forced into this role and away from their happy lives. He had not been that hard to convince, he had always had the feeling his life was meant for more. But what about the versions who were completely happy? Then his train of thought took a turn down a dark tunnel. One that he didn't want to spend too much time in, he decided – what if none of them were truly happy? He looked around at the three other versions of him sat back in the chairs – all of them had messed up in some way. Even Rigsan, who to outsiders would probably be classed as the most 'successful' of them by society's standards, was not *truly* happy. Even if he couldn't see it himself or didn't want to see it. Rigsan had actually done the things that Abel had always lamented *not* doing and yet, he'd still managed to make a Horlicks of it.

"So you go on about choice," he said, through angry, gritted teeth, "and yet you take it away from us!"

"What would have me do?" questioned Jax, rising from the stool and skittering towards him, "I have seen the end of all things. I have a way to stop it, or at the very least postpone it. Surely that is worth the sacrifice of one being's happiness?"

Before Abel, or indeed any of them could answer, the elevator doors opened and a white-sashed Cromulite scientist came gracefully bounding out of the tube towards them. He was clearly perturbed about something.

"Jax, we have a…situation that requires your attention most urgently," the scientist said, its native language being translated by the Agent's SARDOCs.

The Agents all stood up in unison, sure that this would soon involve them somehow.

"Go on". Replied Jax, her hand gestures to the Cromulites clearly informing it that all could be privy to the ensuing conversation.

"It would appear the Wardz have targeted Yicorth 6 again. However, the wormhole signature on this occasion is four times the size of previous instances". The Cromulite was clearly distressed by the information he was imparting, "It would appear the Wardz have enhanced their technology and mean to complete the Entropisation of the planet this time. Gravity would be affected in the six surrounding systems".

"Sounds like it's a mission for more than one Agent". Said Abel, smiling knowingly as he re-joined the group, making eye contact with each of them as he did so. His colleagues joined him in a grin as his inferred suggestion dawned on them. Abel held a fist out in front of the group.

"More than two, by the sound of it…" added Rigsan, looking at the others as his fist joined Abel's.

"The more the merrier," Kinmal pressed his fist into the growing group.

"Well, I can't stay here on my own!" laughed Dofe sarcastically, completing the four-way fist bump.

They each looked at their host, the impossible being from the unlikely place. She returned their smile, wondering in awe once again at the dichotomy of Humans. They had been arguing less than 30 seconds before, questioning everything she had built. But now, with barely a second thought, they had all resolved to put their parallel lives on the line. And none of them had even been to the loo.

"Are you sure, Agents?" These are grave threats that are even unknown to us". Asked Jax.

"Do we have a choice?" Abel asked cheekily, his petulant smile adding itself to all his colleague's faces as they processed his joke.

Jax joined in with the smile. She waved them away proudly.

"Now, before we go," said Abel, as the heroic group headed for the elevator, "Where's the loo? I'm busting!"

CHAPTER 19
THE SATISFACTORY FOUR

"Well, this is nice!" said Abel, in his best 'motherly' voice.

They had decided to share one TTAXI. Partly so that they could talk tactics, but mainly so that two TTAXIs didn't get destroyed in the same place, like last time. Abel and Rigsan had both pointed this out at the same time back at Departures and Jax had concurred with them.

"So, two TTAXIs exploding in the same point in space and time ripped a hole between dimensions?!" Asked Dofe, still scared stiff by the information that his colleagues had relayed before they got in the TTAXI, "I didn't realise these things were so powerful!"

"Oh yeah, tasty bit of kit this, mate," chirped the driver, proudly patting the steering wheel. Everyone had been pleased to see a professional back at the wheel, after their last few 'self-drives'. They all shared a silent joke at his expense through, marvelling at his blue-toned apparel through the use of various facial expressions and eye rolls.

"I don't think I've ever come close to destroying my TTAXI". Said Kinmal, thoughtfully stroking his chin.

"It wasn't the original plan for me, Kinmal!" Abel defended, thinking back to his driver's head exploding in front of him the last time he was on Yicorth.

"Nor mine!" added Rigsan, pretending to himself that it was his driver's fault they hadn't engaged their cloaking device on that fateful mission.

"We need a team name," said Abel excitedly, "We've got to have a team name!"

"How about 'Rigsan Angels'?" said Rigsan, waving his hand across an imaginary billboard as he spelled it out. The silence was as deafening as if they'd just killed one of the Wardz.

"What about Mark Uber Alles?" added Kinmal.

"What about the Fant…" began Dofe.

"That's taken!" Abel stopped him before he could finish his very litigious suggestion, "Although it gives me an idea. What about 'The Satisfactory Four'?"

The varying degrees of disgust registered across their faces, as Abel wiped his hand across his own imaginary billboard.

"Atmospheric entry has begun, gentlemen!" interrupted the driver, as the TTAXI lurched forward, the thickness of the Yicorthite ionosphere beginning to slow them down. The traditional flames licked up over the bonnet, painting a picture in yellow and red on the windscreen. The Agents' suits began to activate their respective Battle modes, as the Agents readied themselves.

"Right, we need to get hidden as quickly as possible when we get in range". Rigsan began, automatically taking charge, "These Yicorthites are nasty and trigger happy, so do not expect any favours from them. Even though we are saving their planet from Entropisation, they'll be quite happy to shoot us. We need to take care of the Wardz as quickly as possible and find a way to destroy that wormhole".

Three determined nods showed Rigsan they were all in agreement.

"I still can't believe you kissed Michelle". Said Abel, shaking his head in mock disgust at Rigsan.

"What was it like?" asked Dofe, sharing in Abel's memory of that night at the Leavers Disco.

"It was…amazing. That night felt like the end of something. The last vestiges of childhood safety, before beginning the journey into the adult world. I just didn't feel ready". Rigsan took on the glassy eyes of reminiscing, as Abel and Dofe remembered the exact same feeling, "but then kissing Michelle…it felt like a beginning. A hello in a night of goodbyes". His jaw stiffened as he realised that not only was he about to cry, but the other Agents were staring at him. His logical brain regained control of his memory and his mouth, "It was all downhill from there really".

Abel and Dofe both wondered what they would have done if that had been them on that night. Would they still have turned out the way their arrogant, job-obsessed reflection had? Maybe. But somewhere there was a version of them that had done it all right. Made all the correct decisions in their vital moments, even though they didn't know it at the time. And logically, for every one of those correct decisions, there had to be a version of Mark that made the wrong one. The number of 'incorrect' Marks would therefore massively outnumber the 'perfect' Marks, making the latter the anomaly. This strength in numbers comforted both of them, but especially Dofe, as he had not felt part of anything for so long.

"She was always a good kisser," added Kinmal, reminding all of them that fate can sometimes take unpredictable turns to bring people to the same point, "I had returned to England to complete my studies at Bristol University. We met at the Gym in the first year and were never apart for the rest of our time there. She begged me to stay in England once our studies were complete, but I could not choose her over my family. I would be intrigued to meet the Mark who did".

"Target approaching in 5000 metres, sir". Interrupted S, "I would suggest stealth mode be engaged immediately".

"Definitely. Hit the stealth mode, driver!" commanded Abel, looking out of the window as they dipped below the cloud level. The driver complied and the TTAXI became a giant Ulian Parrot, the largest bird of prey on Yicorth. The agents would soon see how resplendent its purple and red plumage was when they disembarked, but they would have precious little time to appreciate it fully. They all looked out of different windows and none of them could take in the scene they were presented with. The spaghetti-junction like highways? Gone. In fact, half the city was already gone, with chunks of parts of the other half shimmering and Entropising out of existence as they descended.

"I detect fourteen anti-matter suit signatures and three more coming through the wormhole," instructed S, marking each of them on Abel's HUD. The wormhole was massive, looking even bigger than the four-times the Cromulites had estimated.

This one was horizontal, with the blazing red anti-matter showing up on his visor like a blood-filled bath slushing down a plughole. As S had rightly predicted, Abel saw three more tell-tale signatures emerging from it and running off in various directions.

"Are you seeing all this?" asked Abel, not tearing his view away from the window.

"What's the plan?" shouted Dofe, over the intercom that their SARDOCs had set up without being asked, "I mean, I know the loose plan – go down, kick everyone's butt, win the day. But what's the *actual* plan?!"

Rigsan thought for a minute. He thought back to the last game his studio had been developing before he got abducted, as from the air this very much looked like a real-time strategy game, but in the real world. What would Dirk McEwan, the main character of *Zombie Bashers II*, have done in this scenario?

"How about this?" he replied, turning away from the window as the group's heads met in the centre of the back-seat area, "We'll each start off at a compass point, at the limit of where they've got to. We'll push them back in a spiral pattern towards the wormhole. The energy keeping that thing open must be phenomenal, so it won't be open for long. We need to contain the damage, kill as many as we can and wait for it to run out of juice".

"Sounds good. Did you hear that driver?" asked Abel, turning around.

"Way ahead of you, skip!" shouted the driver from the front, "Coming up on the first drop point in 10 seconds".

"I'll go first!" said Kinmal, moving to the door and placing a determined hand on the door release, "See you after for drinks!"

To the Yicorthite citizens, fleeing an invisible enemy that was making their roads and buildings disappear, the day was just about to get even weirder. To the few who took a short break from running and screaming, looking up at this moment would have presented them the sight of an oversized Ulian Parrot swooping down close to the ground and pooping out a gold, shimmering person. That golden humanoid then appeared to wrestle with itself on the ground, while the Parrot flew off and pooped out another one some distance away, followed by two more. Of course being Yicorthite meant that even the prospect of being wiped from existence didn't stop some of them from getting itchy trigger fingers. In fact, many would consider it an ideal way to go. So it was with depressing inevitability that the big Parrot started flying through a hail of laser fire as it evacuated its last person.

That last Parrot poop was Abel, who landed with a safety roll and thanks to the power of the Nano Bytes, came up running. Trying to ignore how much his knees were hurting, he headed for the nearest Wardz signature. It was too busy aiming its Entropiser at a nearby hut to notice its onrushing doom.

"I'm hit!" shouted the driver over the comm link, "I'm making an emergency landing!"

Abel looked up and sure enough, the wounded Parrot was plummeting to Earth with all the grace of, well, a normal Parrot.

"That's the ride home gone!" shouted Rigsan, the sound of his Matter Cannon firing joining his voice over the airwaves, "One down".

"Make that two!" added Kinmal, the familiar anti-scream making his comment sound like it had been made in a vacuum chamber, "Making for the next target".

"Dofe, you okay? You're quiet over there. Talk to me!" sounded Abel, as he leapt onto the Anti-Matter creature in front of him.

"Uh, yeah, I'm fine," came a quiet, elderly voice, "the suit's doing a grand job!"

"Just hang in there Dofe!" shouted Rigsan, as compassionately as he could. Which wasn't much, "Fourteen more to go".

"Make that sixteen," corrected Kinmal, "Unter reads two more signatures exiting the wormhole!"

Abel looked towards the wormhole and confirmed Kinmal's information. He leapt off the newly-foamed creature below him and began his pursuit of the second target.

"Keep to the plan!" shouted Rigsan, forcefully, "If we keep rotating in the same direction, we'll keep them contained until the power gives out!"

"Driver, you okay?" asked Abel, waiting expectantly for a positive answer, which seemed to take an age to come.

"Yeah, take more than a few pot shots to kill me!" said the driver confidently, "Auto pilot's knackered though".

Having seen what this planet could do, Abel was not nearly as confident in the driver's survival prospects. He had already seen one driver lose his head on this world and he wasn't about to see another one.

"You just stay put where you are. Stay down inside the cab". Commanded Abel.

"Oh don't worry, I got me packed lunch and *the Best of Shakin' Stevens*. I'll be fine right here!" replied the driver, as Abel could hear him munching.

"Two more down!" exclaimed Rigsan. Abel looked in his colleague's direction as he was running and saw a foam statue materialising over his colleague's head. Rigsan must have cracked it in mid-air as it tried to jump over him. He wished his agility was that good and as if fate wished it too, he bumped right into a fleeing Yicorthite and sent both of them sprawling to the ground. As he tried to get up through the forest of panicking legs, he looked towards the wormhole.

"I think my HUD's broken, S" he said, banging the side of his head, "There's a big black splodge in the centre of my visor".

"The suit is undamaged, sir," replied S, "The 'big black splodge' you are referring to is coming out of the wormhole".

The 'big, black splodge' was indeed exiting the wormhole, accompanied by three more normal-sized splodges. This battle was getting out of hand, even for the four of them. It was three times the size of the Wardz they had been battling up to this point. It had four arms as big as wheelie bins and legs the size of Post-boxes. And it was not happy.

"What. The hell. Is that?" screamed Dofe, "It's three times the size of the other ones!"

"Mein gott!" exclaimed Kinmal.

"Okay, plan B," shouted Rigsan hurriedly, changing direction, "Everyone on the big fella first!"

They all complied, changing their own directions and sprinting toward the gargantuan new threat. As Abel approached, the splurge on his visor just kept getting bigger. Rigsan arrived first, naturally, dodging a swipe of its massive arm by sliding under it and began climbing up its arm all in one action. As it reached the creature's back, which was at least fifteen feet off the ground, Kinmal arrived and surrounded his arms around one of the beast's legs. The creature barely broke stride, still firing its much-bigger Entropiser and taking out a whole five storey building with one shot. Dofe, or rather Dofe's suit, arrived next, copying Kinmal's tactics and grabbing the other leg. This slowed the animal, as it decided to stop and remove the irritants just as Abel arrived.

"Scalpel boost on three! Ready?" shouted Rigsan, his hand forming into a trident.

"Ready!" confirmed Kinmal, ducking his head away from the monster's wild swings and preparing his hand for cracking open its armour.

"AAARRRGGGHHH!!!" screamed Dofe, which they all took to mean his suit was ready too.

"THREE!!!" shouted Abel, who was already in mid-air, torpedoing towards the centre of the thrashing Leviathan's chest. The monster was so consumed with removing his unwanted leg warmers, that he hadn't noticed Abel leaping towards his middle. His trident plunged deep into its chest, just as the others did, producing a four-way crack across their collective comms link. The sound produced a feedback loop, bringing the monster down with a loud whistle and healthy dose of anti-scream, as it filled up with purified matter from four injection points.

The petrified foam statue fell forward and whacked against the ground, shaking the four Agents loose and sending them tumbling back. They all took a second to gain their bearings, all scrambling to their feet as quickly as their Nano Bytes would allow.

"Resume plan…" Rigsan began. He stopped as he looked back at the wormhole.

"Which Plan?" asked Abel, not yet seeing what his well-tanned colleague was looking at. "Oh…".

"There's two more of them!" shouted Kinmal, pointing towards the wormhole, which was now almost completely covered with black in his visor.

"How long's that thing staying open?!" questioned Dofe, looking around at the other Agents.

"Too long," Confirmed Rigsan, "We need a plan C".

"How about the TTAXI?" asked Abel, thinking quickly, "When it exploded it ripped a hole in the continuum. Well, maybe on the other side of that wormhole, it'll do the opposite. Maybe self-destructing it on the other side will cause the portal to implode".

The beasts were fast approaching as they each digested Abel's suggestion. It would take far too long for any reinforcements or larger Matter Cannons to reach them. It was down to them and only them.

"That's not how Anti-matter works is it?" asked Kinmal.

The black blobs were almost upon them, starting block out everything behind them.

"Has anyone got a better suggestion at this point?" Rigsan demanded of his colleagues. Their silence was all the confirmation he needed.

"Driver, we need you to pilot the TTAXI into the wormhole and self-destruct it!" Rigsan said over the comms link, in the same way you would ask someone for Chicken Nuggets at a Drive-Thru. The driver, much to Rigsan's surprise, was not keen.

"What, South of the Dimensional axis at this time of night?" asked the driver incredulously, "Nah mate".

There was no time to argue at this point. The first of the two new gargantuan blobs was upon them and they needed to deal with this first.

"Same as before lads," commanded Rigsan, "Dofe you take the right leg, I'll take the back, Abel the front and Kinmal the left leg. On my mark…"

"Ready". Agreed Abel, stepping back a few paces to get in range for his chest jump.

"Jah!" Kinmal ran towards the beast's leg.

"Dofe, you ready?" asked Abel, worried about the silence from his team member. His question was greeted by more worrying silence.

"Where's Dofe?!" shouted Rigsan, running towards the beast's arm as he had done the first time.

Abel looked around and was dismayed with what he saw. In the distance and disappearing as fast as his Nano Bytes would carry him, was Dofe. Running away from them.

"He has disabled his comms link, sir" confirmed S, "I cannot contact him".

"I knew he'd bottle it," exclaimed Rigsan angrily, jumping up the monster's arm.

"I don't understand..." Abel trailed off, surprised that his suit would let him do such a thing, "he said we were like his new family".

"Well, he deserted his family once before," said Kinmal, his voice juddering as he thudded against sprinting monster's leg.

Abel turned away from the departing Dofe and back towards the matter at hand. He managed to jump the same as before, but the beast was not slowed down by two golden, wobbly leg warmers like before. Abel splatted against the beast's chest with the grace of a custard pie hitting a clown's face. Only the quick reactions of his Nano Bytes prevented him from falling off and being trampled underfoot. A three-way Scalpel boost later and they were done with this one.

As they landed, even Rigsan struggled to get up. All three of them were bleeding inside their suits, from the various impacts. The Nano Bytes were good, but even they couldn't protect their wearers from this new, larger threat. As they stood up and readied themselves to face round three, their collective hearts sank as they saw two more giant black splodges appearing out of the wormhole.

"This is hopeless". Kinmal spoke for all of them, even the unnecessarily confident Rigsan.

"One of us is going to have to go and get that TTAXI!" shouted Abel, crouching and readying his aching body to jump at the oncoming monster.

"The auto-pilot's broken. It'll be a suicide mission!" cautioned Kinmal.

"Well it won't be the first time I've wanted to kill myself," came Dofe's voice scratching suddenly over the comms link, "At least this time it'll be for something worth-while!"

"Dofe, what are you doing?!" exclaimed Abel, as Rigsan and Kinmal began his run at the third monster. From his position his peripheral vision picked something up. Stomping resplendently and aggressively towards the Wormhole was a giant Ulian Parrot. It swerved violently as it avoided the escaping locals, its massive wings flapping one way and another to maintain what little balance it had.

Abel readied himself for his chest jump, but his gaze was split between the onrushing monster and the Parrot marching to its doom. He jumped and the three of them completed another successful, painful, exhausting kill. All three of them would run out of energy a long way before that wormhole by the look of it. It didn't stop him from trying to run after Dofe though.

"He's doing his job, Abel!" shouted Rigsan, his voice etched with pain as he jumped on the fourth monster, "I suggest you do yours!"

Abel ignored the beast and carried on running.

"Dofe, there's got to be another way!" Abel shouted after the Parrot, knowing that there wasn't, "You said we were your new family!"

"You are my new family!" shouted Dofe, the self-destruct timer counting down over the comms in the background, "you all sacrificed yourselves for your families when you left Earth. I didn't, not really. I was glad to leave. But now, I have a chance to sacrifice myself for my new family!"

"There's still time!" shouted Abel, as the Parrot's head breached the wormhole.

"We're out of time, Abel". Said Dofe, his voice sounding old and tired, "I'm worn out, Mark. Maybe I'll see you…"

The comms link went dead as the Parrot's tail disappeared through the portal. Abel stopped running and stood watching it, as if expecting the Parrot to reappear. Instead, the wormhole lit up with black light, before collapsing in on itself like someone closing a particularly nasty Duffle bag.

The vacuum sucked in air all around it and expelled it again in an invisible tsunami of pressure. It knocked all three of them off their feet, apart from Rigsan, who fell from the large Wardz' back as it collapsed to the ground.

As Abel looked around, he could see the black splodges all around the mission site expanding. With their anti-matter protection link gone, they began to swell up like over-inflated ghostly balloons, each one expiring in turn with an 'anti-pop', which was both audible and inaudible at the same time.

"He did it," said Abel forlornly, "The stupid old man did it".

"Agreed, a most agreeable outcome". Concurred Kinmal, now lying flat on his back on the ground next to nothing, "maybe that is how anti-matter works after all!"

"First suggestion when we get back," said Rigsan, climbing to his feet and dusting himself off, "better protection on the Auto-pilot circuits!"

"Sounds reasonable," agreed Abel, "Have you called us a new TTAXI, S?"

"Indeed I have sir," confirmed SARDOC, "They will be here shortly".

"Thank god for that, if we stay here much longer, we're bound to get shot!" said Abel, only just noticing that the crowd of Yicorthite that had been running had stopped and were all facing the three off-worlders. But something strange was happening. Or rather, not happening. The Yicorthite weren't shooting at them. But they *were* approaching them.

The Agents began to walk backwards towards each other, until they formed a tight triangle, each of them with their hands out in peace-making fashion. Still the crowd approached, the grunting Yicorthite plodding closer and closer until they were less than a metre away from them on all sides.

"Well, it was nice knowing you guys. Mainly you, Kinmal". said Abel, squinting one eye and preparing for the first shot to ring out.

Except it didn't.

Instead, the Yicorthite nearest to Rigsan clasped his paw into a fist and struck it to his face in what was clearly a gesture of salute. The one next to him did the same, then the next, then the next. Pretty soon, the whole crowd of appreciative locals were all showing their thanks for this band of strange, thinly-legged aliens that wrestled thin air and won. There were only three small face-shootings, but they were at the back of the crowd when a few were accused of trying to push in. But on Yicorth, this was practically a peace rally.

Abel surveyed the crowd and proceeded to replicate the salute. His colleagues did the same. And that was it – as the crowd quietly dispersed, the Agents went back to waiting for their new cab and the Yicorthite went back to shooting at it as it landed. Luckily, no damage was done this time.

"We're going to need to recruit another member". Said Rigsan coldly, as the TTAXI disappeared above the clouds, "either that or a new team name. Or we could go with Rigsan's Angels. There was only three of them".

"Oof," said Kinmal, shocked.

Abel looked at his perfect-teethed reflection and contemplated knocking a few of them out.

"Too soon man," he said, shaking his head and turning away to look out of the window as the orange sunset turned into the blackness of space, "Too soon".

CHAPTER 20
THE CHOICE IS YOURS

As the TTAXI joined the rank and made its way slowly towards the main Arrivals entrance, the Agents could see Jax walk out to meet them, flanked by two white-sashed Cromulites. As they drew closer, they could she was smiling a respectful smile, which to Abel meant she was already more Human than Rigsan. It had been an uncomfortable, yet thankfully-short journey back after Rigsan's comment.

Abel had sat looking out of the window and remembering the short time he had spent with Dofe and the tremendous sacrifice he had made for them. He wondered if he would have had the strength to make such a sacrifice had the opportunity presented itself. He honestly wasn't sure.

Rigsan had spent the journey looking out of the opposite window and wondering what Abel was so upset about. He thought that this version of Mark would have made a perfect partner for Michelle, as she used to react in this surprising manner when he said perfectly reasonable things as well.

Kinmal spent the journey facing forward, watching the stars go past and wondering when he was going to get A BLOODY DRINK!

The flanking Cromulites bowed deeply as the Agents exited the TTAXI. They each returned the bow, all three of making similar 'old man' noises as they straightened back up.

"I have been watching your mission unfold with great interest on the view screens, gentlemen," said Jax, proudly, "It would appear that I have been wrong about a great many things. I believe I owe you all an apology".

"Oh, it's alright," Abel replied, holding up a conciliatory hand, "you were only worried about destroying the continuum if we got together".

"Not about that," corrected Jax, as the Cromulites scanned each Agent for signs of damage, both to them and the Nano Byte suits, "I owe you an apology for pressing all of you into service, without giving you a choice".

Abel was amazed. "13 billion years old," he said, a wry smile developing across his face, "and still learning".

"Indeed, Mark" agreed Jax, matching his smile, "as you would no doubt say, 'you're never too old to learn'".

"Shame about Dofe though. In the end, he was the bravest of us all". Stated Abel, glancing at Rigsan as he said, as he knew it would stick in his throat.

"Agent Dofe was indeed most valiant. His sacrifice will be remembered through the ages. He has once again proved to me what a curious and awesome species Humans are. He will be celebrated as all fallen agents have been".

All three Agents were desperate to ask the obvious question, but they all came to the conclusion that they'd asked enough life-altering questions for one day. 'What happens to fallen Agents and their realities?' Could wait.

"So is this it then?" asked Rigsan, "can we keep working together from now on?"

Abel, Kinmal were all taken aback by Rigsan's request. Of the three of them, he had always been the one who seemed to think he was too good for the others. Like he felt that he was better off alone. Like they were holding him back. Rigsan seemed to realise this outburst was out of character for him as well, as he felt the need to justify his question straight away.

"Well, uh...you know," he stammered, "It's good to have wingmen".

Jax paused and surveyed her Agents, as the Cromulite assistants completed their scans. They busily tapped away on their Data pads, before returning to their leader's side.

"It would seem that the forces of chaos have started to increase their firepower," Jax replied finally, "It would therefore be logical for us to do the same. I will make the necessary arrangements for your SARDOCs to have inter-dimensional communication subroutines added. You will all be able to contact each other at any time".

"Excellent!" exclaimed Kinmal, clapping his hands together in excitement, "this calls for a drink or two, surely?"

"Oh, now that sounds like a great idea!" concurred Abel, as the group began to walk inside, "Let's go back to the Observation Deck and make a toast to Dofe".

And so that's exactly what they did. They toasted their fallen comrade, they toasted success, they toasted their new team, they even toasted Jax's previous universe. And as the oldest sentient civilisation in the multiverse, the Cromulites provided excellent nibbles.

-

"I can't believe how tasty that Flurbian Brandy is!" slurred Kinmal, as Abel and Rigsan helped their sozzled colleague out of the Departures door and dragged him towards his awaiting TTAXI.

"Yeah, I'm sure it would have been," replied Abel, Kinmal's hand patting him lightly on the cheek from the outside, "if there'd been any left".

"Maybe we can help you with your drinking, huh?" said Rigsan, ever the focused, self-appointed leader, "You're not alone now. We can help you cut down".

"Nonsense!" shouted Kinmal, who was as shocked as everyone else at how loud he'd just spoke and whispering the next bit to make up for it, "more reasons to celebrate now, Hee Hee".

"Come on, in you go," puffed Abel, protecting the top of his Kinmal's head as he pushed it into the back of the TTAXI.

As the reactor began to power up and the TTAXI pulled away from the side of the rank, Kinmal stuck his head out of the window and smiled a well-lubricated grin at his fellow Agents.

"See you later, TEAM!" he shouted, his fingers waving at them whilst simultaneously grabbing the top of the window glass. The window rolled up automatically as the TTAXI prepared for its jump, sending Kinmal's hand and face sliding up the inside of the window, "Here's to next time!" They barely made out the last bit, as his face was still sandwiched against the glass.

Abel and Rigsan waved the TTAXI off. They both gave each other a playful, tutting grin, like the proud owners of a puppy that had just weed on the carpet but was still too cute to tell off.

The next TTAXI, this one for Rigsan, pulled to the front of the rank.

"Well, this is me," said Rigsan, his white teeth glistening in the starlight. He held out his tanned hand for Abel to shake.

"Do you believe in fate, Rigsan?" asked Abel, as he reached out and shook his team mate's hand.

"Fate? Nope. Nooooo. Girl's stuff," said Rigsan, deepening his voice as if hardening himself against the idea, "Life is what you make it. You are the decisions you make".

"Or the ones you don't" replied Abel, smiling, as Rigsan pulled his hand away and started to head to his TTAXI, "If those TTAXIs hadn't blown up when they did, we wouldn't…"

Rigsan was almost in his cab by now. He cupped his hand to hear, as if pretending he couldn't hear what Abel was saying.

"Until the next mission!" He shouted, ignoring Abel's musings. As the TTAXI started to pull away, Rigsan looked like he was searching in his pockets for something. Which was weird as his suit didn't have any. Abel knew what was coming but let him carry on his comedic routine. Just as the TTAXI pulled away,

Rigsan pretended to find what he was looking for – a hearty middle finger, accompanied with a wide, juvenile grin. He continued the rude gesture through the back window until the cab jumped, leaving Abel smiling in his wake and shaking his head.

"I will give them all a choice from now on, you know". Said Jax's familiar voice behind him, as his TTAXI started to roll towards them.

"I know, but what about the ones already in service?" he asked, turning around to face her, "what about them?" Will you tell them the truth, or will I have to do it for you?"

"Maybe we could do it together?" suggested Jax, "it might sound better coming from someone they know".

"Oh I'm not sure that's true". Replied Abel with a chuckle, "I didn't know any of the other three me's I've met today".

"Yes you did," corrected Jax sagely, "you knew all of them. You have the most self-awareness. It's your gift and your curse. You saw parts of your personality in each of them, just a different dominant facet in each. It's what makes you who you are".

Abel knew she was right of course.

"Can I ask you a question, Agent Abel?"

"By all means," he replied, aware that she was probably owed a few questions.

"What if some of them say no? What happens to their realities?"

"I used to work in a supermarket, Jax," Abel shot back, "I'm not afraid of a bit of overtime".

He got in his waiting cab and rolled down the window.

"Can I make one request?" he asked, as Jax approached the TTAXI slightly.

Jax nodded agreeably.

"Can I have a proper sky? Around my base I mean". He asked, as the window began to roll up, "You guys can do that right? I'm tired at looking at space all the time".

The window was all the way up now and so he couldn't hear her answer. He took the nod he saw out of the back window as a sign his wish would be granted though.

"Good day, skip?" asked the driver, the soft rock-based tones of *Status Quo* filtering through the hole in the plastiglass barrier.

"You wouldn't believe it if I told you!" replied Abel, "I should write a book…"

Abel's voice trailed off as he realised that was actually quite a good idea, given the time. He resolved to start a plan for one.

"Now don't spare the horses – I'm busting for a cup of tea!"

EPILOGUE
WHAT GOES AROUND...

Jax waved off Abel's TTAXI away and returned inside the complex. She made her way to her office on the top floor of the complex, just below the Observation Deck. She could hear the clean-up operation from the celebration was still in progress.

The office was surprisingly small for the office of someone who is as old as time itself, but she had decided long ago that grandeur was for beings who needed to make a good impression and she was past all that. The room was home to an ancient wooden desk, carved from the first tree ever grown and three large sentient Blofo Trees from the swamps of Pioll II. The trees would sing soothingly of home whenever requested. Thirty-six large monitor screens filled the wall opposite, controlled from the terminal on the timeworn desk. Jax rounded the resting stool and crossed four of her legs as she liked to do. She tapped a few commands into the console and four live feeds flickered into life on the middle four view screens.

In the top left, the CRC (Colin Retrieval Crew) team were busying themselves chasing the black and white cat around the sofa, attempting to take him for rehoming with the next

available Mark to be recruited.

In the top right, Kinmal could be seen flat out asleep on his sofa, snoring loudly as the television played away to nobody. The Nano Bytes had once again carried him there and retired to their tube to heal. His Colin could be seen relaxing on the drunk Agent's back.

In the bottom left, Rigsan was already doing his warm-down routine in the living area, Colin watching disgustedly from his cushion, wondering what the hell was going on. *Runaway* by Bon Jovi could be heard playing over the speaker system, as Sarge boomed out commands for his 'maggot'. He was furiously doing sit-ups, trying to sweat out the events of the day.

And in the bottom right screen was Abel. Already in his pyjamas, bowl of popcorn on his lap, happily watching Paintless. Colin could be seen sauntering into the picture and letting out a silent meow, as if asking permission to hop onto his Human's lap. A confirming pat on the leg and Colin was quickly up and doing the familiar cat thing of turning around at least ten times before coming back to the first spot to settle down. The contented cat got an appreciative head tickle from his owner.

Jax smiled as she turned the view screens onto other channels, to view other Marks. Some were TTAXI cams of Marks being abducted, some were helmet cams of Marks deep in pursuit of various targets, some Marks were even climbing trees to set traps. This job would end one day, she thought, but today had been one of those days that made her realise why she was doing it.

She opened the word processor app on her console and started to type a memo to the Recruitment stations, advising them to change their recruitment speeches, just as she'd promised Abel she would. From tomorrow, all Marks would have a choice. She then drafted a request for her science division to look into the reasons behind the shared dream phenomenon.

For now, she had had quite enough excitement for one day for someone almost 14 billion years old. She would retire to her bed chamber and ruminate on the day's momentous and potentially reality-altering events.

-

Jax awoke from her slumber with what she could only describe as a 'jolt'. She was not used to waking up like this – being as old as the universe meant that most things were usually quite simple to put into perspective. Events that would make lesser, younger, less experienced beings stress themselves out were but 'weeing in a well' to Jax. She couldn't remember the last time she had had what was commonly referred to as 'a bad dream'. Even the dreams she had about trying to get eight-legged leather trousers on had been met with quiet consternation and a leisurely waking. No, something really quite disturbing must have wrested her from her slumber. At this moment, she was still in that state of confusion one is in when they are woken before they should be.

"Are you alright, Madam Jax?" asked the orange-sashed Cromulite, who had run into the bedroom upon hearing his leader's subconscious scream, "You're sweating profusely. Would you like me to get you a towel?"

She looked down at her nightgown. She was soaked through with perspiration, another occurrence of which she couldn't remember the last instance.

"I believe I had a bad dream," she stuttered, taking the offered towel from her assistant and pressing it gently to her brow.

"What about?" asked the perturbed assistant, offering Jax a glass of rehydration liquid, "Was it the leather trousers again?"

She gave him an admonishing look. She had told that story to one assistant, in confidence and it was still being brought up to her five million years later. Would it ever be forgotten, she wondered?

"No," she replied firmly, as her assistant looked away guiltily, "I can't quite remember it to be honest. I think," her memory started to coalesce as she gulped the rehydration liquid and pass her assistant the glass for a refill.

"I think I was laying on a table. Or rather it wasn't a table," the assistant passed her the refill and she took a sip, "It was a metal surgical table of some kind. And this other being was there, but I couldn't move because I was incapacitated in some way".

She took another sip from the glass as her subconscious memories began to become more vivid in her mind's eye. She squinted as if to get a better look at them.

"Behind me, there were…there were cupboards of some kind. My table was attached to one of the cupboards. The being came into view and spoke into a listening device that was hanging from the ceiling. He was wearing a white coat and had bright blue glasses on. Then he rolled my table back into the cupboard and that's when I woke up".

By now the assistant was tidying the moist towel and the empty glass away into the recycler. He had his back to his leader, so he could not see her reaction when he said what he said.

"Oh, how strange," he said, calmly placing the items in the open wall-flap, before closing it and pressing the red button, "Sounds like a morgue…"

Jax got her second fright in the last ten minutes and realised she was about to need another towel…

"Oh bugger!"

END

APPENDIX
WARNING – SPOILERS AHEAD
– READ THE BOOK FIRST!!!!

MARK FARRINGDON TIMELINE – ABEL EDITION

1980   Mark's Dad is offered a promotion in Bielefeld, Germany. He decides against taking it.

1985   Buys all-time favourite graphic novel, *Watchmen*.

1986   Has brace fitted to correct teeth. Has it taken off less than six months later as it 'felt weird in his mouth'.

1990   Completes sixth form. Fails to dance with Michelle Evans. She dances with John instead.

1991   Drops out of University before and of first year. Fails to complete the end of year exams, meaning he cannot go back.

1992   Gets first full-time position at the supermarket. Beaten up on night out to celebrate but is rescued by his friends.

1994   Meets Jenny at work and begins a relationship with her.

1996   Gets job in stock department. Finds his 'niche'.

1998   He and Jenny buy first house together.

1999	Marries Jenny.
31/12/99	He and Jenny have a massive argument about a sarcastic comment he made.
2001	Gets first managerial job at supermarket. Moves away from Plymouth for first time.
2003	Grandfather dies. Moves home to Plymouth soon after.
2005	He and Jenny have their first child, Anastasia.
2008	He and Jenny have their second child, George.
2011	Has midlife crisis. Divorces Jenny. Moves back in with Mum and Dad.
2012	Abducted by Cromulites. Takes the TTAXI as he's too lazy to walk to the bus stop in the rain.

MARK FARRINGDON TIMELINE – RIGSAN EDITION

1980   Mark's Dad is offered a promotion in Bielefeld, Germany. He decides against taking it.

1985   Buys all-time favourite graphic novel, *Watchmen*.

1986   Has brace fitted to correct teeth. Has it taken off less than six months later as it 'felt weird in his mouth'.

1990   Completes sixth form. Dances with Michelle Evans. They begin a relationship. She talks him into going travelling around Australia for a year with her.

1991   Mark and Michelle return from Australia. They attend Bristol University together – he studies Computer Science, she studies Social Work.

1992   They join the University running club together. Michelle has to give up running due to injury.

1994   Runs his first of three London Marathons for the British Diabetic Association (His Dad is Diabetic).

1995   Graduates with a first. Gets a job with Exeter-based software firm, *Ex-ecute*.

1998   Leaves job and sets up his own software studio, *RockHard Softworks*.

1999   Marries Michelle. Has teeth fixed privately in preparation for the wedding.

31/12/99   He and Michelle have a massive argument about how much time he spends at work.

2003	Grandfather dies. He does not make the funeral due to work commitments.
2005	He and Michelle have their first child, Anastasia.
2008	He and Michelle have their second child, George.
2011	Michelle has an affair and leaves him.
2012	Abducted by Cromulites. Takes the TTAXI as he's in too much pain to jog home.

MARK FARRINGDON TIMELINE - DOFE EDITION

1980   Mark's Dad is offered a promotion in Bielefeld, Germany. He decides against taking it.

1985   Buys all-time favourite graphic novel, *Watchmen*.

1986   Has brace fitted to correct teeth. Has it taken off less than six months later as it 'felt weird in his mouth'.

1990   Completes sixth form. Fails to dance with Michelle Evans. She dances with John instead.

1991   Drops out of University before and of first year. Fails to complete the end of year exams, meaning he cannot go back.

1992   Gets first full-time position at the supermarket. Beaten up on night out to celebrate. His friends run away rather than help.

1993   Loses his job at the supermarket due to appalling absence record. Never meets Jenny, who starts the week after he is sacked.

1996   Gets a council flat. Becomes a recluse. Loses contact with friends and only has sporadic contact with Mum and Dad.

1998   Tries Marijuana for the first time 'for his nerves'. It helps. A lot.

1999   Michelle Evans becomes his case worker. He remembers her from school and quickly becomes obsessed.

31/12/99	Has a massive argument with a stranger online over who the best version *Green Lantern* is.
2000	Given restraining order barring him from seeing Michelle. Given new case worker, Dave.
2003	Grandfather dies. Makes up with parents at funeral.
2004	Begins Computer Science degree through Open University.
2005	Starts 'his first child', a conspiracy website, *TheGreyhammer.com*.
2007	Graduates his OU course with a first. Does not attend the Graduation ceremony.
2008	Starts 'his second child', his *TGH* YouTube channel.
2012	Abducted by Cromulites. Takes the TTAXI as he's too scared to walk past a gang of youths at a bus stop.

MARK FARRINGDON TIMELINE – KINMAL EDITION

1980	Mark's Dad is offered a promotion in Bielefeld, Germany. He convinces Mark's Mum to move.
1985	Buys all-time favourite graphic novel, *Watchmen*.
1986	Has brace fitted to correct teeth. Keeps it on.
1991	Graduates from school. Attends Bristol University to study Computer Science. Meets Michelle Evans in fresher's week and they begin a relationship after she dumps her previous boyfriend, John.
1995	Graduates with a first. Splits up with Michelle as she won't move to Germany with him.
1996	Starts working for *SAP SE* in Bielefeld. Finds his 'niche'. Joins company Handball team.
1997	Meets Nicole in work. They begin a relationship.
1999	Marries Nicole.
31/12/99	He and Nicole have a massive argument about his drinking problem.
2003	Grandfather dies. Travels home for funeral. Thinks about moving to England but decides against it.
2005	He and Nicole have their first child, Anastasia.
2008	He and Nicole have their second child, Dietmar.
2011	Nicole leaves him because of his worsening drink problem.

2012   Abducted by Cromulites. Takes the TTAXI as he's
            too drunk to drive home.

Printed in Poland
by Amazon Fulfillment
Poland Sp. z o.o., Wrocław

53335974R00204